Dead Town

ALSO BY STEPHEN WILLIAMS

RAINE AND HUME SERIES
Book 1: The Skin Code
Book 2: A Bloodstained Coat
Book 3: Dead Town

DEAD TOWN

STEPHEN WILLIAMS

Raine and Hume Series Book 3

Joffe Books, London
www.joffebooks.com

First published in Great Britain in 2024

© Stephen Williams 2024

This book is a work of fiction. Names, characters, businesses, organizations, places and events are either the product of the author's imagination or are used fictitiously. Any resemblance to actual persons, living or dead, events or locales is entirely coincidental. The spelling used is British English except where fidelity to the author's rendering of accent or dialect supersedes this. The right of Stephen Williams to be identified as author of this work has been asserted in accordance with the Copyright, Designs and Patents Act 1988.

Cover art by Nick Castle

ISBN: 978-1-83526-698-4

For Josephine.
From a tree to now, then on to forever.

CHAPTER 1

With her feet spread apart to maintain balance, Raine moved along the aisle of the first-class compartment, studying the digital reservation numbers displayed in the overhead hoarding. Finally, with a grunt of satisfaction, she flumped into a seat.

'That was close,' she said, smiling across the table at the middle-aged man sitting opposite. 'Only just made it before the doors locked. If I'd missed this train, I'd have been fucked, big time.' She placed her mobile on the table between them, unfolded it, and began to type.

The man peered at her over the lid of his laptop, with a look of mild disgust. His skin was smooth and pale, his eyes somehow blank behind his glasses. 'Do you mind not swearing?' he asked softly.

Raine glanced up from her phone. 'I'm sorry?'

The man twitched an on-off smile. 'I said do you mind not swearing?'

Raine cocked her head slightly, taking in the designer suit with the jacket hung on the window hanger and the neatly folded paper beside his laptop. On the other side of the device was a bowl of salted peanuts.

'I'm not sure,' she mused. 'I *might* mind. I've never tried not swearing.' She smiled at him. 'But as we're in first class, I'll give it a go.'

The man gazed at her for a long second, then sighed and turned back to his screen. After a moment, he began typing.

'Nice laptop,' said Raine. 'Very swanky. I bet it cost a lot of money.'

The man stopped typing. He took in her black cotton shirt and waistcoat topped off with a black leather beret, as if they were a personal affront to his professional environment. 'Are you talking to me?'

'I've got a friend who advises me on all the techy stuff,' Raine said, taking off her beret and putting it on the table. The choppy, dark blonde hair that had been contained underneath now stuck out in all directions. ''Cos I'm useless with that stuff. Couldn't encrypt anything to save my life. He's always going on at me.' She pointed a finger at the man's device. 'That looks like it could encrypt in its sleep. I bet those switches on the side turn off the camera and microphone. Maybe even the Wi-Fi. Am I right?' She smiled at him brightly, then pointed at the bowl of nuts. 'Can I have one of those?'

He looked down at the bowl, then back at her, his expression incredulous. 'You want my—'

'No, I don't want yours. That would be weird. I mean, can I get my own bowl? For free? My friend Betty says that in first class everything is free. The drinks, the snacks. Everything.'

'I don't mean to be rude, but maybe you should sit somewhere else?' The man gestured to his laptop. 'We pull into King's Cross in half an hour, and I have a lot of work to do.'

'Oh, don't mind me,' said Raine breezily, scooting herself over to the window and putting her feet on the seat next to her. 'You won't even know I'm here.' She grabbed her phone, and to the man's astonishment, levered herself up and sat on the table. 'Actually, do you think we could take a selfie? Betty will never believe I've travelled first class.' She held out her phone and took a shot, holding up her other hand in a peace sign. 'Cheers. I'll drop it on the gram; my friends will go mental. They've never seen me outside London.' Raine threw herself back into the seat again. 'How do you order the nuts? Is there a button or something, or do you have to go to the little shop like the people in the cattle class?'

The man glowered at her. 'I'd like you to move.'

Raine smiled at him and waved her phone. 'Can't, mate. Reservation. This is my seat. They'd probably arrest me if I was somewhere else, yeah?'

'Why are you even here?' the man asked, a look of horrified fascination on his face. As if he was staring at a petri dish full of bacteria.

Raine leaned forward on her seat and placed her hands on the table. 'Nothing special. Just the normal. My wife died, and between you and me I lost it. Went a bit *Spiders from Mars*, if you get my drift. Had to leave my job. Personal development issues. Difficulty controlling my anger.'

'That's not what I mean—' began the man, but Raine cut across him.

'Then I set myself up as a PI. Private Investigator. Took this job to find a young woman, Heather Salim, only she turned up dead in the street with her face blown off.' Raine leaned in conspiratorially. 'Only it wasn't Heather, because I got a text message from her later asking for my help. It was a stooge body. A Fake-Heather.'

The man opened his mouth to speak, alarm now written on his face, but Raine cut him off again.

'Then, on another job, I helped Clara's mum. She's a detective for the Met, by the way. Clara's mum. Not Clara. She's my wife. And dead. Anyhow, I met this guy called Frankie Ridgeway. Absolute tosser. Complete scum. We never used to get on, but we do now.'

'What are you talking about?' said the man, increasingly agitated.

'Not Ridgeway. Me and Mary, Clara's mum. She used to think I was bad for her daughter. And then she died — Clara,

I mean — and I kind of hated her. Felt she had let us down. But now . . .' Raine made a see-saw gesture with her hand. 'Anyway, this guy, Ridgeway, was into some serious shit. Trafficking. Prostitution. Abuse. And it turned out that he had something to do with Fake-Heather, this woman who supposedly got shotgunned in the street. They found traces of her blood in his van.'

'What happened to him?' asked the man, his anger seemingly forgotten.

'He disappeared before I could question him.' She clicked her fingers. 'Just like that.' Raine held out her arm and pulled the shirt sleeve up. Running down the skin was a white scar, mottled and ribbed like an engraving. 'I never even got to pay him back for this.'

'How did—' began the man.

'Hit me with a hammer. But I stabbed him with a mooring spike so I suppose fair's fair. Although I'm pretty certain he murdered my cat.'

There was an awkward silence as the train pulled into Stevenage. On the platform, a group of youths stared sullenly at her while angrily vaping below the no-smoking sign. The setting sun behind them, red and swollen, added a sinister sheen to the setting. Raine gave them a cheery wave.

'Anyhow, I'm on the hunt for him, as well as trying to rebuild my relationship with Mary, Clara's mum.' Raine gazed earnestly at the man. 'Really, how do you get the nuts?'

The man's patience was wearing thin. 'Listen, I have a very important meeting in . . .' he glanced at the laptop screen, 'less than an hour, so I need to—'

'I also had to move my accommodation, literally,' continued Raine as if the man hadn't spoken. 'Because Frankie knew where I lived. It's a canal boat, did I mention?'

The man sighed, increasingly aggravated.

'My parents used to run warehouse parties out of King's Cross, so we had a canal boat there. When they passed on, I kind of took it over. The boat, not the parties. I don't do drugs. Not for moral reasons; I just don't like the lack of control.' Raine shrugged her shoulders. 'Sorry. Not relevant. Once the bad guys knew where I lived, I had to move. Luckily, in a boat, that's no big deal.'

'Your parents were drug dealers?'

'Nah,' said Raine, helping herself to some nuts. The man's mouth pinched, but he said nothing. 'But I'm certain they dabbled. I mean it was the nineties rave scene, right? Ecstasy was everywhere. Even the rats were on disco biscuits. The point is, I had to move, and so for the first time I had neighbours.'

'Look, whatever your name is, I don't really—'

'Raine. Like the weather only with an "e" at the end.'

'Sorry?'

'That's my name, Adam. Raine. Like I was saying, I had to move, so I rocked up in Little Venice. It's busy there. Not just like a few boats. There's oodles! It's like Piccadilly sodding Circus!'

The man just stared at her.

'So for the first time since forever, I had a neighbour, right? And she's a bit of an old hippy. We're talking cardigans and chakras, you get me?'

'You called me Adam,' he said, his eyes hard. 'How do you know my name?'

'Doesn't matter,' said Raine, batting the question away. 'The important thing is this old lady, Jolene, kind of adopted me. Would cook for me and that. She even gave me a pot plant once.' Raine's brow creased. 'Or at least I think it was a pot plant. It was a pot and had earth in it. Nothing ever grew from it, though.'

'I asked you how you know my name,' said Adam, his voice tight.

'And I said it doesn't matter. What matters is Jolene's grandniece. That's what you need to zoom in on.'

Adam looked past her down the carriage. It was almost empty. The people that were there were all focused on laptops or phones. Business people doing business things in a portable intercity office. He returned his gaze to Raine. 'I've no idea where you got my name or what you're doing at this table but—'

'I got it off the guard,' said Raine pleasantly.

'The guard?'

'Conductor. Ticket woman. Whatever they're called. She says you travel this route a lot. Like every week.'

'And why did you ask her for my name? Are you some sort of stalker?'

'Pay attention, Adam. I've already told you. I'm a private investigator. What did you think about those boys?' said Raine, smiling at him.

'What boys? What are you talking about?'

'The boys at the station. The ones pretending to be gangsters. You must have seen them.'

'No,' said Adam, shutting his laptop and standing. 'I'm going to get the guard. You're harassing me and—'

'Come on, Adam, you must have seen them. They were dropping off your money.'

Adam, in the process of walking away, turned back. 'What money?'

'It's in the sports bag over there,' said Raine, pointing past him to the carriage entrance. 'In the rack. One of the boys put it on the train while the others stood around looking hard. Although it's quite difficult to look hard when your vape smells of candy floss, but fair play, they were giving it a good go.'

Adam slowly sat down and placed his hands on the table. 'Go on,' he said lightly.

Raine smiled widely. 'See, I knew you'd be interested! Jolene's such a lovely lady, even if she does paint rainbows all over her boat. Where did I get to?' Raine clicked her fingers. 'That's right. Elizabeth, but she goes by the name Libby. Fourteen years old. Super-pretty in a street way. You know how kids are.' Raine picked up her phone and fully opened the screen. 'Here, I've got a picture of her somewhere.' She swiped at the device until she found what she wanted, then turned the phone so Adam could see. 'Of course, it's hard to tell because of the bruising and cuts, but underneath all the damage she's gorgeous.'

Adam's face remained impassive.

'This was taken just after she was admitted to hospital,' said Raine softly. 'She's going to be left with scars, of course, but I reckon she'll be able to rock them. Jolene says she's the type. Someone who owns the scars. Wears their battles, you know what I mean?'

A smirk butterflied around the man's lips. 'Why are you showing me this?'

Raine closed her phone and placed it on the table. 'Do you know how county lines work, Adam? The drug trafficking business? They use kids to transport the drugs from the big cities to the provinces. Young teenagers. They go for children because they're easy to control. Find the vulnerable ones. The ones they can manipulate. Get them addicted then use them to courier for you. Maybe intimidate them a little. Sometimes a bit of peer pressure.'

'Fascinating. Does this story have a point?'

'I can't believe nobody has come down and offered me some nuts,' said Raine, looking around. 'What's the point of first class if you have to go and get your own?'

'Forget the nuts and get to the end of the story. I take it this Libby was in a gang? Was a junkie?'

Raine turned back to face him. 'No. That's the thing. That's what makes county lines such a bastard. They don't just use gangs. Not for the transport. They use citizens. Kids who you wouldn't even expect. Because they only need to make them do it once. If they can get a kid to agree, through intimidation or bribery or whatever, that's all they need, because they've got this extra scam up their sleeve. They get the kid to do the drop, saying they only need to do it once. But then they hire someone to rob them. Either of the drugs or the money. The kid thinks it's a rival gang or whatever, but really it's the guy who's paying them. And when they return without the drugs or with no cash, the guy says they owe him. Have to work it off or he'll do them some damage.'

Adam shrugged and glanced at his watch. Over the intercom an automated voice informed them the train was pulling into King's Cross. 'It's a tough old world.'

'And sometimes,' continued Raine, 'to hammer the point home, so to speak, they'll do some damage anyway, but not to the kid they're using. They do it to the kid's friend. Like Libby. Jolene was in bits when she told me. About how her grandniece's best friend had been caught up and then robbed. About how Libby tried to get her out. About how the guy, the one who ran the line, had her beaten up to keep her friend in check. To make sure she did what she was supposed to. Libby said he even watched. Maybe to show his henchmen he was one of them or some such bollocks. Those boys have been picked up, by the way. The ones at Stevenage who dropped off the swag bag. And the ones before. Leeds. Wakefield. All of them.'

Adam's face, amused a moment before, hardened. 'What are you talking about?'

'I'm shutting down the line, mate. I've been following you for two weeks. Watching the kids sell the drugs from the cuckoo houses. Watching them drop off the money on the train. Watching your partner in the next carriage pick it up and take it to your little safe house in Deptford. He's sleeping, in case you wondered where he is.' She paused. 'Well, sort of sleeping. Not awake, anyhow.' Her face took on an expression of outrage. 'He tried to zap me with a stun gun!'

Raine's phone pinged. Adam snaked out his hand and gripped her wrist, her skin whitening with the force of his grasp. 'You bitch. You have no idea who I am. What I can do to you.'

Under the table, Raine pressed the Vipertek stun gun she'd taken from Adam's partner against his leg and pulled the trigger. The man immediately let go of her as his nervous system overloaded.

'You know, I've been trying to cut down on the violence in my life,' sighed Raine, watching the man's eyelids flicker. 'For my karma, you know? Try to live more harmoniously with the universe. Problem is, the universe I live in is full of fuckleberries like you, Adam. Don't call me bitch. It isn't very polite.' Raine picked up his phone and pointed it at his face. The device unlocked and Raine glanced at it. 'I mean, I'd told you my name so you don't really have an excuse.' She smiled. 'Whoops. Your phone seems to be unlocked. I hope there's not lots of juicy numbers for the police to munch on.' Adam stared back at her, unable to move as his nerves fizzled inside his skin. 'All those contacts. All those drug houses. All those bank accounts. Between the phone and the laptop, you're proper fucked, mate.'

'You have no idea . . .' the gangster slurred, saliva dribbling down his chin.

'Try not to talk. The effects of the electricity are more painful if you move. Strictly speaking, the stun gun is illegal, but as it belongs to your henchman in the next carriage, I'll let myself off with a warning. I told you he tried to zap me? That notification I got, by the way? That was Libby. I sent her the selfie because she said you were there at the beating. Said you ordered it. I went and saw her in the hospital.' Raine stood as the train came to a stop, wiping down the stun gun and dropping it in Adam's jacket pocket. On the platform outside were several police officers. Raine gave them a little finger wave. 'She was battered half to death, with tubes coming out of her. The bruises and cuts on her face were an entire rainbow of hurt. She looked like she'd been beaten up by a bus.' Raine leaned down and whispered in his ear. 'But I'll tell you one thing: she wasn't frightened. She was angry.'

There was a triple beep, and then the doors opened with a hiss. Several police officers stepped aboard, followed by a well-groomed man in a charcoal suit.

'Detective Inspector Conner!' said Raine, walking towards him. 'Even dishier in the flesh than you sound on the phone. I swear if I were into men I'd swoon into your arms.'

'Raine.'

'The man dribbling behind me is Adam Pirie, of Deptford county lines fame. His laptop is unlocked and I'm pretty certain the spreadsheets on it are for the drug houses he keeps in the north of England. Also, there's a bag full of money in the rack and an unconscious gangster in the next carriage. I have a client who's willing to identify him for abduction, GBH and drug trafficking.'

DI Conner looked past her at the man spasming slightly in his seat, 'What's the matter with him?'

Raine glanced over her shoulder, cocking her head in thought.

'I think it's just nerves,' she said brightly. 'Probably. I'm going to buy some nuts. I'll meet you outside the station.' She stepped off the train and breathed in the London air.

As she walked up the platform, her phone buzzed. Raine tapped her earbud, answering the call.

'How's tricks?' said a deep, nicotine-tuned voice.

'Jasper!' Raine smiled. 'How's the sketching?'

Jasper, a dinosaur left over from the days when her parents used to run warehouse parties throughout London. A forever outlaw, he had known every shady club and gathering in the capital. These days, he spent his time doing exquisite line drawings of the city he loved. Or at least he had until he had been beaten up and left for dead while he was helping on one of Raine's cases.

'I've got some information.'

Raine slowed to a stroll, forcing the river of commuters to flow around her. 'Regarding?'

'Ridgeway.'

Frankie Ridgeway. The gun for hire who had tried to kill Raine. Had murdered her cat. Had possibly abducted Heather Salim, a woman she had been hired to find and bring home. The woman who had begged her for help.

'Well, well. What do you have?'

'Can you meet me tomorrow?'

Raine stepped out of the station into the London night. The air was bitterly cold, causing her breath to mist as it left her body. 'Sure,' she said. The scar that snaked down her arm seemed to throb in symphony to the beat of the city. 'Where?'

CHAPTER 2

As soon as she stepped out of the car Mary Hume felt the cold bite of the wind. The late October air was crisp and sharp, with an acrid hint of smoke from early fireworks. DS Etera Echo stood waiting for her outside a small, terraced house, arms wrapped around himself in a futile attempt to ward off the bitterness of the night.

'Nice holiday, boss?' he enquired.

Hume and Robert, her husband, had spent a week in Prague, ambling through the medieval courtyards and labyrinthine alleys that make up the city, before taking a slow train through Europe. It had been so long since they had had time away from London.

'Too short,' she replied, while gazing at the exterior of the house.

'The place is unoccupied,' offered Echo, as she took in the unkempt exterior. They were in Aquinas Street, behind Waterloo East station. Hume guessed the block would be worth several million pounds, even in its dilapidated state. The entrance door was open, with SOCOs moving in and out.

'I see you've already attracted the ghoul squad,' she said, indicating a group of civilians standing behind the hazard tape, phones in hand.

Echo glanced across at the throng. 'You know the public, guv; anything with a hint of the grisly and they're on it like flies.'

Hume moved rapidly towards the entrance. 'Well, get them moved on; I don't want this all over social media before I've even had a chance to investigate.'

Echo nodded, calling over a PC and giving her instructions to push back the perimeter.

'Tell me about the body,' said Hume when he'd finished.

'There is no body.'

She paused at the threshold, lifting an eyebrow at her sergeant. 'No body? Then why am I here, Etera? I might remind you that you had me picked up from the sodding airport. My holiday hasn't technically finished.'

'Sorry about that,' said Echo cheerfully. 'It's complicated.'

'Complicated how?'

'Better if I show you.'

Hume gazed at Echo for a moment. It suddenly dawned on her that he seemed a little jittery. Moving from foot to foot. 'Something got you spooked?' she asked, a smile fluttering around her mouth.

'You won't be saying that in a minute,' he replied. 'This one is proper weird.'

Hume had never known Echo to be nervous, except maybe when talking about Bitz, his might-be girlfriend. 'Show me.'

As soon as they entered the ground-floor flat, Hume felt it. A coldness that had nothing to do with the autumn air. An emptiness. An absence.

'The primary scene's through the back,' said Echo quietly.

'I thought you said there wasn't a body?'

'There isn't. Not anymore.'

'Removed?' asked Hume, intrigued. 'The pathologist has been and gone? Echo, you know I like to—'

'No pathologist. Not yet. As I said, it's complicated. This way.'

Echo led her through the flat, walking on the metal treads the CSI team had erected. It was in a poor state, the wallpaper peeling and mildewed.

'Creepy,' muttered Hume, eyeing a massive spider's web in the corner of the ceiling.

'That's nothing,' said Echo as they entered the back room. Although the light was on and the overhead bulb was bare, its feeble wattage barely illuminated the space. The floor was littered with autumn leaves, brown and skeletal.

'They were here already,' said Echo, reading her thoughts.

'Blew in from outside?' suggested Hume, but she knew that was unlikely. There were too many, and too far into the property. Bizarrely, these seemed to have been brought in deliberately.

'The trees outside are birch. Different leaf shapes. I'm not sure what tree these came from.' Echo walked on, passing through a doorway into the next room. There were more leaves on the floor, and also a chair, set square in the centre and facing the corner. There was no other furniture.

Hume studied the room. Once again, the wallpaper was peeling. The chair was wooden, like a kitchen chair, with rodded arms. Attached to the arms were tatters of grey duct tape. A spark of anticipation lit in Hume's brain. 'Hostage?' she said aloud. The floor around the chair was hidden under a carpet of leaves. Hume pointed at the chair. There were dark mottled stains on it. 'Are you going to tell me that's blood?'

'Probably, but not confirmed yet. There's also mould on the legs and back. Forensics think that it might have come from a skip or wasteland.'

'That would explain the smell of decay, then.' There was also another smell, high and coppery. Hume had attended enough murder scenes to recognise it. 'And there's no body in the flat?'

'No, boss.'

'Basement? Attic? Buried in the garden?'

'We've had the cadaver dogs out. Nothing.'

'Then, once again, why am I here instead of with Robert?'

Robert, her husband, had kissed her goodbye at the airport and promised to wait up.

'Because you like to see the murder scene before SOCOs start to process it.'

Hume glanced back at the chair. Surveyed the walls and the floor and the ceiling. 'What am I missing?'

Echo held up his tablet. 'Do you like horror films?'

'Not since I was a teenager. Explain.'

'Step onto the spur,' he said, pointing.

Hume saw that the technicians had laid an offshoot. A little metal walkway branched towards the back corner of the room. Hume walked onto it.

'A little further,' said Echo. 'I've marked the place with tape.'

Hume looked down. There was a piece of duct tape stuck to the metal. She stood on it.

'Echo, just tell me what—'

'Now face the chair and hold the tablet in front of your face.'

Sighing, Hume did so. Echo leaned in and swiped the device. Hume stared at the screen.

'Jesus,' she whispered.

On the tablet was an image of the room. It must have been taken from exactly where Hume was positioned because everything was perfectly proportioned. The chair. The bulb. The leaves. Everything. As if she was just looking through the screen at the actual room.

Except in the image on the tablet, there was a woman tied to the chair with a carving knife pressed against her throat. Echo reached across and tapped the screen again. The image immediately came to life, and Hume realised it was a video feed of some sort. The knife was held in a black-gloved hand. All that could be seen of the wielder was the hand and arm, covered by a black sleeve. As Hume viewed the scene, the woman's throat was cut, the knife slashing across the exposed skin. Hume watched, shocked, as the woman tried to scream. There was only silence.

'What's wrong with the audio?' Hume asked. She couldn't look away from the dying woman. Her eyes behind her glasses were full of terror as the blood rivered down the front of her dress. The hand holding the knife disappeared out of shot. Hume moved the tablet aside. The same image, but without the woman, was in front of her. Just the chair with its stains and its smell. She brought the tablet back. The woman's eyes stared sightlessly out at her, then her head fell forward, her black hair covering her face.

'Nothing. When he slashed her throat, he must have severed her vocal cords.'

Hume nodded. Placed in the woman's lap was a piece of cardboard about a foot square, like it had been torn from the lid of a packing box. Written on it in blood-red capitals was one word:

DEADTOWN

'The video is time-stamped with yesterday's date,' said Echo.

'How did we get it?' asked Hume. 'Was it sent to us?'

'No. A couple found a bag dumped outside a pub in Soho. They handed it in at Charing Cross Police Station.'

'Very public-spirited of them,' commented Hume.

'It was covered in blood.'

'Ah.'

'Seemed like a robbery. No wallet. Just a busted-up phone. We managed to extract this from it.' He pointed at the image of the woman staring, petrified, out at them.

'Can we track the SIM? Find out who the bag belongs to?'

'No. One-use burner phone, looks like. Bought from Camden Market. No chance of establishing ownership. We're running the blood.'

They both stared at the empty chair and then at the dead woman on the tablet.

'Creepy, yes?' said Echo.

Hume held up the tablet again. The chair looked the same, as did the peeling wallpaper behind it. The only difference when she put the tablet down was the absence of the body.

'Who is she? Do we have an ID yet?' asked Hume, squinting at the image; the shot re-cued with the knife poised to cut. Before the blood. Before the light went from the woman's eyes.

'Melissa Clarke. Has a regular show; quite popular.'

Hume nodded, her mind focusing in. Now Echo had said her name, she recognised her. Melissa Clarke, blogger of unusual historical murders around the capital. An internet sensation. 'Of course. And her show is called . . . ?'

'*Deadtown*,' confirmed Echo.

Hume nodded again. 'And so close to Halloween.' She handed back the tablet. 'Okay, It's ours. Set up the hub and get the SOCOs to send everything to us first thing in the morning.'

CHAPTER 3

By the time Raine stepped back onto her boat it was nearly eleven o'clock. The air had turned from merely cold to freezing, and she took a moment to warm her hands by blowing on them before tapping the code into the lock pad. Pressing her fingerprint to complete the verification, the safe opened and she removed the key. After the last attempted break-in, she was extra careful. She hadn't intended to be this late; the unofficial statement she had given DI Conner had taken longer than she wanted. Still, she thought, unlocking the door that led down below deck, at least she'd got a meal out of it. He had bought her a burger at Five Guys outside King's Cross.

'You put this guy in my lap, the least I can do,' he had said as she dictated her statement and blue-toothed across her report. She had no client to show it to. Jolene had not technically employed her.

Disarming the alarm and relocking the door, Raine flicked on the light. The interior was sparsely furnished, with just a queen-sized bed against one wall and a small gym set-up. The stern of the vessel housed a shower room and toilet. The rest of the space was taken up with a tiny sink and table beneath the canal-side window. On the table was a coffee pod machine and a single cup. There was also a micro-fridge. Raine did not own a cooker. She firmly believed life was too short for cooking, and her previous berth, on the Regent's Canal, had been within walking distance of any type of food she could think of, from anywhere in the world. Further along the bulkhead, she had a fold-down table she used for her laptop. All her files were kept digitally on a remote server. Any physical records were in a storage facility in Shoreditch. If her boat was stolen or torched tomorrow, she could be up and running somewhere else within a day.

Raine opened the fridge. In front of her were several protein drinks, some turmeric and mango shots, and a Mars bar. She took out the Mars bar.

The phone call from Jasper had fired her up. Usually, after a job ended, she would crash. She had been following Pirie for weeks, getting the lay of his organisation. Occasionally she would use Danny Brin — the twilight bouncer who had helped her on a previous assignment — to share the legwork, but he had been unavailable. Raine didn't mind. She'd enjoyed the job. Travelling to the north by train. Watching the scenery tick by. The last job she had done had nearly killed her. She had thrown herself into needless danger, intent on . . . what? Raine peeled back the wrapper and took a bite.

If she was honest with herself, she'd been intent on self-destruction. Putting herself in the way of trouble. Being unprofessional.

If she was really honest with herself, she had not yet processed the death of her wife. Clara had been the love of her life, the only person she could conceive of living with, and without her, she was lost. Had been lost.

But now she thought there was a glimmer. Of a future. It wouldn't be easy, and was probably going to be lonely, but there were small gaps in the fog of destruction that had seemed to envelop her for so long.

And one of those gaps was finding Heather Salim.

And finding Heather Salim began with finding Frankie Ridgeway. Jasper had been putting out some feelers, and now had some news for her.

As Raine munched methodically through her Mars bar she heard someone stepping onto the boat. Grabbing her phone, she scrolled to the security app that accessed the door camera. Outside was an anxious-looking woman in her sixties, wearing a pair of battered dungarees and a shapeless cardigan. She knocked tentatively on the door.

'Raine? Are you home?'

Raine shut her mobile and walked to the door, sliding back the bolts. She opened it, smiling at the startled woman.

'Jolene,' she said. 'Come in. I've got some good news for you.'

CHAPTER 4

Frankie Ridgeway regarded the man opposite him with disdain, watching as he sucked on the shisha pipe.

'You know those things are bacteria-collectors, right? Every bastard who tokes on it breathes their germs down.'

'Nah, man. They completely sanitise them after use.'

Ridgeway barked a laugh, sandpaper on metal. He took a drag on his own cigarette. 'Look around you, mate. You're in a backstreet shithole in Hastings, not some swanky Soho number. I doubt they even wipe them, let alone sanitise them.'

Even with the electric heaters, the tiny outside space hidden behind a high fence was freezing. Everything about Hastings was freezing. Dirty and cold and empty of any joy, as far as Ridgeway could see. He hated it. But business was business, and as London was a dead zone for him at present, he had to deal with the cards he had. The man on the other side of the table, deep-throating his infection pipe, was the contact for a speedboat coming in from France in the next few days. Most of the small boats would be stopped, of course. Or would sink. Whatever. But a few high-payers would make it through to this man, and the punters were paying extra for identity documents to validate their immigration status. Passports for a different origin country. Resident-status. Whatever was needed to let them stay. And Ridgeway could get them. Hence the meet. Beyond the small space he could hear the sea, the tide scritching and scraping the pebbles of the stony beach. Unending in its noise and pressure. Ridgeway loathed it. The sooner he could sod off back to civilisation the better.

'So, we have a deal?' he asked.

'Yeah, bruv,' said Shisha-man. Ridgeway hadn't even bothered to get his name. He took out his mobile phone and looked at him expectantly. Shisha reached up and pulled at a leather thong around his neck. Attached was a Ledge Nano X crypto wallet — a stick-like electronic storage device. Shisha folded back the metal covering to reveal an LED screen. With a few touches and swipes, a large sum of cryptocurrency was transferred into Ridgeway's Zengo account — a secure online vault.

Ridgeway nodded, taking a final draw of his fag and discarding it, grinding the butt under his boot as he stood. 'Cool. Send me through names, ages and photos. I'll message you when the documents are ready.'

Shisha nodded, smiling, but his eyes were concrete. 'That's a lot of money, bruv. Hard coin. You come recommended but don't fuck me about, yeah? I've got a rep to keep.' He leaned forward to take a pull on his pipe.

Ridgeway resisted the urge to rabbit-punch him, even though it would give him great satisfaction to watch the would-be gangster's head smash into the table.

'No problem,' was all he said, his voice light and pleasant. 'You'll have the papers. I've been doing this sort of thing a long time.'

CHAPTER 5

Hume entered the combined living room and kitchen of the third-floor flat she shared with her husband. A brittle light sliced across the apartment through the glass door that led to the balcony. Her skin still tingling from the shower, she surveyed her partner as he spooned porridge into a bowl. As well as the bacon and sliced banana, there was a plate of what seemed to be baked strawberries. The city beyond glittered in the late October air.

'Morning, darling,' said Robert cheerfully as he poured the orange juice. He leaned forward and kissed her gently on the neck. 'You smell nice.'

'I smell of coal-tar soap,' said Hume, drying off her grey crew cut with a towel and sitting at the table. 'And only you could think that smells nice. Sorry I was so late last night.'

'At least we managed most of our holiday before you were summoned. What do you want on your porridge; fruit, bacon . . .' Robert paused for a moment, one eyebrow arched. 'Both?'

Hume sighed. 'You've really got to stop watching cookery programmes.' She took the offered bowl of porridge and spooned the strawberries into it. She tried a tentative mouthful, nibbling at the fruit. Some of her husband's recent culinary efforts had been verging on the avant-garde and were barely food. The fruit was sweet and sticky and blended perfectly with the porridge. She raised her glass of orange juice to him. 'Delicious.'

'Thank you. Was it a bad one?' Robert dipped a bit of crispy bacon into his porridge, using it like a spoon. 'It must have been, to call you in straight from the airport.'

'I don't know about bad. It's a weird one, though.'

'Murder?'

'There was no body at the scene and no sign of a struggle.'

Robert looked at her in surprise, bacon poised between plate and mouth. 'Then why did Detective Echo need you?'

Hume gave him the rundown of her night at Aquinas Street. The leaves and the chair and the short video clip depicting the woman's murder.

'But surely there would be blood splatters and things? If she'd had her throat cut?'

'A lot of it,' agreed Hume. 'In the video, she was upright, bound to the chair . . .' Hume paused, looking at the porridge with swirls of pink strawberry through it. Carefully she pushed the bowl away. 'Well, let's just say at the very least the leaves should have been sodden with the stuff.'

'And they weren't?'

'Dry as a bone.'

'Weird. And you say they couldn't have blown in?'

'No. The leaves didn't come from the immediate area. Different tree varieties, apparently.'

'So they were what — transported there? Are you sure it isn't some sort of prank? Kids messing with you? It's only a few days until Halloween . . .'

'You know I'd probably go with that,' agreed Hume. 'But the video looked real. The woman appeared terrified.'

'But no body, no blood and no explanation?'

'That about sums it up, yes.'

'So why call you in?' asked Robert. 'There must have been something else to create this amount of urgency. You were VIP'd off the plane.'

Hume took a sip of her coffee. It was bitter and black and hit her like a punch. She felt her throat contracting. 'How much caffeine is in this?' she hissed, staring at it. Her heart felt like it was making a run for the door.

'Do you like it?' said Robert, beaming. 'I found it at Borough Market. It's made from the Robusta bean. Triple roasted and twice as strong as the Arabica, the woman said.'

Hume put the tiny cup down cautiously, as if it might explode. 'I think I might need to call in Environmental Services. This isn't coffee; it's nuclear waste.'

'I'm thinking of taking a barista course there. They do a morning taster session.'

Hume looked at her husband. 'Do you actually do any work at the museum, or do they just pay you for your looks? Because you seem to have endless amounts of time off.'

'Well that's the thing with extreme specialisms, isn't it? You are only needed periodically, but when you are, they have to pay through the back teeth.'

Hume arched an eyebrow. 'Oh yes? And what extreme specialisms are we talking about?' She was delighted to see that her husband actually blushed. 'It was the woman. The victim.'

'What was?' asked Robert, taking a hefty sip of his own coffee. Hume thought his stomach must be constructed of metal.

'The thing that made Echo call me in. It was the woman.'

'What about her?'

'It's Melissa Clarke.'

It took a few seconds for the name to register, and then Robert's eyes widened.

'Melissa Clarke? The woman who—'

Hume nodded, standing up. 'So you see why the screws were turned. I need to get to the office. There was plenty of material at the house to be analysed. Plus blood from a shoulder bag. Maybe Echo has got some DNA hits.'

As Hume stood and turned to get dressed, Robert said: 'I've booked us in for Friday, by the way. The usual table.'

Hume nodded. Friday would be her daughter's birthday. If she had lived. 'Good.'

'I wondered.' Robert's expression was tentative. 'Whether you wanted to ask Raine to join us?'

Hume kept her face neutral but felt her heart slip. 'I don't know, Robert. She's . . . It's complicated how I feel about her. I'm not sure it would be the right thing.'

'I know,' he said softly. 'But I think it's worth mulling over. It's been five years since Clara died. She was Raine's wife, as well as your daughter. I thought as you've been getting on so much better these last months . . .' Robert let the sentence hang, a question on his face.

Hume cocked her head. 'Did you just dot dot dot me?'

'Darling, you are a Detective Inspector of the Met. I would never dot dot dot you.'

Hume nodded. 'Good, because I'd have to leave you if you did. And I'll think about Friday.'

Robert watched her go before beginning to clear up the breakfast things.

'Melissa Clarke,' he muttered to himself as he loaded up the dishwasher. 'The papers are going to go insane.'

CHAPTER 6

Raine stepped out of Embankment tube station onto Villiers Street and climbed the steps to the Golden Jubilee Bridge. The morning air was crisp, and she felt it bite in her lungs. As she crossed over the Thames, Raine pulled out her phone. 'Wildfell!' she said cheerily when the bouncer answered. 'How's tricks?'

'Fine,' said Danny Brin. His weary sigh was clear over the ether. Raine had given him the nickname when she had discovered he was a fan of the Bronte sisters' books, *The Tenant of Wildfell Hall* being a favourite. 'And stop calling me Wildfell. What do you want, Raine? I'm working tonight and need to get some sleep.' Danny was employed as a door enforcer for several twilight clubs; venues that were not quite legitimate but were not fully criminal either. That was how he and Raine had met on a previous case. After a vicious attack that put Raine in hospital, Danny had taken on her recovery training, returning the detective to full fitness.

'Why do I have to want something?' she said. 'Maybe I just wish to share a moment with my friend.'

'Then phone one of them up and stop bothering me.' His voice was gruff, but the warmth in it was unmistakable.

'How rude,' said Raine, gazing out over the Thames as she walked. The weak sunlight skidded across the river's surface, making it shimmer. There was a skin of white mist snaking around the supporting piles of Hungerford Bridge to her left. 'But while we're chatting so nicely, I wonder how you're fixed for next Monday?'

'What's happening next Monday?' said Brin, sounding confused. 'I don't remember—'

'You wouldn't, because I've only just thought of it.' Raine neatly sidestepped a gaggle of tourists, who were looking at everything except where they were going. 'Can you meet me?'

'Why?'

'I've got a job for you.'

Brin's voice immediately became clearer. More focused. 'What sort of job?'

'I'd rather discuss it in person. Do you want to meet at my gaff? I'll do nibbles and everything.'

'Raine, it's nearly bloody winter. Your boat will be Baltic.'

'I'll put the heaters on; it will be warm as toast.'

There was a long pause, then: 'Is it a paying job?'

'Absolutely. Will you come?'

Another pause, before Brin finally spoke. 'What time?'

Raine smiled. 'Come at five and try not to look too scary.' She shut the phone, crashing the call, then took the steps down off the bridge. Under the structure, skate punks were practising their moves, the sound of their wheels and the clack of their boards echoing off the metal and concrete. She crossed over the road to the yellow entrance that led to the roof garden of the Queen Elizabeth Hall. The door at the top of the stairs was secured, but after tapping in the code Jasper had given her, there was a click and it unlocked. Raine stepped through. The garden was deserted, which, coupled with the cold air and her frosted breath, gave an unworldliness to the scene. Beyond the garden's boundary, Raine could see the London Eye, Portcullis House and St Stephen's Tower. A bustling London that housed nine million people. But from her vantage point, it was as if the city was empty. Like only she existed. For a second she thought she could feel a cool breath on her neck. A familiar scent caressing her. A welcome tightening of her heart that Clara always brought. Raine closed her eyes. When she opened them again, the feeling was gone. She stepped forward and looked around the garden. Jasper was sitting on one of the stone benches facing the north wall, a digital sketchpad in his hand. Beside him on a small table, a cigarette burned lazily in the battered sweet tin he used as an ashtray. He was dressed in his customary jeans and duster coat, like an urban cowboy. Only the slight tremble in his hand as it hovered above the pad gave away the brain trauma that had resulted from his recent beating. Raine smiled and strolled towards him.

'How come they let you up here, old man? The gardens are meant to be closed until next spring, no?'

Jasper ignored her, concentrating on the stylus as he shaded in a small area of his sketch. Satisfied, he put it down on the table and picked up his smoke. 'I'm thinking of hosting an event up here. The manager knows me from the old days.'

'The bad old days?' said Raine, her eyes fixed on what he was sketching. It was the garden, only covered in a blanket of snow, with fairy lights strewn around on posts.

Jasper nodded happily. 'He once put on a rave in the Docklands development. Over two thousand punters.'

'My mum and dad involved in that one?'

'Nah, they were in India.'

Raine nodded. There were large periods of her childhood when her parents disappeared, leaving her with friends in the bustling water-community behind King's Cross. She had once even spent a summer travelling the waterways of south England on a Romany barge, delivering coal to the boats that were wild-mooring. 'You said you had some information about Ridgeway?'

Jasper examined his cigarette, turning it in his fingers. Blue smoke snaked up from his gnarled hand. Even after the beating; even though he must be skirting seventy; even though he had spent a lifetime walking hard roads and dealing with even harder people, his eyes were clear. Lined and flecked with muddy pearls in his sclera, but clear. He still looked dangerous. 'Do you know what he was doing for Green, before you took him down?'

Raine shrugged. 'Collecting takings. Prostitution. Gambling. Drugs. He was the bag man.'

'And you stole it off him,' Jasper smiled. 'Which was why he had to leave London.'

'I wish I hadn't,' said Raine. 'If I'd left well alone, Green wouldn't have had you nearly battered to death.'

'If you hadn't, those women would have been killed,' said Jasper flatly. 'That was worth a slap or two.'

'I only saved one woman,' said Raine grimly.

'And all the ones who would have come after. Give yourself a break. And you're wrong. That wasn't all Ridgeway was doing for Green.'

'No? What else?'

'Seems sometimes Green couldn't source homegrown bait for his business and got Ridgeway to supply him with another body-stream. Not up to his normal spec, but would do in a pinch.'

'Where from?'

'Where do you think?'

Raine didn't have to think; the answer was pitifully obvious. 'Runaways. Sex workers. People under the radar.'

'All of the above,' agreed Jasper. 'But he also had contacts in the trafficking networks. Had done for years, my understanding. Seems Frankie was one of the OGs, way before the boats. Used to run the road routes in from Amsterdam when the drugs dried up. Containers full of human cargo.'

Raine remembered seeing the images on the news. Frightened and dehydrated people crammed into refrigerated lorries, blinking under the police torchlight. She also remembered cases of vehicles found abandoned on roadsides, their trailers packed with the desperate dead. Her mouth hardened. 'Why doesn't that surprise me?'

'Quite. Well, it seems that now you've burned London for him, he's relocated to the coast.'

Raine's eyes unfocused for a moment, then she nodded. 'In the boat business.'

'Possibly, but more likely the back end. My acquaintance used to be in the forgery business.'

'Why did you need a forger? Your gig was always clubs and raves.'

'Permits. Clone security passes. Sometimes even warrant badges.'

'What — police warrant badges? Why?'

Jasper grinned. 'Because arresting ourselves in front of actual police was a blast.'

'Don't forget I was a police officer once,' warned Raine, but she was smiling.

'Yes, but you're better now.' Jasper smiled back, but then the smile slipped from his face. 'Point is, my friend says a guy with a scar, like the one you gave Ridgeway, is new on the scene down on the coast. Comes connected with some nasty people up north. A player, my friend says. Not someone you mess with.'

'Sounds like my date,' agreed Raine. 'Where on the coast?'

'Hastings. He operates all across the South East, apparently, but his base is Hastings.'

'Brilliant. Thanks, Jasper. Ping me over what you have.'

'You really think he knows about this woman, Heather? The one who asked for your help?'

'Yes. I really think he does.'

Raine held out her elbow for him to bump, then started back to the gate.

'You seem better, you know,' said the old man.

She turned. 'Yeah?'

'Yeah. More yourself. Less careless. Before, you'd have made me tell you his address, then got straight on a train. No thought of personal safety. No consideration of consequences.'

'Well, I'm a more rounded human individual, now,' said Raine. 'I like to think really hard before I start hitting people's fists with my face.'

Jasper laughed. 'Look after yourself, Raine. I promised your folks I'd keep you safe but I'm too old to do anything but talk.'

Raine tipped two fingers to her forehead, turned and walked through the gate. As she strolled back across the bridge, she thought about what Jasper had said. Then she thought about her parents, both long gone.

Her phone buzzed. A message from Jolene. Raine read the message, pocketed the phone, and continued walking.

CHAPTER 7

Hume hung her jacket on the back of her chair and handed DS Echo a small glass bottle containing a murky liquid. 'Here. I know you want to live forever so I picked this up for you.'

'What is it?'

'I don't know, but it contains ginger and cost me five pounds, so you'd better drink it and feel brilliant.'

'Cheers, boss,' said Echo, taking the proffered gift with a smile. The room seemed to brighten from the reflection off his perfect teeth. As usual, his hair was stylishly mussy, framing his face along with the black rimmed round glasses. A koru, the small spiral tattoo Echo sported as a reminder of his Maori heritage, was clearly visible on the inside of his ear.

Hume sat on the edge of her desk and sipped her green tea. She could still feel the effects of Robert's death-coffee buzzing through her system. The day beyond the window was mortuary-grey. She shivered and turned her attention to the large smart screen on the office wall. All it contained at present was a headshot of Melissa Clarke. 'Bring me up to date. Have we got any DNA or fingerprints from the scene?'

'Lots,' said Echo. 'But nothing that says "Murderer".' He paused while he emptied the contents of the shot. 'Or "Murderee" for that matter.'

'Okay. But are we certain this is for us? Melissa Clarke is still missing, right?'

'Since two weeks ago. Missing Persons have her as an active case.'

'Which has nothing to do with her celebrity status, I'm sure.'

Echo picked up his tablet and began shifting data to the large screen. Hume thought of it as the Murder Screen. Back when she had started at the Met, they used to have a Murder Book: a folder where all the information that had been read and sorted by the investigative team would end up, ready for a detective to read. Now it was on an interactive smart screen where data could be moved about, edited and added to at the press of a button or the swipe of a hand. Hume knew it was better. More connected and comprehensive. But sometimes she felt overwhelmed by the sheer weight of the information that could be gathered. And as the data increased, the staff available seemed to decrease as budgets were squeezed. She was just grateful she had Echo there to decode everything for her.

'Sequence it out for me,' she said, sitting down.

Echo nodded. 'The bag was handed in at 3 p.m. yesterday. It was an hour before the footage was discovered and passed on to us. The clip was an MP4 video file. The metadata showed the approximate location of the shoot, but everything else was corrupted.'

'How did you get to the correct house?'

'It was the only one in the street not occupied. We got the key from the estate agent.'

'Okay. Check with them. See who's viewed the property recently. What can we get from the clip itself?'

'Not much. Digital forensics has had it, but so far can't tell if the footage is staged or real.' He swiped again, sending the video file onto the screen. He separated an image of the woman's face mid knife-stroke.

Hume winced. 'Looks pretty real to me.'

'When we gained access, it was clear the property had already been compromised.'

'Compromised? You mean someone had already broken in. Really, Etera, way too many American TV shows.'

Echo smiled. 'What can I say? I have no social life.'

'What about Bitz? I thought you and she were an item.'

Bitz was a software developer who coded for some hi-tech company in Shoreditch and lived in the same uber-modern housing block as Echo. Bitz was also a skater and culture-punk and Hume was pretty sure that she was using the wrong gender pronoun when talking about her, but didn't quite know how to ask.

Echo laughed. 'Bitz is nobody's item. If she heard you say that she'd accuse you of the commodification of romance.'

'Thank God I've got Robert,' muttered Hume. 'He *likes* being commodified. Life's already too complicated without having to double-think your love life.' She pointed at the screen with her drink. 'Tell me about Melissa Clarke.'

Echo nodded, happy to be off the subject of Bitz. 'Melissa Clarke. Investigative internet journalist. Host of *Deadtown*, an online interactive podcast. She's a new breed of true-crime blogger: she digs up some of the wilder cold-case murders in London and repackages them into a multi-interfaced experience for a mobile platform.'

Hume stared at him, stony-faced. 'And without the bollocks?'

'You can walk round the area with your phone and receive audio and visual material about the murders,' explained Echo. 'As if you're inside a TV documentary. She released one last year on the shooting outside the King's Arms in New Cross.'

'The rival drug firms from a couple of years back? Nasty.'

'Right. Melissa compiled all the data: interviews, photos, news snippets. Anything that existed in the public domain. Then she made an interactive narrative out of it, so that if you subscribed to her channel, you could walk around the murder scene and access the stuff all neatly packaged for infotainment.'

'Like a guided tour.'

'Exactly. You could stand outside the pub while an audio reel told you what had happened, then click on your phone to see actual images of the shooting. Police photos. Bystanders' commentary. Anything she could get her hands on.'

'Seems a bit ghoulish.'

'Murder tourism,' said Echo. 'She's very popular.'

'And then she disappeared, and the trolls came out of the woodwork,' said Hume. 'I remember the reports coming through.'

'Missing Persons have sent over the file. They couldn't wait to get rid of it, to be honest. As soon as her disappearance was made public, the internet theories began.' Echo held up his hand and began counting points off with his fingers. 'One of her old cases had pissed someone off and she had been abducted. One of her *new* cases had touched a nerve and she had been taken. She had faked her abduction for publicity. She was in rehab. She'd committed suicide.'

'How the internet loves to fill a void,' commented Hume, as a document box containing the Missing Persons files joined the board below the image of Melissa. In the photo she was staring straight at the camera, her black hair tied back in a professional, no-nonsense ponytail. Hume guessed it must be a publicity shot from her website. The woman seemed to be in her late twenties, with hard eyes behind round glasses. She wasn't smiling in the shot. Hume imagined that smiling in a murder blog was probably counter-productive to the mood. 'Refresh me. I didn't really follow it at the time.' She waved a hand in the vague direction of the window. 'Robert and I were on the way to Paddington.'

'I still can't believe you decided to just go on a train for your holiday.'

Hume smiled. She and Robert had caught the Eurostar to Paris for the evening, then taken the sleeper to Berlin. Then Prague. After that they had worked their way by train down to Barcelona. The slow pace of the holiday had been a welcome change from her job in London.

'We got a plane back,' said Hume. 'Luckily for you.'

'And don't think I'm not grateful. No way would I have wanted to explain this to a temp DI.' Echo made a face.

'Melissa,' Hume prompted.

'It was big news for a couple of days. The disappearance. The media speculated whether it might be a gangland hit. Or perhaps a mental health issue. They dug up an old flame who said she suffered from depressive episodes. Maybe self-harmed. But as the days went on with no leads, and no sign of foul play, the media lost interest. Or at least the heritage media. The internet warriors continued with the conspiracy chatter.'

'But it was never pushed our way? No one ever suspected she'd been murdered?'

'Nope. She was kept with Missing Persons, although the thinking was, behind closed doors, that she'd done a runner. There had been some online talk about her faking a couple of leads. Staging a couple of found footage clips of some old cases to bump up her profile.'

Hume studied the photograph. 'She doesn't look like a faker.'

'The good ones never do. That's why they're good at it.'

'Fair point. So no suggestion that she was being targeted by someone. That she was under threat?'

'No. Just missing. And not even for that long.'

Hume clicked her teeth together. 'DNA at our scene? On the door?'

'There's a lot of biological material to process. Both DNA and prints. We're getting everyone from the estate agent's to give samples so we can rule them out. Missing Persons have sent through Melissa's DNA for comparison but nothing yet. The labs are backed up.'

'Of course they are. What about the blood from the bag?'

'Same thing. Hopefully have the results today.'

'Fine. Run the clip again.'

They watched as the tied and gagged woman's eyes pleaded to the camera. Watched the blood tide out of the cut across her neck and down her front. Hume felt a tightness at her scalp and a throb deep in her chest as she watched the light dim, then finally go out in the woman's eyes. Hume watched, mouth drawn tight, as the young woman's head fell forward, her glasses falling off her face.

'The glasses were there, by the way,' said Echo, freezing the feed. 'Next to the chair, just where they would have fallen. There was no DNA or fingerprints on them. They had been wiped clean.'

'No body,' said Hume.

'No body.'

'So the killer moved it after filming her death?'

'I don't see how. That amount of blood would be impossible to clear up.'

'Maybe a spill sheet was hidden under the leaves,' mused Hume. 'So that afterwards the whole mess could be folded away.'

'And then the killer set down a new set of leaves to replace them?'

Hume shook her head. 'It doesn't make sense.'

'A hoax, maybe? Sick publicity stunt? Something to bump the clicks?'

Hume didn't think so. The terror in the woman's face leaked out of the screen.

'Find out what she was working on, as well as what she'd published recently,' said Hume. 'Maybe she rattled the wrong person's cage.'

'Boss.'

Echo continued uploading data onto the screen. Photos of the house. Of the chair. Of the glasses.

'How about CCTV of the area?' asked Hume, sipping at her tea.

'None of the street itself. We're checking the surrounding area but without an exact time there is a lot of footage to go through. We're also knocking on doors and collecting streams from door cameras.'

Hume glanced through the internal glass wall to the open office space beyond. 'Where's Jonas? Shouldn't he be dealing with this?'

'On loan to Woolwich,' said Echo. 'Since the cutbacks we're having to share him with other boroughs. We've got a couple of uniforms doing the donkey work, and the data trawling has gone to the digital department upstairs. Unless something breaks, like we get an actual body, then we're in the queue, I'm afraid. No body, no budget.'

'Okay. What about the leaves?'

Hume watched as several images of the house arrived on the screen. The hallway, with its dim lighting. The peeling wallpaper. The room with the chair was brightly lit by lamps brought in by SOCO. The leaves on the floor were a greyish brown and reminded Hume of shed skin. They looked as if they would crackle if you walked through them. There was something deeply disconcerting in their presence. They just shouldn't be there. She remembered how she'd felt on seeing them last night. The house had been tomb-cold, and the leaves were like dead insects on the floor.

'Well, they were not from any of the trees on the street. Wrong shape.'

Hume frowned. 'So the killer, or hoaxer, or whatever this is, brought them and planted them there. Why?'

Echo didn't answer. The question wasn't directed at him.

'Find out whose bag it is. And see if you can identify the leaves; they're creeping me out. Do we have an address for any friends or work colleagues? Maybe her parents?'

'We have the mother and Melissa's work partner.'

'Right. We'll start with the mother. Get on to the paper that printed the old flame story. Get an address. Let's see if she's faking it and is holed up somewhere.'

'Do you think it's a hoax, boss?'

Hume thought about the video clip of Melissa having her throat cut and shook her head.

'No, but we need to check.'

CHAPTER 8

Raine whistled appreciatively at the girl in front of her. 'Nice set of rails!'

Libby smiled shyly, her lips pressed tightly together. Jolene had told Raine that several of the girl's teeth had been broken in the assault; one completely knocked out. The rails were the parallel scars that ran from above the girl's left collarbone, down her chest to just below her right breast. Raine could see the top of the wounds protruding from her baggy tee. The scars were new; red and raised. Libby reached out and touched them gingerly.

'The doctors think they will fade a little in time, but they'll always be there, yeah? That fucker put a permanent mark on me.'

The girl's accent wasn't London street, but had a lilt of the capital to it. Raine caught the glimpse of a jagged tooth when she spoke.

'Libby!' admonished Jolene. 'Watch your language.'

'I'd say "fucker" was about right,' said Raine, matter-of-factly, keeping her eyes on the young woman. 'You're being let out today?'

'Just been signed off. I can go home.'

Raine saw the determination in her face. In the set of her small shoulders. But underneath, a shadow of fear seemed to flow, causing her to shuffle and twitch. Alert to every sound and movement.

'It will take a while,' said Raine softly. 'To feel safe. But the more you take control of your recovery, the more you lay plans for the future, the easier it will get.'

Libby nodded, the thin smile back again, but Raine could see it was only holding on by a thread.

'Thank you so much for your help,' said Jolene. 'Just knowing that . . . that—'

'Fucker,' said Raine and Libby at the same time. Libby giggled, putting a hand to her ruined mouth, and Raine gun-cocked a thumb and finger at her.

'Yes. He's not on the streets anymore. It's something. It's a start.'

'Where are you staying?' Raine asked Libby.

'She's not going back to that estate,' said Jolene firmly. 'Not yet. She's coming to live with me for a while. Until she feels strong.'

Raine heard the steel in the old woman's voice. Saw the metal determination in her kind face. Raine knew that you didn't survive living on a boat in central London for years by being soft, no matter how much of a hippy librarian you seemed. 'Good for you,' she said. 'Do you need me to get a lift for you?'

'I've ordered an Uber. You've done enough.'

Raine nodded at Jolene and offered a fist to Libby. After a moment's hesitation, she bumped it. Jolene didn't. Instead, she gave Raine a hug that threatened to break her ribs.

'Thank you,' she whispered in her ear, before letting her go and walking slowly away down the corridor, her grandniece at her side.

Raine watched them for a moment. The young woman's back was straight, but she moved warily, as if at any minute she might be attacked. Raine took out her phone and unfolded it.

'Mary!' she said, when Hume answered. 'How was the Orient Express? Did you and Robert dress up as Marple and Poirot? 'Cos if you did, I want pictures.'

'Raine.' Hume's voice was clipped, but even through the airwaves, the DI's voice held a thread of warmth. 'It wasn't the Orient Express and I'm working. What do you want?'

'Lunch. Specifically, with you. I've got some information.'

'I heard about the county lines. DI Conner is just about ready to name his next child after you.'

'And what a lucky child that would be. But no, not that. Different information. Are you available?'

'As long as it's central, I can probably manage a quick bite in an hour or so.'

'Great. How about I meet you at Brick Lane Community Gardens?'

'Raine, it's bloody freezing.'

'Honestly, it will be fine. I'll buy you a bagel.'

Raine closed the phone, ending the call.

CHAPTER 9

Hume and Echo stood shivering on the doorstep of a small house in Sudbury. It looked exactly like the other houses on this estate. Clean and functional, thrown up in the eighties, with no stamp of individual design. A place to exist when not at work.

'Should we show her the image from Aquinas Street?' asked Echo, as they waited for the door to be answered. 'I could crop it to just the face.'

'Not yet,' said Hume. 'Without a body or a ransom note, I don't think it would serve any purpose. We don't need a formal identification. But maybe we ask about the house itself. See if there is a connection.'

'Understood.'

Hume was about to knock on the door again when it was flung open by a woman in her mid-forties. Her nostrils flared as she glared at them. Hume thought she looked ready for a fight.

'Yes?'

'Mrs Pauline Clarke?' Echo held up his warrant card. 'DS Etera Echo and DI Mary Hume. I wonder if we could come in?'

'This is about my bloody daughter, isn't it? Have you found her?'

Echo blinked, recalibrating. 'Sorry, no.'

The woman's face remained hostile. 'Then why are you here?'

'Just following up on enquiries, Mrs Clarke,' said Hume smoothly. 'I take it she hasn't been in touch?'

'Of course not. Why would she? She knows she's not welcome.' The woman began to close the door.

'Mrs Clarke,' cut in Hume, smiling her most professional smile. 'Pauline. We would appreciate a moment of your time. Melissa might be in trouble.'

The woman glared at them for a moment longer, then sighed, grudgingly opening the door. 'If you must.'

She led them through a bare corridor to a small kitchen. The inside of the flat was clean to the point of cruelty. Every surface seemed to have been scrubbed or polished to within an inch of its life. There was no sense of comfort or warmth in the space.

'I haven't got long,' said Pauline, standing with her arms crossed. 'What is it you want?'

'When was the last time you saw your daughter?' asked Hume.

'A couple of years ago. She called round trying to tap me for money.' The woman let out a dismissive breath. 'Bloody scrounger. I told her to go and get a proper job, instead of messing about trying to be an influencer or whatever.'

'You weren't a fan of her podcast?' asked Hume, interested. 'It was my understanding the show was well received.'

'By kids, maybe,' sneered Mrs Clarke. 'Sitting in the dark staring at their laptops. If she was a real journalist she'd be working for a newspaper or something. Not that anybody would have her.'

Hume studied the woman. She sounded like she was reading from a script, or spouting somebody else's opinion. But whose?

'Are you in touch by phone or online? Do you know if she's had any problems recently?' asked Echo. 'Perhaps with somebody from one of her pieces? Somebody she'd upset?'

Mrs Clarke gave a harsh laugh. It sounded like she'd swallowed a cup of wasps. 'No, we're not in touch, and as for upsetting people I imagine there's a waiting list. Problems stick to her like glue. Stuck-up bitch never knew when to shut up. That's why Derek left.'

'Who's Derek?'

'Derek Evans, my partner. Ex-partner now.' Mrs Clarke pulled out a pack of smokes from her shirt pocket, screwing one between her lips and firing it up. She didn't ask if the detectives minded. 'Melissa drove him away.'

'Really? How?'

Mrs Clarke's eyes cut sideways. 'It doesn't matter. She accused him of certain things. In one of the internet things she did. All lies, of course. That girl couldn't tell the truth if she swallowed it.'

'What did she accuse him of?' asked Echo.

Mrs Clarke sucked on her cigarette, not meeting his eyes. 'Like I say, it doesn't matter now. What's she done, anyhow? You said she might be in trouble. What does that mean?'

'She hasn't been seen for a few days,' said Echo. 'And there are indications that she could be in danger.'

'Oh that,' said Mrs Clarke dismissively. 'Yeah, I saw it in the news. Probably one of her scams. The girl was always scheming. Ever since she was at school. Spying on her classmates. Spying on Derek. She used to run away regularly. Always trouble.'

A sense of outrage and defiance shone out of this woman, but underneath was the sheen of despair. Hume wondered what had happened with Derek, and made a mental note to look him up later.

'Has anybody called for her? Or perhaps phoned to ask where she was living now?'

'I told you already. I don't have anything to do with her.'

'I understand. I wonder if we could see a recent photograph of Melissa? If we could scan a copy, that would be very helpful.'

'Do you know what that little bitch did?' Mrs Clarke's voice had become quiet. Venomous. 'She stole Derek's phone. Sent horrible stories to all his contacts. Lies about what he was like.'

'When was this?'

'As if I wouldn't know what my man was like. She was just jealous.'

'How old was she when she moved out, Mrs Clarke?'

'Sixteen. But even then she went on causing trouble. Bombarding Derek with emails and that. Accusing him of all sorts.'

'Like what?'

'It doesn't matter. It was all made up. But it took its toll on Derek. In the end, he couldn't take any more.' She stubbed the cigarette out violently in the ashtray. 'Left me. She drove him out. I hope the slag gets a proper comeuppance.'

Be careful what you wish for, thought Hume, as she gazed at Melissa's mother lighting another cigarette.

* * *

'Well, that was fun,' said Echo, as they made their way off the small cul-de-sac. 'But at least we know Melissa's not hiding out there.'

'I don't think she's hiding out anywhere, but we have to check. See if you can find this Derek,' said Hume, her tone clipped, white breath punching out into the cold air. 'Find out if he's on any register. The way Mrs Clarke was talking it sounds like he might have been abusing Melissa.'

'And she fought back? Exposed him to his friends and workmates?'

'Maybe. And if she did, I wouldn't have thought he'd have taken it well.'

'Enough to kill her?' said Echo doubtfully. 'And mock her by doing it like one of her podcasts?'

'Seems a bit over the top,' admitted Hume, 'but let's check him out.'

Echo unfolded his phone and made notes as they walked back to the car.

'Okay,' she said, as they climbed into the vehicle. 'You go back to the station and start collating what we have so far. You can drop me at Melissa's flat. Call for a uniform to meet me there. I want to take a look at where she lived. Viewing things from a different perspective might throw up something new.'

* * *

Drake House, a shabby post-war apartment block, couldn't have been more different from Pauline Clarke's house. It was chasing shabby and running hard at dilapidated. But the man standing in the doorway of the ground-floor flat gave almost exactly the same response as Pauline Clarke had.

'What do you want?'

Melissa's flatmate was not in a good mood. When Hume showed him her warrant card, she could see his features pinching in distaste. It appeared she had woken him. His hair was dishevelled and there were bed creases in his face. Hume would put him in his early thirties, but it was hard to tell. His face seemed older. Or maybe, she thought, it was just his persona that had seeped out of his pores. As he had opened the door and seen the policeman standing next to her, Hume had got a whiff of old sweat and ganja.

'Sir, I am Detective Inspector Hume and this is Constable Marsh. We would like—'

'She's not here. I don't know where she is. I've told you lot again and again, if she comes back, I'll let you know.' He made to shut the door, but Hume put a hand up to stop him.

'Yes, sir, I understand. Please could you tell me your name?'

'My name?' The young man looked at her suspiciously. 'Why do you want my name?'

'Because I expected to find the flat empty. It was my understanding Melissa lived alone. Are you her partner?'

There had been no partner listed on the Missing Persons file. Hume had only called round to make sure Melissa hadn't returned. She was still waiting on a warrant to search the property.

The man smirked. 'Yes I'm her partner, but not in the fuck-buddy sense. We work together.'

'And your name?' repeated Hume politely. The man looked slightly disappointed she hadn't reacted to the provocative language.

'Oliver Bell,' he said after a pause.

'Thank you, Oliver. Could you tell me when was the last time you saw Melissa?'

'I don't know. Maybe a month ago. Your lot interviewed me.'

'Here?' said Hume.

Oliver was clearly uneasy. 'No. I wasn't living here then.'

It was Hume's turn to pause. 'You mean you've moved in here since she disappeared?'

'No,' said Oliver, an indignant expression on his face. Then: 'Well, yes. But I often stay here. Like when we're working on an episode and stuff. I sleep on the sofa.' He reached into the pocket of his jeans. 'I have my own key.'

'Right. Do you mind if we come in, Oliver?'

'Why? I've told you she's not here.'

Hume took a deep breath, before explaining. 'Oliver. You are residing in the property of someone who is missing. You have no legal right to be here. Two police officers have arrived at Melissa's door, only to find it answered by a stranger. What do you think we should do?'

He hesitated for a moment, calculating. *I bet he's left his drugs on the table*, thought Hume. *Or maybe on the floor next to the sofa.*

'Okay,' he said. 'But give me a minute to tidy up.'

'It's all right, Oliver,' said Hume, stepping past him into the flat. 'We're police officers. We don't mind a little mess.'

'Wait, what?' Alarmed, Oliver rushed past her, leaving the uniformed officer to close the door. By the time Hume entered the living room Oliver was hurriedly stuffing something into his pocket while trying hard to seem nonchalant.

'Sorry. I only got in at four. Pulled a skeleton shift at the warehouse.'

'I thought you worked on the show? Or guide. Whatever it is,' asked Hume, as her eyes quickly took in the surroundings.

'I did. Do. But London's so sodding expensive.' He shrugged.

The flat was small and barely furnished. There was the sofa, with a duvet slipping off it onto the wooden planked floor, a TV, and that was it. On the wall was a poster that proclaimed:

WELCOME TO DEADTOWN

Hume guessed it was a promotional poster Melissa had commissioned. The Ws were crossed curved swords, the Os made to look like bullet-holes, and blood dripped down from the L and the T.

'Yeah. I designed that,' said Oliver, following her gaze, a hint of pride in his voice. 'It's a still from the show's promo. We put it out on YouTube.'

'Right,' said Hume. She pointed at the sofa. 'And this is where you sleep?'

Oliver nodded. He looked tired. Not the sort of tired you get when you've pulled an all-nighter, but the sort of tired you get when you've been worrying about something. The sort of tired you get when you haven't been sleeping well for a while.

'And where were you before? When Melissa went missing? You said you weren't here.'

'In a van. I've got a spot on Tressillian Road.'

Hume glanced sideways at the constable, who nodded. 'In South London, ma'am. A couple of minutes from Brockley tube. Lots of vans there.'

'You sleep in a van?' asked Hume, turning back to Oliver.

'I *live* in a van,' corrected Oliver. 'About the only affordable option in this city. It's a nice little community. In the summer the park's a blast, but now, in the winter . . . Well, my power runs off solar. If I need to get work done, I have to rent space in an office. I'm a freelance audio editor. When I started collaborating with Mel on *Deadtown*, I worked from here. Like I say, I've got a key and she lets me stay over.'

'But unofficially. You're not paying rent.'

'No. It's just a bit of sofa-surfing.'

'And so when she went missing, you what, moved in?'

'You're making it into something it's not,' protested Oliver. 'When I came round to do work a couple of weeks ago and found—' He glanced at the officer examining the ashtray on the floor. Hume saw there was the nub of a blunt in there. '—a bunch of uniforms along with the landlord, I was freaked. They asked me a bundle of questions, but you're barking up the wrong tree. Mel sometimes goes away for a few days. Couple of weeks even. Chasing down a story or whatever. It's no big deal.'

'So why was it this time?' asked Hume. 'What was different?' She realised that she hadn't actually asked Echo how Melissa's disappearance had been reported. Why it had caught the media's imagination.

Oliver's gaze slid to the poster on the wall. 'Well, it was the fans, wasn't it? The subscribers. They started posting that she had been abducted or whatever. The whole thing just spiralled.'

'But you think there's no problem. And you just moved in here to keep the place warm until she comes back?'

Oliver said nothing. Just shrugged insolently once again. *Like a teenager who'd been caught stealing money from his mother's purse,* Hume thought.

'Could we see Melissa's room?'

'What, you think I'm hiding her or something?' Some of Oliver's arrogance returned.

'She's missing, Oliver. People are worried. We turn up and find a man occupying her flat with no legal grounds to be here. We find drugs being consumed. And—'

'Hey! What drugs? You mean a couple of spliffs? For fuck's sake—'

'And when we ask to check her room, we find that person doesn't seem to want us to investigate. That makes us curious.'

Suddenly, there was a new light in his eye. It took Hume a moment to work out what it was: excitement.

'Something must have happened. Not an accident or anything. Something that you're not telling me.' He looked at the uniformed officer, then back at Hume. Taking in her lack of uniform. Reassessing. 'You're a detective, right? You're not just here because she broke the law or something. You said you were worried about her. What's happened?'

'Could we see her bedroom please, Oliver? We really need to know where Melissa is.'

'She's not in there. I told you.'

Hume could have said that most violent crime was domestic, carried out by people the victim knew. Even had an intimate relationship with. Instead, she said: 'Melissa is missing, Oliver, and it's vital we find her as soon as possible. We are concerned that something may have happened to her. We would like to have a quick look in her room to see if there's anything that could shed some light on where she is now.'

'Don't you need a warrant or something?'

'Actually, no. Not when we think someone might be in danger. Plus, you invited us in. But I really would like your cooperation. You seem to be someone close to her. A friend and work colleague who could help us understand her movements over the last few weeks.' Hume spun him a smile. 'Someone who has the inside track, as it were . . .'

Oliver glanced at the bedroom door, then out of the window, then back to Hume. He shrugged his thin shoulders again. 'Yeah, whatever, man. If Mel is in trouble, anything I can do to help.'

'Thank you,' she said. 'You know, I'd love a cup of tea.'

'Sure,' said the young man after a beat. She could tell he didn't want to leave her. Wanted to go into the room with her. She was under no illusions. Oliver Bell had got the scent. He smelled a story. No way did Hume want him around while she surveyed Melissa's room. She smiled as he left for the kitchen, then she walked across the room, slipping a pair of nitrile gloves out of her pocket. Opening Melissa's bedroom door, she stood and took in the small space. The neatly made single bed. The laptop open on the desk, screen dead. The micro studio set-up. Hume saw that rails hung all around the room with floor-length curtains. She guessed it was for when Melissa was recording, to deaden the sound. *Melissa clearly lives and breathes her work*, thought Hume, before correcting herself. Lived.

Because even though there was no body, Hume believed the young woman was dead. Murdered on camera for reasons unknown. She didn't know why, and she didn't know by whom, but she felt in her bones that Melissa Clarke was no longer alive.

In Melissa's bedroom Hume first checked the items on the desk. There was a professional make-up set in a rolled leather case; a discreet vape device and a tube of mints. There was also a selection of batteries and a portable Tascam recording unit. Hume nodded to herself. Any reporter or journalist worth their salt would have a fully charged supply of replacement batteries. There would be nothing worse than running out of power at the crucial moment.

Apart from having your throat sliced open, of course.

Hume absently opened a drawer, but was uncertain what she was looking for. A diary maybe, but she suspected Melissa would use something a bit more digital. Something on her phone. A calendar app. Hume turned and walked back into the living room. Oliver was sitting on the sofa, three cups of tea on the table. He was messaging on his phone. Hume had a pretty good idea of what he was writing.

'Could you tell me what you and Melissa are working on right now, Oliver?'

'Sorry, that's confidential. Ongoing, you get me?'

Hume nodded. 'Fair enough. When was the last time you saw Melissa?'

'What's happened to her, Detective Inspector . . . Hume, is it?' He pointed at the pocket she had returned her warrant card to. 'What do you believe has happened to Melissa? Are the rumours true then? Is she in danger?'

Hume had no doubt she was being recorded. Possibly filmed.

'We are just concerned, Oliver. Surely you are too?'

'Of course, but you have barged your way into her home—'

'Sir, I hardly think—' began the uniformed constable, walking forward, but Hume stopped him.

'How many coats does Melissa have?'

'What?'

'Coats,' said Hume patiently. 'How many does she have? It's freezing out there.'

'One,' said Oliver, a puzzled frown on his face. 'An old army coat. It's good for the optics.'

'Would she have gone out without her coat on?'

'No, of course not,' said Oliver, baffled. 'She's a reporter.'

'What about batteries? Spare batteries for the equipment? Would she have left them behind?'

For the first time since they had arrived, Oliver seemed worried. 'No way. You never know—'

'What about her recording device? How many does she have?'

'One. Plus her phone. Look, can you—'

'Thank you,' Hume cut him off again, and moved back into the bedroom. The batteries in their charging nest blinked back at her, all the lights green. The charger was full, with no empty spaces. Hanging on the back of the door was a camouflage army jacket, old and faded but clean. Plenty of pockets. Good for the optics. She stared at it for a moment as the room ticked around her. She could hear the two men talking in the other room but didn't pay them any attention. She turned back and examined the desk. Something was nagging at her. Something that set her brain tingling. The desk wasn't cluttered, but it was untidy. The rest of the room was neat, but everything on the desk looked like it had just been dumped haphazardly.

By the side of the desk was a wastebin full of sweet wrappers and balled-up pieces of paper. Empty vape packets. Sitting on top was a blue asthma inhaler. Hume picked it up and examined it. She pushed in the cylinder and a puff of vapour shot out of the nozzle. She put it back in the bin and scrutinised the desk again. Eventually, she saw it. The thing that had bitten into her subconscious. A hangnail, snagged in the cracked veneer of the desk, near the side of the battery pack, sticking up like it wanted to ask her a question.

Hume returned to the living room. 'Oliver, did Melissa have asthma? Some breathing difficulties?'

Oliver looked at her like she was insane. 'This is London, yeah? The levels of airborne toxins are way above what is legal. If we were still in the—'

'Would she go out without her inhaler,' Hume interrupted, the urgency in her voice cutting through.

'No. Course not.'

Hume turned to the uniformed officer. 'Call in forensics. She was snatched from here. This is the primary location.'

'What?' said Oliver. 'What do you mean "snatched"?'

The officer began speaking into his lapel mic while Hume focused on Oliver. 'I'm afraid you'll have to come with us, Oliver.'

'No way,' began Oliver, incredulity in his voice. 'You're arresting me?'

'Not at all,' smiled Hume. 'We just need to interview you formally to establish what you know.'

'Right,' said Oliver. 'And then I can come back?'

'I'm afraid not. Not here. This site is now a crime scene.'

Hume turned away from the protesting Oliver and walked out of the flat, pulling her phone out of her jacket.

'Boss,' Echo said, when the call connected. 'We've got preliminary DNA back from Aquinas Street. There's no way anybody was murdered there. Maybe the hoax theory—'

'She's dead,' said Hume. 'I know it. Check the records from Missing Persons. Did they search the flat?'

'Hang on.' There was a pause and the sound of tapping. 'Landlord let them in. There was no sign of a struggle. They did a welfare search to make sure no one was in trouble and then left.'

'It's been cleaned up, but she was definitely taken from here against her will. I want you to get a team down here and take it apart. Also, there's a lodger here, of sorts. I need you to interview him at—' Hume poked her head back round the door.

'Where are you based?'

'Whitechapel, ma'am.'

'At Whitechapel station,' Hume relayed to Echo.

'We can't interview him at Melissa's flat?'

'No, and he has no permanent address. It needs to be the station.'

'Will you wait for me at the site?'

'I need to be somewhere else. I'll meet you at Whitechapel. If I'm not there, start without me. We need to know what story Melissa was working on.'

CHAPTER 10

Hume spotted Raine immediately as she entered the Brick Lane Community Gardens. She was sitting on a bench staring into the flames crackling in the firepit. Hume held back, watching her for a moment. In the shimmer of the heated air, the woman seemed to go in and out of focus. Hume felt a weight as time seemed to fracture.

'I love her, Mum. She just gets me.'

The words Clara, her daughter, had said to her a few weeks before she'd married Raine. Barely a year before she had died. Even from this distance Hume could see the metal key cache Raine kept attached to a belt loop in her cargo pants. Hume knew what was inside. The ashes of her daughter. The last physical remains, the rest scattered and lost. Hume took a deep breath and stepped forward.

'I could invoke the 1990 Environmental Protection Act and have that fire put out,' she said, taking a seat next to Raine.

'Nah. The *Raine-is-bloody-freezing Act* supersedes it. I've brought you a bagel. Salt beef.' She reached down and picked up a greasy brown paper bag. Hume reached in and took out the sandwich. Raine removed hers and they sat in silence for a few moments, eating and staring at the embers as they sparked into the sky like fireflies.

'These are from the shop on Brick Lane,' said Raine eventually, examining her food. 'Do you know they've been there since before Hitler? Survived two world wars without shutting. Open 24/7 all year round.'

'They must be tired,' said Hume. The bagel was delicious. She made a mental note to pick some up for Robert.

'All the antisemitism riots of the early twentieth century and they kept going. That's dedication for you.'

'Why am I here, Raine?'

'Two reasons. Three if you count the fact that you crave my company. Number one: Heather Salim.'

'You've found out about her? What happened?' said Hume, surprised. Secretly she believed the woman to be dead.

'No, but I've got a lead on Frankie Ridgeway, and I'm hoping he'll help me find her.'

'And why would he do that?' said Hume. 'The last time you saw him you knocked him out with a brick.'

'Half brick, and it was just a love-tap,' countered Raine.

'He's dangerous, Raine. If you do find him, you need to take back-up. Like the police.'

'I was the police, Mary. Remember?'

Hume nodded. Before Raine became a private detective she had been a police officer. Then came the death of Clara. The mental breakdown. The instability that had placed her on a permanent hiatus from the force.

'I remember. Why are you telling me, then? What can I do to help?'

'Heather's parents. Don't you think it was weird that they arranged for her body to be cremated? That's just not a Muslim thing.'

'Agreed, but not illegal. There was no reason not to release her body into their custody.'

'Yes, but it's *really really* not a Muslim thing. Could you check it out again for me, please? Chase them up or whatever. It nags at me.'

Hume sighed. 'We're short-staffed as it is, but I'll see if Echo can spare an email or two. What's the other reason? You said two.'

'What was the name of the dentist who fixed my tooth? The Goth one.'

Hume gave an inward shudder. Although the dentist had taken a shine to her and Echo on a previous case, the woman still sent a shiver down her spine. There was something vampiric about her. 'Ms Arnold.'

'That's it!' said Raine, smiling. 'Do you know if she does any *pro bono* work?'

'Why? Are you that poor?'

'The county lines bust you mentioned? The reason I got involved was because the grandniece of a friend of mine got battered for standing up to them.'

'How bad?'

'Hospital bad. She'll be okay but her teeth got trashed. I thought Lady Dracula might be able to help.'

A wicked smile spread across Hume's face. 'I'll get Echo to pop over. Ask her in person.' Echo had been afraid of the dentist ever since she'd shown an almost arachnid interest in him when they first met.

'That's great, Mary. She's a good kid, trying to do the right thing. I want to help. So what's going on with you?'

Hume gave her a brief synopsis of what had happened since her return. The house on Aquinas Street and the missing body.

'Wow,' said Raine when she had finished. 'Melissa Clarke. I wouldn't want to be you when the media gets wind. It'll be a fuckstorm.'

A couple of middle-aged men in painfully on-brand ethical identi-clothes tutted from further down the bench. Raine smiled at them and stuffed the rest of her bagel in her mouth, throwing the packaging in the firepit.

'I'm hoping to close it off before then,' said Hume. 'If it goes public then it will be a mess. It's already got the conspiracy junkies sniffing around.'

'Let me know if I can help,' said Raine, as she rose to her feet. 'I need to boogie. Got to see a man about a pier.'

As she began walking away, Hume called out: 'About number three . . .'

Raine turned and looked back at her. 'What?'

'Number three on your list.'

Raine cocked her head, her eyes wide. 'Yes?'

Hume took a deep breath. 'I do. I do crave your company.'

The two women locked eyes. Hume's heart hammered in her chest. She wanted to say more. More about how she was sorry. How the years of continued love for her daughter that Raine felt was clear to her. How she couldn't bear to see Raine hurt. How she just wanted to be able to sit by this fire and talk about Clara with her until all the pain had run out of their bodies. But instead, she held her breath.

Raine remained motionless. Finally, she smiled. 'Clara really loved you. You know that?'

Hume felt like crying. 'I really loved her. And I'm sorry we—'

'Even when you were being an arse.'

Hume blinked, but before she could reply Raine had turned and strolled away, hands in pockets. Her hair was crammed beneath her beret, and from behind she could have been any age. Any sex. Hume stayed watching as she slipped between the gates to the garden. Even when she could no longer see her, Hume stayed watching.

CHAPTER 11

She looks nice.

Well, not nice. Even in the cold she's beginning to decay. There's not much to do about that. Not without a lot of intervention.

Embalming. Replacing the eyes with glass. Sewing her up so the insides don't fall out.

Uh-uh. Not worth it. She's only meat. Just a red flag on a board. Anything that was her, actually her, is gone.

I'll burn her soon.

Still. Better her than me.

CHAPTER 12

'We got the cell number for Melissa from Missing Persons. I've confirmed that it was the same one Oliver had. Made sure there wasn't another she used for work.'

Hume and Echo were in their office behind Charing Cross Road. By the time she had left Raine, her DS had messaged to say they had let Oliver Bell go.

'All I could do was confirm he was who he said he was, take his contact details and let him go. I've arranged a time for him to come back for a formal interview.'

'But he'd moved into her flat without permission,' protested Hume. She wasn't happy with the young journalist. Her instinct told her he knew things he wasn't telling them.

'He had texts on his phone validating his story. Melissa saying he could stay over whenever he wanted. We've confirmed that the texts came from her.'

'Or at least from her phone. Do we know where her phone is now?'

Echo shook his head. 'It hasn't been active since she went missing. But the good news is that Oliver and Melissa had a link on their map app.'

'What sort of link?'

'When they were working together they would location-share. Just in case one of them got into trouble, Oliver says.'

Hume's face creased. 'What, like Google maps or something?'

'Exactly. Each of them could see where the other's phone was in real time. He said Melissa insisted on it. Because of the cold cases they'd investigated for the *Deadtown* podcast, she thought it was a necessary safety precaution.'

Not so flaky, then, thought Hume. *Taking safety precautions and thinking about the team. Not just herself.* Aloud she asked: 'Are the routes archived on the app?'

'Absolutely.'

'So we can see where she's been?' said Hume excitedly.

'Yes. But don't get your hopes up. I've had a cursory glance. On the surface there's nothing untoward. Short trips around Whitechapel, presumably shopping. A journey to Brockley.'

'Where Oliver keeps his van,' nodded Hume. 'Who lives in a van, anyway?' She waved a hand dismissively, as if the concept offended her.

'Well, Raine lives in a boat. That's just a van without wheels.'

'Don't be smart.'

Echo smiled innocently.

'Speaking of Raine,' said Hume, 'she's asked if you could do her a favour.' Hume went on to explain Raine's request for a follow-up about Heather Salim's parents.

'No problem,' said Echo, making a note on his tablet. 'I'll fire off an email later to the station that made the original contact with them. See what information they can give me.'

'Great, thanks.' Hume glanced at the board. Melissa's image stared back. 'Where else did Melissa go, other than the van?'

'She spent some time in King's Cross. Upton. A trip to Basingstoke. Looks like she visited the National Archives in Richmond, presumably for research. I'm cross-referencing with the back catalogue from the *Deadtown* productions

— and I've asked Oliver to compile a list of upcoming projects. Between them I hope to eliminate most of the journeys.'

'But nothing is standing out? What about the final location?'

'Her flat, I'm afraid.'

'And do we know where Oliver was at that time?'

'At work in the warehouse.'

Hume gazed at the smart board. 'And he couldn't have nipped out on a break or anything helpful?'

'Nope. It's one of those places where you're constantly performance-monitored. No way could he leave without there being a record of it.'

'So what else do we have?'

'Melissa recently had her front-door locks changed.'

Hume looked away from the board and glared at her sergeant.

'Really? You waited this long to tell me that?'

Echo grinned. It made him look like a child. 'I knew you'd like it. A week before she went missing. Oliver never shared that with the original investigators. As far as he was concerned, she was just away; everything else was internet bullshit.'

Hume guessed that when you worked in entertainment cold cases, internet bullshit was a given. 'So do we have her emails? Was she receiving threatening messages?'

'Her emails are not available to us. I'm chasing the tech companies but . . .' Echo grimaced.

Hume nodded. Even with a digital search warrant it was debatable, and they weren't anywhere near that yet. All they had was a possible faked video and a feeling.

'We do have her internet search history,' said Echo.

'And? Presumably Missing Persons had it too so it can't have anything interesting on it.'

Echo swiped at his tablet again. 'Three days before she disappeared Melissa Clarke was researching islands off the coast of California.'

'Interesting,' said Hume slowly. 'A holiday?'

'Not really holiday destinations.'

'So a work thing? Are there any retired drug lords on these islands?'

'Again, no. They're known more for their fauna and flora.'

'A bolthole, then? Maybe she went there on a false passport. A journalist who investigates crime wouldn't have too much trouble accessing sketchy paperwork.'

'I'm checking the flight passenger lists. There's only one flight from Heathrow to Long Beach airport per day, so there's not many.'

'Right. Any news on Aquinas Street?'

'Still chasing the owner.'

'Too much for just you. Compile everything we've got and I'll contact the DCI. With two potential sites we could really do with Jonas back.'

Echo shrugged. 'No body, no budget.'

Hume nodded, standing. 'Don't forget to chase up that thing for Raine. I'll see you tomorrow.' She waited until she had almost reached the door before turning back and smiling at him.

'What?' he said. Hume's smile had a malicious quality about it.

'I need you to pass on a message to Ms Arnold.'

'The dentist?' said Echo, a touch of alarm in his voice. 'Why?'

'Raine needs a favour from her, and I know she has a soft spot for you.'

'But boss, she—'

'It's for a good cause.' Hume explained the reason Raine wanted her. Echo nodded reluctantly.

'Okay. But if I don't turn up in the morning it will be because I'm in a cocoon.'

Hume was grinning broadly as she closed the door.

* * *

Later that night, Mary and Robert sat on their balcony gazing out over the city, drinking hot chocolate. Although it was over a week before bonfire night, fireworks could be seen exploding in the distance. In the crisp air, the colours of the rockets as they showered back down to the ground were amazing. Dotted in the distance were small fires. Practice fires before the big event.

'You know,' said Robert, 'even though it happens every year, I love sitting out here and watching the fireworks. Especially on a night like this.'

Hume knew what he meant. The weather had turned unseasonably wintery in the last few days. The air was so cold she felt she could snap bits of it off. Her breath misted out of her mouth and hung in front of her face. The hot chocolate was both bitter and sweet, with just a hint of cinnamon.

'I saw Raine today,' she said softly.

'Oh yes?' said Robert, his voice neutral. 'How was it?'

'Good. She's looking much better. Still edgy, but not as self-destructive as she was. I really think she might at last be coming to terms with what happened to Clara.'

Robert reached out and stroked her hand. 'Did she say anything?'

The sky stutter-flashed as some sort of firework exploded. A nano-second later there was a deep percussive *thrump*.

'Blimey,' murmured Robert. 'I swear these fireworks get bigger every year. It's like a warzone.'

'It is a warzone,' said Hume plainly. 'For some, anyway.'

Robert squeezed her hand. Hume had shared enough stories from her job with him; he was under no illusions as to what she meant.

'I told her I crave her company,' said Hume quietly. 'Raine. She didn't ask. Or maybe she did, in that throwaway banter she does. But I told her anyway.'

'Wow,' said Robert gently. 'That was very brave of you.'

Hume let out a shaky breath. 'It just slipped out. I was thinking about Clara and . . . I don't know. There were bagels involved.'

Hume didn't realise she was crying until Robert leaned over and kissed one of her tears away. 'I'm very proud of you,' he whispered in her ear.

Hume sniffed, then turned around and looked into his eyes. They were full of love and the reflected light of exploding rockets. 'How proud?'

'Enough to get you a bowl of the bedtime trifle I made earlier?'

Hume raised her eyebrows. 'Trifle? You haven't been to work at all, have you?'

'Nothing is more important than trifle,' he said gravely.

Hume stood up, pulling Robert with her.

'Agreed, but I've already done the washing up. I don't want to dirty another plate.'

'So no trifle?' he said, slightly deflated.

Hume's mouth curved in a crooked smile.

'I didn't say that.'

'Then how will—?'

'If you lie very still, I won't need a plate, will I?'

'Ah,' said Robert.

* * *

Echo stretched in his chair, feeling his bones crackle and pop as he crossed his arms over his head. It had been a long day following a long night. The Aquinas Street scene had freaked him a little. There was something almost cultish about the way the chair had been set in the middle of the room. The way the leaves had covered the floor. Like it was a forest altar or something. It gave him horror film vibes, especially so close to Halloween.

And now he was going to go home to his microflat — a tiny space in a modern concrete and glass block along with a hundred others, with leisure areas on the ground floor, including a gym, restaurants and next-generation Wi-Fi.

And Bitz. His maybe girlfriend/something friend; the person who seemed to occupy more and more of his thoughts.

His phone buzzed. 'Speak of the devil,' he murmured, when Bitz's picture popped up. He swiped to open the message.

hi. Up for a late night galaxian sesh?
If you win i'll give you a prize

Echo's and Bitz's block had a retro arcade room in its basement.
What's the prize? he thumb-typed.

A tee shirt.

Echo pictured Bitz's tee shirts. The obscure quotes or strange pictures. They were unique.

Which one?

The one i'm wearing

He thought of the implications of what she'd typed. His relationship with Bitz was a minefield for him to navigate. But she was worth it. He'd never met anybody like her. Grinning, he typed that he'd be there in twenty minutes.

As he was leaving his phone buzzed again, indicating an email. It was from the Leicester PC who had accompanied the Family Liaison Officer when they had broken the news of Heather Salim's death to her parents.

'Well, well,' he mused as he read. His phone buzzed again. Bitz telling him to pick up crisps. He quickly fired off a message to Raine, attaching the email, then shut off his computer and left the office. Once he had gone, the only light remaining came from the smart board. The photograph of Melissa Clarke, staring out of the screen at nothing.

CHAPTER 13

Hume's breath came out in hazy white clouds as she pounded the dark streets around the small park outside her maisonette. Susan, her normal training partner, was away, so she was running solo. She didn't run with headphones. As a police officer she was well aware of the dangers that could befall a lone runner who couldn't hear someone approaching. As a woman she was even more heightened to what could happen. Which was why she ran with a live phone tracker and two cylindrical one-kilogramme hand weights. They sat snug in her palms, attached with Velcro clasps around her knuckles. They were designed to increase strength over time, but Hume knew they would be ideal for adding an extra punch if she ever needed it. She also carried a Defender rape alarm. The small device released over 140 decibels at the pull of a pin, and as far as Hume was concerned, nothing said defence like the bleeding ears of a predator.

As she ran, she thought over the case. There was something sinister about it. The absence of a body that should have been there. On the video clip lifted from the phone it was clearly, gruesomely, there; but the physical evidence was confusing to say the least. The Aquinas Street flat had definitely been broken into and the tape attached to the arm of the chair had seemingly been used to bind someone to it. Yet there was no blood beneath the chair when there should have been buckets of the stuff. And those leaves were just plain odd. What was the purpose of them? The person who had planned whatever this was, had clearly brought them in for a reason. Hume considered again that they were there to cover a spill sheet underneath. At a stretch it might explain the lack of any blood, but it didn't explain why it had been done at all.

What was the point?

Her phone, strapped to her arm, flashed as a call came in. She stopped, resting her back against a fence so she had a good view of the street, and answered.

'Guv. Sleep well?'

'Echo,' said Hume. 'It's not decent that you sound so bloody cheery at this time in the morning. It's still dark.'

'Not in my soul.'

'One more comment like that and you're sacked,' Hume said as she started gently jogging on the spot so as not to seize up. 'Why are you ringing?'

'Couple of things. The lab has confirmed that the biological material attached to the chair straps belonged to Melissa, as did the blood on the bag and chair. We've compared it with samples taken from her flat.'

Hume closed her eyes for a second. She had known in her heart that Melissa was dead. The look in her eyes on the video clip as the life bled out of her couldn't be faked. That, coupled with the nail Hume had found wedged in the surface of her desk, made it almost a certainty, but this seemed to confirm it.

'We need to find her body,' said Hume.

'But that's not all. Along with Melissa's biological identifiers — hair and skin samples — there was DNA from someone else on the tape. Also on the door handle and the light switch in the room.'

'Really?' said Hume, feeling a tingle of excitement. 'The killer left their print? That was clumsy.'

'Well, someone did, and they were the last ones to touch the switch, so they must have turned it off. The prints and DNA are being run through the various databases but no hits yet.'

'Good work. With any luck we'll get a match and be able to get this closed off. Any luck with the CCTV?'

'We've managed to track down the owner of the house opposite, who had a door camera set up. They're away in the Seychelles at the moment but have promised to download the footage and send it to us. I should have that by the time you come in.'

'Excellent. I'll be at the office in an hour or so. See you there.'

Hume closed the call, then checked her watch. If she was quick she'd have time for one more lap of the park and a shower before the car came to pick her up.

Fifty minutes later she was once again outside her maisonette, standing in the grim grey light of a London dawn when her phone rang.

'Give me a break, Echo,' she groaned into the mouthpiece, 'I'm literally waiting for the car to turn up. Although if it doesn't come soon I'm going to be dead from hypothermia.'

'She's on the move.' Echo's voice was tense. Excited.

'Who is?' asked Hume. The grey light gave a hint of the day to come. A coldness to the sky. A grittiness to the air, like it had dirty ice in it.

'Melissa.'

An unmarked police car, Hume's ride to the office, pulled in smoothly by the curb in front of her, but Hume didn't see it, her vision momentarily full of the journalist, blood ribboning down her front. 'What?'

'Melissa Clarke is on the move. She's walking down Old Compton Street as we speak.'

'Melissa Clarke is dead. There's no way she's walking around London.'

'Her phone,' Echo clarified. 'Remember I said that she had an app linked to Oliver Bell's phone?'

'I remember,' said Hume, stepping down into the back of the car. 'A mapping app.'

'Well, it's just been activated. Not Oliver's, but Melissa's. She, or someone, has turned on the phone and is heading . . .' There was a pause, then: 'towards Soho.'

'But . . .' began Hume. 'Actually, never mind. Are there any patrol officers nearby?'

'Yes. Two beat officers. I've alerted them. They're a couple of minutes away.'

'Right. When they get there, tell them to just observe. Not to engage. If it is the same person who murdered Melissa, they are clearly dangerous.' She leaned forward and told her driver to head for Soho.

'Boss.'

Echo relayed the information while Hume's car sped silently through the grainy light. After what seemed an age Echo came back on the line.

'The signal's gone. We've lost tracking.'

'What do you mean? Has the phone been turned off?'

'That or they've gone into a dead zone with no data connection. Hang on, the officers are just coming into range.'

Another long pause.

'Jesus, Echo, tell me what's going on! Are they there?'

'The officers are at the scene, but there's no target,' said Echo, his voice slightly metallic in her ear. 'All they can see is a couple of street cleaners and a homeless woman with a shopping trolley.'

'Bugger,' said Hume under her breath. 'Okay. Get one of them to make sure the woman doesn't have the phone and see if the cleaners saw anything. The other can scout the area.'

'Wilco,' said Echo. 'But there are a lot of lanes and alleys around there. They could be anywhere.'

'Agreed, but we can't cordon off central London on a couple of minutes of footage from a phone app. Are we sure it's not a glitch or something? Maybe an old journey that's been saved?'

'No, it was definitely live.' Although Echo sounded firm, Hume thought there might be a small edge of doubt in his voice.

'Check it out anyway. There's no point in me going to Soho. I'll be with you in twenty.'

Hume ended the call, told her driver to take her to the office instead, and sat back in her seat. A tension headache was forming at the base of her skull. The day hadn't even made it to full light, and she felt like she was fighting through sludge.

CHAPTER 14

Raine woke, as she always woke, alone. She stretched out her hand across the queen-sized bed to the space where Clara once lay.

'Morning, darling,' she said quietly. She gave herself a moment, a small space in time to remember her wife. The way her skin had smelled first thing in the morning. The first flash of her green eyes when they opened. The way her fingers intertwined with her own. The way her body fitted into Raine's like that was what it had been designed for.

And then she got up, took a hot mango shot out of the mini-fridge, and downed it. Out of the window she gazed at the other vessels around her in Little Venice. Narrow boats of various sizes and colours, as unique as the people residing on them. Raine wasn't used to neighbours and found it unsettling. So many people living nearby knocked her off kilter. With Clara it hadn't been like living with another person at all. It had been . . . inevitable. As if she had been a jigsaw piece in the puzzle of Raine's life that had been missing. Not that there hadn't been arguments and disagreements. Of course there had. But they hadn't mattered, somehow. Because deep down Raine knew they would be resolved. That eventually everything would be all right and they would continue together, hand in hand.

And that was how it had been, for almost a year of marriage. Until it wasn't, and Clara had been ripped from her.

Raine blinked. She slipped a pod into the Nespresso machine and switched it on. While she waited for it to brew, she took a cold shower and dressed. Attaching the key cache containing Clara's ashes to her cargoes, she sat down with her coffee and read her emails. She had a follow-up from DI Conner updating her on the county lines bust. Not only was the case against Pirie strong, but the henchman who had beaten up Libby was also in custody and looking at hard time. Conner asked if Libby would be willing to go to court should she be needed.

Raine typed back an answer, promising to ask.

Next was a work enquiry. Raine saw that it had been forwarded from one of her archived addresses. Every year Raine changed email addresses and phone numbers. In fact, all her contact details. The type of people she dealt with — hardcore criminals, gangbangers and abusers of every stripe — did not forget, and it was best not to leave a digital trail of breadcrumbs that led back to her. Although, she noted wryly to herself, Frankie Ridgeway had managed it.

So she set up new addresses, new message services, and archived all the old ones, leaving a forwarding service in case any former clients needed to reach her. This person had clearly got her email from one of those.

Dear Ms Raine, it began.

'Well that's wrong for a start,' murmured Raine, taking a sip of her coffee, but she read on.

> *Please excuse me for reaching out with no introduction, but I'm so desperate. I was given this address from someone you'd helped in the past. A woman who was trapped in a situation that, as far as I understand, you deal with often. Her name was Chloé Jones. She has changed it now. Forgive me if I don't give you her new name. I'm sure you will understand.*

She tells me to thank you and they are doing fine. Still healing, but have found a sense of themselves again.

Raine did understand. Her eyes unfocused for a moment as she remembered Chloé. It had been a few years ago. The woman had been an aspiring actor. Not much older than a girl. She had answered an ad for models and the inevitable had happened. A few candid shots had turned into blackmail, with a threat to show them to her friends and family unless she posed for more. Things had continued to escalate until she was forced into webcam pornography. Live shows. Eventually prostitution. When Raine had found her she was being kept in a flea-infested basement in Canning Town with six other women, addicted to heroin and unable to even remember a life before the abuse. Raine had got her out and handed her back to her parents, who had immediately uprooted to Europe in the hope of separating themselves completely from the past. The last time Raine had seen them they had waved to her from the window of a Eurostar train, their broken daughter between them. They had insisted Raine come to Paddington station with them, not feeling safe until the train was actually pulling away.

'Well, well,' said Raine softly, reading on.

If you remember them, then you will know where they moved to. That is where I met Chloé. Her parents had signed her up for a circus skills course. Not only to help build up her strength, but to give her a sense of community and confidence in herself. There is nothing like the trapeze to help a person learn self-reliance!

'I bet,' said Raine. She pictured the emaciated young woman she had rescued fit and healthy and high above the ground. Raine raised her coffee cup in salute.

Sorry. I am rambling. I was Chloé's teacher at this place. I am myself a member of a travelling circus. Aerial and acrobatic skills. My circus also has high wire and silks.

After teaching Chloé to trust herself, which is essential if one is to walk the wire, she eventually opened up to me about her past. I can say I was honoured to be her confidante and have not spoken about her early life to anyone until now, as I write to you. To have overcome such odds and become the person she is today. Strong and fierce, loyal and protective. All I can say is she is a special soul, as you must be, to have freed her from such a life as she had before.

Raine took a sip of her coffee. 'Not really. She did it all herself. You go, Chloé.'

Now I find myself in need of someone like you. An investigator who can go where the police cannot. Places where I could not. I will be in London next week with my circus. I wonder if you have space in your schedule to see me so I can explain what has happened? I understand if the answer is no. You do not know me and I have not given you a clue as to why I might have need of your services. All I can hope is that you remember Chloé and still feel the same way about helping those who find themselves in a position where they cannot help themselves.
 Yours,
 Felice

Raine read the email again, then wrote a short message back conveying that she would be glad to meet, and was delighted Chloé was doing so well. She asked for a time, place, phone number and photograph, then moved on to the next email. It was from Echo.

Raine. Attached is info re. Heather Salim case.
Cheers, Echo.

'Short and sweet,' smiled Raine, opening the attachment. She read a report that had been sent through from the

Family Liaison Officer who had dealt with Heather's parents. When she had finished reading she made herself another cup of coffee and stared out of the window. The canal was slate grey, with a toxic-looking froth of scum at its edge. A swan glided by, showing absolutely no interest in her whatsoever. She followed it with her eyes for a few moments longer, then unfolded her phone.

'It's me,' she said when the call was answered. 'Change of plan. What are you doing tonight?'

CHAPTER 15

'Okay, so where exactly did they go?'

'The phone went live on Old Compton Street then headed down Greek Street,' said Echo, sending a map of central London onto the smart board. 'It was stationary for a minute, then turned off onto Romilly Street. From there it turned again onto Moor Street which took it back to Old Compton. Then it disappeared.'

'And after that?'

'Nothing. The officers searched the surrounding streets and alleys but they were empty. Or at least empty of anything suspicious. Nobody acting in a covert way. Nobody running or being evasive.' Echo shrugged. 'A turned-off phone in a pocket. It could be anyone.'

'And the street cleaners?'

'They didn't see anything out of the ordinary, and they're pretty observant. There are often muggings in that area. The carts they use are electric and the batteries have a resale value on the streets so they keep their eyes open. They said it was a normal Soho morning. Couple of drug deals. Couple of skin deals. Nothing to report.'

Hume took a moment to acknowledge the sad fact that drugs and prostitution didn't raise any alarm bells before continuing. 'And the homeless person? The woman?'

'Same. She didn't see anything. Although it's unclear that what she sees IRL is what everyone else sees. The officers said she appeared to have some mental health issues.'

Hume didn't ask what IRL meant, mainly to annoy Echo, who clearly wanted her to. 'Did they search her for a phone?'

He nodded. 'They bought her breakfast in exchange for checking her trolley and pockets. Apparently she's well known in the area. If she had the phone, she'd have happily sold it to them. She's not a person of interest.'

'Which kind of sums up the state's view on the homeless, doesn't it?' said Hume grimly. She scanned the map. 'So, what's so interesting about this area? Why was the phone turned on here?'

'Well, the route is circling the Coach and Horses pub. It's a known hangout for journalists and media types.' Echo brought up a picture of the old building. 'Lots of history. Jeffrey Bernard and John Hurt used to drink there.'

'They used to drink everywhere,' muttered Hume. 'What about Melissa? Do we know if she hung out there?'

'More than likely. There'd been several murders there or nearby over the years.'

'Interesting,' mused Hume. She could immediately see the appeal. The link to celebrities. The rich salacious history of the area. It was a journalist's dream. The hashtags alone would pull in the keyboard browsers. 'So whoever was carrying the phone could have been meeting someone there. Or outside there, as it would be closed now. Is there any CCTV?'

'Loads. The landlord doesn't live-in, but we tracked him down through the brewery. He's meeting an officer there and will allow access. We should have it soon.'

'Great.' Hume picked up her own phone and typed into it. After a moment she looked up. 'Any advance on the dead leaves?'

'I've sent an enquiry to Kew Gardens. Apparently it's hard to identify from a photograph and they would like to see the leaf in the flesh, as it were.'

'IRL,' said Hume triumphantly. 'In Real Life.'

'You just got that off the Net, didn't you,' said Echo.

'No,' lied Hume, pocketing her phone and standing. 'Have we got any further with the bag?'

'We've checked with Oliver. It's not Melissa's.'

'Well she'd hardly be filming her own death,' said Hume. 'Any idea who it could belong to?'

'No, it's just a bag from a high-street shop. Not designer. Nothing individual about it. All it contained was the busted phone.'

'Have we checked with whoever handed it in? Maybe they lifted the wallet or purse.'

Echo shook his head. 'It was just handed in to an officer. No way to find them.'

Hume cursed under her breath. 'Brilliant. Have we got a name?'

'A name? I said—'

'Not for the bag. For Kew Gardens.'

'Right.' Echo glanced at his tablet. 'Professor Davies. He's the one who requested the sample. He's based on site.'

'Come on, then. Might as well go and see him while we're waiting for the CCTV.'

* * *

The library at Kew Gardens was surprisingly modern inside; open plan and, despite the early hour, already occupied by several studious-looking individuals working away on laptops or consulting books. Professor Davies was waiting for them in reception.

'Thank you for seeing us at such short notice,' said Hume as he offered her an elbow to bump.

'Not at all! The leaf looked interesting. And you say there were a number of them?'

'Several thousand, at a guess,' agreed Hume.

'How odd. Well, from the image I would definitely say it was not a native of London. Did you bring a sample with you?'

'My colleague, Detective Sergeant Echo, has it.'

Echo patted the satchel hanging from his shoulder.

'Fabulous,' said the professor, leading them into one of the glass-walled meeting rooms at the back of the library. 'We can examine it back here.'

Once they were in the room, Echo unclasped the satchel and removed a clear envelope. Inside, a selection of the leaves was clearly visible. He placed it on the table and Professor Davies leaned forward.

'Yes, definitely not native to this climate.' He took out a pen from his jacket pocket.

Hume noted that it had leaked, creating a stain in the material.

'You see the length of the body? And the angle of the edging. This leaf is from a fern tree of some variety. Pine perhaps. Definitely not plane or elm. Not local.'

'But aren't ferns evergreen?' said Hume uncertainly, eyeing the dead leaf. 'Would it go this colour?'

'Oh, contrary to popular belief, Officer, evergreens can turn brown,' said the professor breezily. 'They don't shed like their deciduous cousins, but they do occasionally drop. When the leaf becomes damaged, for example. Or diseased. Although . . .' his brow furrowed. 'Hundreds, you say?'

'Possibly thousands. Enough to cover the average sitting-room floor.'

'A sitting room . . .' The professor was confused. 'But why would you need to cover—?'

'Not important,' said Hume smoothly, not wanting to get into a discussion of the case with a civilian. 'Could you tell us where they might have come from?'

Professor Davies studied the leaves for another long moment, then peered through the glass walls of the office. His eyes lit up. 'There's Anita.'

'I'm sorry?' Both Hume and Echo followed the professor's gaze. He was looking at a woman in her thirties with serious dark blonde hair and round glasses worn on a chain around her neck. She appeared to be wearing both a jumper and a cardigan. 'Who's Anita?'

'Anita Straw. She's a PhD student on loan to us from St Andrew's. Her specialism is in evergreens.' He looked at Hume, eyebrows raised in a question.

'By all means,' encouraged Hume.

Professor Davies nodded and called the young woman in. Once he explained the situation, Anita leaned down to look at the sample. Frowning, she glanced at Hume. 'May I?'

Hume nodded, and Anita picked up the envelope and turned it, examining both sides of the leaf.

'*Lyonothamnus floribundus*,' she said after a moment.

'Wow,' said Echo, impressed. 'You know your stuff.'

'Specifically, subspecies *aspleniifolius*. Catalina Ironwood.'

'That's very . . . exact,' said Hume slowly, looking at the envelope. 'Is the leaf structure unique, then?'

'Every plant species is unique, Officer,' said Anita. 'Each with its own individual signature and components. Shape and texture. Mesophyll and veins. My thesis was on the epidermis of the—'

'But you can tell just by looking?' interrupted Hume. 'You don't need a microscope or anything?'

'Well, normally I would require some time to reference,' admitted Anita. 'But not in this case.'

Hume eyed her with interest. 'Why not?'

'Another sample was brought to me just a few weeks ago, actually,' said the student, glancing nervously at the detective. There had been a sliver of steel in Hume's voice.

'Really?' said Professor Davies. 'How extraordinary. Who was it?'

'Elizabeth Stride,' said Anita. 'She's a student with the Eden Project. They have college placements. She told me they had a hitchhiker and needed identification. She was in

London and . . .' Anita's voice petered out as she looked at the police officers.

'Elizabeth Stride?' said Hume, her voice flat. 'Are you sure?'

Anita nodded. 'Have I done something wrong?'

'No, no,' said Echo gently. 'What's a hitchhiker?'

'It's when an unidentified plant comes in with another batch. One you weren't expecting.' She spread her hands. 'A hitchhiker.'

'Got it,' said Echo, smiling. Anita smiled back. 'And could you tell me. Is this Elizabeth?' He held out his tablet, showing the PhD student the publicity picture of Melissa Clarke.

'Yes,' said Anita, nodding. 'Only her hair was a different colour and she didn't have glasses. She seems older here.'

'That's really helpful,' said Hume. 'And did she have a sample too? Of the leaf?'

'Yes. It's actually quite interesting. The tree is quite rare. Well, not rare exactly, but quite specific to a few islands off the coast of America.'

'Which coast?' Hume asked, feeling the familiar tickle of excitement at the back of her neck.

'West,' said Anita. 'Santa Catalina, mainly. Hence the name.'

Hume thought of Melissa's search history. 'And this island is off the coast of California?'

'Yes,' said Anita again, clearly impressed.

'And once you'd identified it for her, did she ask anything else?'

'No. She just said she wanted to know what it was as she hadn't seen one before.'

'Right,' said Hume. 'Well, thank you for your time.' She turned to the professor. 'And yours. It's been very educational.'

'Not at all. Could I ask what this is about. Identification of a leaf hardly seems to require the presence of two detectives.'

'We were in the area,' said Hume. She thanked them again and began walking towards the door.

'Actually, now that I think about it, I *did* tell her one other thing,' said Anita as they moved to leave.

'Oh yes, and what was that?'

'I told her I thought it was odd.'

'Why odd?'

'Well, the leaf she presented was from a well-established tree. It seemed unlikely that it came from a hitchhiker. They are normally young. Thrown in with other starter plants and such.'

'Ah. And what did she say?'

'Not much. She just said that the Eden Project receives fully grown trees for conservation, and it must have come with those.'

'Right.'

'But as it was clearly dead, I told her that she could see a real live one if she wanted.'

The air seemed to still around Hume as she took in the guileless expression on Anita's face. 'But I thought you said they're rare? Native to those islands in America?'

'They are, but there's a few in London.'

'In London?' Hume looked out at the grey, cold day. 'Really? In a greenhouse, I suppose?'

'No,' beamed Anita. 'Well, yes. You can buy starter plants and such from nurseries specialising in exotic plants, but there are a few examples of fully grown trees, too.'

'Wow,' said Echo. 'Where?'

'Well, there's one in Cannizaro Park, of course: they have everything there. And I believe there's another within the gardens of the Inner Temple.'

'What's the Inner Temple?' asked Echo.

'It's one of the four Inns of Court,' said Hume. 'Private buildings in the centre of London. If someone started taking lots of leaves or tree branches from the Temple Gardens, I think it would be noticed.'

'And then there's the one in Chelsea,' continued Anita. 'It's the only mature example on a public street in the capital, or at least the only one that's been catalogued. A bit of a freak, really.'

Hume stared at her for a beat, then asked: 'Do you have an address?'

Five minutes later, as they walked to their car, Echo said: 'On Melissa's map history it shows her visiting Richmond. I thought she was going to the National Archives, but she was coming here. Sorry, boss. I should have checked.'

'Maybe she was doing both,' said Hume grimly. 'The point is, she had been sent a leaf. Or discovered a story involving the tree.'

'The tree in Chelsea?' He checked his tablet. 'In Wilbraham Place?'

'Maybe,' said Hume. 'Whatever, it's a connection, and where there's a connection there's something for us to pick at.'

'Why did you react like that, by the way?'

'Like what?'

They had reached the car, and Hume waited for Echo to unlock it.

'Like you were angry. When Anita Straw gave Melissa's false name.'

'Elizabeth Stride,' said Hume, climbing into the passenger seat.

'Yes,' said Echo, starting the car. 'Who is she?'

Hume pulled on the safety belt, clunking it in with a harshness it didn't deserve. 'Elizabeth Stride was the third victim of Jack the Ripper.'

* * *

Hume and Echo gazed up at the tree, taking in the fern leaves and the strange, strap-like bark.

'And this is the only one on London's streets, she said?'

'According to *London is a Forest*, at least,' said Echo.

'London is a forest?' Hume was seriously confused.

'It's a book. I've just looked it up,' said Echo, slightly sheepishly, holding his tablet in front of him.

'London isn't a forest,' muttered Hume, looking back up at the tree. 'It's a bloody swamp.'

'Not round here it's not,' quipped Echo.

Hume nodded, taking in the surroundings. The properties of Wilbraham Place, upmarket even for the heady air of Chelsea. The feeling you were in a gated community with nothing so common as actual gates.

'Don't these people feel important enough without having their own exclusive tree?' said Hume.

'I don't think it was on purpose,' said Echo. 'I mean it's a street tree. It just does what it wants.'

'This is an evergreen, right? So the leaves don't fall off in the autumn?'

'Right. It's green all year round. The leaves would have to be physically removed if you wanted them to desiccate. It wouldn't happen by itself.'

Hume gazed at the tree. It was in a line on the street with the other trees but looked nothing like them. Not a huge tree by London standards, around twenty feet tall, but it was nevertheless impressive. The trunk seemed to be made up of a multitude of overlapping grey straps, as if the bark had been lashed there. Hume walked forward and touched it. The texture was brittle and dry. The canopy formed a little haven of gloom.

'I don't believe someone could take a thousand leaves from this tree without it being noticed,' Hume mused, looking up and down the pavement. Nothing unusual about the street. Plenty of similar ones in this part of London.

'No. But as a lure for a journalist, it's pretty good,' said Echo. 'Like a treasure map.'

Hume nodded. 'Get sent a leaf with a cryptic message. Do the research and find that there's only one of them in London. Did we check whether her map history brought her here?'

'Not yet.' Echo made a note on his tablet.

'Take some pictures,' said Hume. 'I'll check for CCTV.'

Hume walked across the street to the edge of a small park. It was surrounded by iron railings and appeared to be locked. She wondered if it was privately owned. Leaves from the normal London trees scuttled across the cold ground. Brown and insectoid in their movement. Like dried skin. Hume shivered in the cold. She scanned the surroundings but couldn't see any cameras.

'Probably have their own security drones,' muttered Hume as she kicked at the leaves.

'Boss!' shouted Echo, excitement in his voice.

'What?'

'There's something up there. In the tree.'

Hume crossed back over the road and joined him. 'Where?'

Echo pointed up into the mass of the Ironwood. 'About five branches up, to the right. Can you see it?'

Hume tipped her head back. It took her several seconds before she realised what Echo was pointing at. A piece of cloth. A grey rag tied to the branch. The colour was so similar to the colour of the bark, it was very hard to spot. 'Is that a piece of shirt?'

'Not sure. Should we call for back-up?'

Hume stared at him. 'Are you insane? If we call a team out and it's just a rag that's blown up there, we'll be a laughing stock.' She paused. 'You look quite fit. Why don't you shimmy up and see what it is?'

Echo looked up, then back at Hume.

'What if I fall?'

'I'll catch you.'

'Of course you will.' Echo slid his satchel off his shoulder.

'Put some bloody gloves on first!' said Hume quickly. 'Unlikely, but it might be evidence.'

'Or a material witness.'

'Sorry?'

'It's a rag,' explained Echo. 'So, a *material* witness.'

'I take it back. I won't catch you. You've already fallen about as far as you can with that joke.'

Grinning, Echo began climbing up the tree.

Hume watched her sergeant's progress from branch to branch. 'Be careful!' she said, as his foot slipped off the bark.

'Excuse me.'

Hume's attention was diverted from Echo by a small woman wearing an expression of outrage beneath a bobble hat and full-length coat.

'I'm sorry. Were you speaking to me?'

'Yes I was speaking to you. What the hell do you think you're doing?'

Sighing, Hume reached into her jacket for her warrant card. 'Madam, I'm a police—'

The woman took a step back and held up her phone. 'I'm filming you!' she shouted. 'If you try anything, you'll be doing it live on the web!'

Slowly, Hume removed her wallet and flipped it open. 'As I was saying, madam, I'm a police officer.'

'So what? It was a police officer who beat up that woman in Brixton. He was filmed too.'

Hume couldn't argue with that. It was a sad day, Hume mused, when even little old ladies in Chelsea didn't trust the police. 'Well, I'm not beating anyone up,' she said. 'Although I think my sergeant's having a good go at this tree.'

There was the muffled sound of swearing above them, followed by Echo shouting, 'Got it!'

The two women looked up as Echo began to descend.

'I really think you should be doing more important things than climbing trees in your stormtrooper boots,' muttered the woman, turning away. 'There's real crime in this city. Like rape and murder and environmental atrocities. You bloody policemen are all the same.'

Hume watched in mild astonishment as the woman walked across the road, still muttering. She moved so smoothly under the massive coat, she appeared to be on wheels. She was just turning the corner when Echo landed back on the pavement with a thump. In his hand he held the grey material.

'It's a scarf,' he said.

Hume put on her own pair of nitrile gloves and took it from him. She held it up to the pale light. The scarf seemed expensive. Perhaps silk. 'Could it have blown up there?'

'Not a chance. It was tied around the branch. It was put there deliberately.'

Hume frowned. 'So why would someone climb a tree in Chelsea and tie a grey scarf to it?'

'Not sure,' said Echo, unfolding his phone. 'But the scarf wasn't all that was there.'

'What do you mean?'

Echo didn't answer. Instead, he handed her his phone. On it was a photograph of the scarf, in situ, tied to the branch of the tree.

'What am I—' began Hume, then she saw it. The brewing flutter of electricity tickled the back of her neck again as she stared. Beneath the scarf, carved into the wood of the bark, was a word.

DEADTOWN

* * *

Later that afternoon Hume stood by their office window, watching the light bleed from the London sky. It was like watching a bruise discolour. Pale yellows smeared into orange and fever-red to end in ink-blues and black. She turned away and faced her colleague.

'I'm really not liking this.'

'There's no CCTV footage that has a good angle on the tree. We've canvassed the area but no news so far.'

'Any identification on the scarf?'

'Yes. There's DNA that matches what we found on the light switch at the house on Aquinas Street, but it's not on any databases. The etching of "DEADTOWN" into the tree was done recently, perhaps in the last few days, according to forensics.'

'How can they tell?'

'The colour of the exposed flesh, apparently. Plus the viscosity of the sap.'

'Check the Aquinas Street site again. See if there are any carvings there we missed. In the wall or something.'

'Will do. Speaking of which, the estate agent's been on to us.'

'What estate agent?' asked Hume.

'Garratts. The agency dealing with the Aquinas Street property. They're on the high street in Deptford. I sent a picture of Melissa through to them.'

Hume nodded. 'Good. There must be some reason that house was chosen. Did they recognise her?'

'No one there had seen her.'

'Damn. Can they put us in touch with the owner?'

'There isn't one. They were asked to sell the property by a surviving relative who lives abroad. The person who deals with it is on leave at the moment. They're trying to track her down.'

'Good. Stay on it. We need a list of anybody who has shown an interest in the building over the last, say, six months.'

'Boss.'

'How about Melissa and Oliver's map sharing?'

'I've set up an alert in case it repeats again. It will ping directly to my phone.'

'Excellent. Did we get the footage from the pub? The Coach and Horses?'

'Yes, but there's nothing useful on there. The cameras are on rotation, so it's possible that whoever had the phone avoided being on screen, but they'd have had to know the set-up.'

'Did the landlord recognise Melissa? We showed him a picture, yes?'

'Yes, and yes. She was a regular, apparently. In fact, turns out she did a *Deadtown* piece from there. A murder a few years back.'

Hume sighed. 'It seems we're getting lots of data without much meaning.'

'I've checked back through the *Deadtown* archives. There's nothing on that particular tree, or Aquinas Street.'

'Okay,' said Hume, putting on her coat. 'Let's call it a night. I'm going to speak to the DCI tomorrow. We really need some help to catalogue the data. Three possible abduction slash murder sites. We can't handle it all ourselves.'

'No body . . .' began Echo.

'No budget,' finished Hume, her tone signalling her frustration. 'I know.'

CHAPTER 16

Raine knocked on the door of Jolene's boat. It was red and crudely painted with white birds. Raine suspected they were doves.

'Raine!' said Jolene, smiling. 'What a lovely surprise, please come in. We've just finished supper.'

'Cheers,' said Raine, ducking as she entered. Although Jolene appeared much the same, dressed in baggy painter's dungarees and a sludge green shapeless cardigan, she radiated tiredness. Raine thought there was a tension about her. A wariness. The set-up inside Jolene's boat couldn't have been further from Raine's. Where the detective went for minimalism, Jolene's looked like she had once had a much bigger boat that had shrunk. Bookshelves lined the bulkhead. In the centre of the living space was a wood burner, kiln-dried logs burning cheerily inside. A kettle sat on the plate above.

'Wow,' said Raine. 'I don't think I've seen so many throw cushions since . . . Actually I don't think I've ever seen so many.'

'Would you like a cup of tea? Libby's just having a lie down.' She raised her chin, indicating a door in the partition beyond the sink and small breakfast table. 'I've given her my room. This sofa folds out into a bed.' She patted the settee she was sitting on, smiling. 'I think it's good to give her some space while she adjusts to . . .' Jolene's words petered out. Fat tears slid out of her eyes and down her lined face. More lines than had been there a month ago. Deeper. Probably permanent. Her hair was dimmer, too. Her bones more pronounced through her skin.

'You need to take care of yourself, Jolene,' said Raine softly. 'So you can take care of Libby. What about her parents?'

Jolene shook her head. 'They can't cope. They can barely keep themselves together. That estate . . .'

Raine nodded. Jolene didn't need to spell it out. Postcode gangs. Want-to-be roadmen. Drugs and violence, fed by poverty and prejudice, all wrapped up in housing that was decades past its sell-by date.

Jolene picked the metal kettle up off the hotplate and poured Raine's tea into a cracked cup. They sat in silence on the sofa, sipping the tea.

'So, Jolene,' said Raine, after several minutes had passed. She carefully put her tea down on the table. She had no intention of picking it up again; it tasted of nettles and earnestness. 'Can you give Libby a knock? I need to talk to her.'

'It's not about the man who hurt her, is it?' Jolene's hand went to her mouth, a look of fear flashing across her face. 'He's not got out?'

'No, nothing like that. I just want to see how she's doing.'

Jolene nodded. 'I'll see if she's awake.'

'If not, wake her.'

Jolene hesitated a moment longer, the fear still swimming behind her gaze, then nodded and went to knock on the door. Raine's phone vibrated in her pocket. She glanced at the text and fired a quick message back. As she put the device back into her waistcoat pocket, Jolene returned, followed by Libby.

'Hi!' said Raine, smiling. The girl seemed worse than last time, in the hospital. Not physically, but inside. Her skin seemed duller. She held her arms across herself, as if she was scared she might fall apart. Only her eyes were the same. Beaten but with a spark still evident.

'Hi,' she said softly. 'Thanks for . . . well, you know. I didn't get a chance to say it at the hospital. I was still quite doped up. You really a private investigator?'

'I really am,' smiled Raine. 'I've got a trilby and everything.' She frowned. 'Well, not exactly a trilby. More of a gothy beret. And I don't smoke or carry a gun or drink whisky in shady bars.' She brightened. 'But I have snogged enigmatic, beautiful women and beaten the fuck out of loads of bad guys, if that's any good?'

Libby's lips crept into a smile, exposing her shattered teeth. She put a hand over her mouth.

'About that,' said Raine, making a circle around her own mouth. 'I've got some good news. There's a dentist I know who can fit you in to fix those. It's the same dentist who fixed my teeth.' She opened her mouth. 'See? A few months ago somebody threw me out of a van and I face-bombed a lamp-post. My gnashers were a mess.'

Libby stared at Raine's mouth. 'I can't even tell. They look . . . normal.'

'She's really good,' agreed Raine. 'I didn't feel a thing.' In her peripheral vision Raine could see Jolene looking anxious. 'Plus she's free. She does test-case dentistry. Writes papers on the work she does. It won't cost anything and you get to have a mouth like a film star, only without the scary glow-in-the-dark white thing they have going on.'

'Raine, that's amazing!' said Jolene, relaxing visibly. 'We were worried. It's so hard to find an NHS dentist, especially when—'

'No sweat,' said Raine. 'Like I say, you'd be doing her a favour. Helping her research.'

'What's your name?' said Libby suddenly. 'I mean, I know it's Raine, but what's your full name?'

'Libby!' said Jolene. 'I told you. Raine doesn't talk about her—'

'No, it's fine,' said Raine. 'Perfectly sensible question. And it's good to ask questions. Helps you stay in control.'

'So, what is it?' The girl was eager. Like she'd been saving up the question. Holding on to it. Turning it into a talisman.

The logs in the wood burner crackled in the silence. Finally, Raine shrugged. 'It's—'

There was a gentle knock on the door. Raine clapped her hands together.

'Saved by the bell!'

Libby suddenly looked scared.

'No, it's okay,' said Raine. 'It's for me.' She turned to Jolene apologetically. 'I got a text a few minutes ago, while you were fetching Libby. It's from a colleague. I was meant to meet him but forgot he was coming. I told him I was next door. Sorry.' She got up and walked to the steps leading up to the door. 'Down here!' she called, then seemed to think better of it. 'Actually, stay where you are! We'll come to you.' She turned round and sat on the steps. 'The man up there is called Danny Brin. He works as a bouncer in some scary clubs but that's not what he's really about. Mainly, he wants to be Heathcliff.' She paused, thinking. 'Or he might want to be Cathy; he's quite sensitive. Point is that the person responsible for knocking my mouth about. The person who gave me this.' She rolled up the sleeve of her army shirt and showed the scar. 'Well, Danny came along and helped me sort it. Get even.' She gazed directly into Libby's wide eyes. 'Helped me not be scared. He didn't protect me, but he showed me some moves so that I could protect myself. Got me fighting fit, you might say.'

'So, he teaches self-defence?' said Jolene, sounding doubtful.

'Not really. He teaches how to survive.' She pointed a gun hand at Libby. 'Would you like to meet him?'

Libby nodded.

'I'm not sure,' said Jolene, doubtfully. 'Libby's still recovering.'

'I want to,' cut in Libby.

'You're still not healed—' began Jolene.

'I want to,' said Libby, more forcibly this time.

Raine nodded. She understood. It was about taking responsibility. Taking control. Not letting the fear move you like a puppet. 'Great,' she said, standing. 'Let's go and meet Brin.'

Outside, on the wooden jetty, Brin waited silently for them, dressed in scuffed jeans, long-sleeved black shirt and a hoodie. The gold cap on his left incisor glinted dully as he smiled at them.

'Danny, thanks for coming. This is Libby. She's fourteen years old and has been beaten up protecting her friend from a county lines gang. She'd like not to get beaten up again.'

Danny nodded at Libby, then turned back to the detective, a puzzled expression on his face.

'Raine, I don't teach self-defence . . .' he began.

'I know, that's what made it special when you trained me,' smiled Raine. 'Libby, show him your trams.'

'I don't think—' began Jolene.

Without taking her eyes off the bouncer, Libby pulled down her top slightly to reveal the two parallel scars. Danny peered at them.

'How?' he asked.

'Grapple hook. Double pronged and serrated, for climbing. It scraped her all the way to the bone.'

'They'll look cool as hell once they heal,' he said, smiling at the girl warmly. He turned back to Raine, the smile switching off. 'I still don't do self-defence.'

'Show him your teeth,' Raine urged softly.

This time there was a longer pause. When Libby eventually opened her mouth in a humourless grin, showing the ruin within, Danny whistled.

'Why?' was all he asked.

'I bit the man who was attacking my friend,' said Libby, a note of defiance in her voice.

Brin chuckled. 'Nice one.' He held out his scarred knuckles for a bump. After a moment's hesitation Libby touched her own fist against his. He turned back to Raine. 'I still don't teach self-defence.'

'That's good, because she doesn't want to learn. What she wants is not to feel frightened when she leaves her flat. Or boat, in this case.'

Brin stayed looking at Raine for a beat, then back at Libby. 'What are you scared of?'

'She just got assaulted, for God's sake!' said Jolene. 'What do you think she's afraid of?'

'Why I'm asking her,' said Brin evenly, not taking his eyes off the girl.

'That I'll be too frightened,' she whispered. She was trying not to cry, but a lone tear treasoned its way out of her.

'Too frightened of what?'

'Too frightened to help. Next time.'

'She's a fighter, Danny. Like you. Help her get back up from what they did to her,' encouraged Raine.

Brin nodded slowly. 'Yeah. I could do that. Is that what you want?'

'Yes.' Libby's voice was small but firm.

'Prepared to work for it?'

Libby didn't say anything, just kept her head high and steady. She didn't need to answer him.

'Where'd you bite him?'

'His fingers. He had his hand over my mouth.'

'Proper,' said Brin appreciatively.

'Then his nose when he took his hand away. I think I swallowed a bit.'

Brin gave her an elbow to bump this time. 'You're like Emily. "No coward soul is mine."'

'Emily?' said Jolene, looking confused.

'Emily Bronte. Woman was hard as concrete.' He turned back to Raine. 'All right. I'm in.'

'Good,' said Raine brightly. 'Now that that's sorted, I've got work to do. I'll ping Brin's number over to you and you can fix up a time.' Raine gave a wave to Jolene and Libby, then took Brin's arm, leading him away.

'You completely set me up,' he said, as soon as they were out of earshot. 'You said you had a job for me.'

'That is a job,' said Raine. 'You're helping to shape the next generation.'

'You said it was a paying job.'

'You're getting paid with love.'

'A paying job that involves hard cash.'

'Oh, that job.' Raine stepped onto the gravel path that led towards Warwick Ave. 'No, that's a different job. That one definitely pays hard cash.'

'Okay,' said Brin, slightly mollified. 'What is it?'

Raine opened the gate leading on to the road. 'Come on. There's a pretty good diner round the corner. I'll let you buy me a burger while I tell you all about it.'

CHAPTER 17

'But she's not even a proper woman,' said Echo's mother, staring out of the screen in consternation. 'She's got a skateboard! What sort of future could you have with someone like that?'

'Skaters are real people too, Mum,' sighed Echo, wondering how on earth they had got onto the subject of Bitz. 'And we're not getting married, just trying out a few dates. She's fun to be with.'

'Maybe if you like pretending to be a teenager,' scoffed the woman staring out of the screen. Even though she was twelve thousand miles away and talking through a screen, Echo felt his mother's scorn. 'Does she even have a proper job?'

Echo sighed. 'I've told you before, Mum. She programs for a gaming company.'

'Ha!' said his mother triumphantly. 'See?'

'She earns at least three times as much as me, and her brain is double the size of mine. Really, Mum, if you let go of your prejudice—'

'I'm not prejudiced,' sighed his mother. 'I'm just your mother. I don't want you to get hurt. I'm sure Bitz is a nice person but . . .' She paused, suddenly looking older. 'It just seems so complicated. All the gender stuff. It was so much easier when everybody knew what to expect.'

Echo smiled at his mother. He thought of his own mixed heritage. Part Maori and part European. His own struggles with identity and representation. 'It was always complicated, Mum. We just pretended it wasn't.'

Echo's door burst open and Bitz bounded in, throwing herself onto the bed next to Echo. She was wearing a baggy pair of black combat shorts and a grey tee shirt that proclaimed:

don't blame the letters
blame the alphabet

'Hi, Mrs Echo!' said Bitz brightly, planting a kiss on Echo's cheek. 'How's tricks?'

'Hello, Bitz,' said the woman evenly, eyeing Bitz's tee shirt with slight confusion. 'My son has just been telling me that you and he are—'

'Going,' said Echo firmly. He did not want a three-way discussion about his and Bitz's relationship with his mother. Not now, when it was still so fragile. Probably not ever. Definitely not ever. 'I'll call you again next week.'

'Bye!' said Bitz, giving a side-to-side wave with one fingerless-gloved hand.

Echo pulled down the lid of his laptop, ending the call, and turned to face Bitz. She leaned in and kissed him, this time on the lips. He felt the coldness of her spider-bite piercings and the hardness of her compression vest beneath her tee.

'What was that for?' he asked when she pulled away. Bitz rarely did physical contact.

'For telling your mother I'm complicated. I'm not really, but it's cool that you think I am. Do you want to go out for pizza and a beer?'

Melissa Clarke flashed across his brain, the light from her eyes slowly fading. DEADTOWN etched in the strange tree like a Halloween promise. He wiped his hands across his face, scrubbing the image. In its place was Bitz, smiling at him.

'You know, I can't think of anything better,' he said, grabbing his jacket.

CHAPTER 18

Frankie Ridgeway stood halfway along Hastings Pier, gazing out into the grey, miserable morning. The sun had barely bothered to rise and a bitter wind blew salt in from the sea, giving the air a gritty feel. Beneath him the water seethed, hissing around the supports that held the structure in place. It was not a good day to be in a boat, trying to reach the Kent coastline from France. Still, that wasn't his problem. The people had already paid. His end was eight grand a pop. What did he care if they made it or not? There were always more. Syrian. Turkish. Albanian. There was an ever-growing list of countries lined up to supply people desperate enough to pay. Like the tide pounding against the pebbled shore behind him, it was unstoppable.

Frankie lit a cigarette. His skin crinkled as he sucked in the smoke, white and shiny along the scar Raine had left him. A physical reminder of why he was standing here on this freezing shit-stick of a pier staring out at the cold sea. The detective had burned London for him, at least for a while.

A seagull landed on the rail a few feet away, its black-button eyes fixed on the cigarette in his hand. Maybe it thought it was a chip, mused Frankie. He returned his gaze to the sea and smiled. In a way he should be grateful. Raine getting his boss Green arrested had given him an out. The man had been seriously psychotic. Frankie was a businessman, pure and simple. It just so happened that his business was . . . ideologically fluid. He didn't care what he did as long as he got paid. He took a final drag on his smoke and flicked the butt at the seagull, which duly flapped out of the way, only to settle a little further down the rail. *You're like me*, he thought, as he stared at the creature. *A survivor. Take any shit that's thrown at you and just move down the rail and scavenge off the next one in line. Because ultimately there is only yourself. Nobody else matters.*

'You know, The Sex Pistols once played on this pier, before they were famous.'

Frankie blinked. He didn't turn around but felt the skin between his shoulder blades tighten.

'Of course, that was before it got burned down and rebuilt again. I'd have loved to have seen Johnny and the boys ripping it up.'

Frankie took a long, slow breath. The skin around the scar on his face tingled. Carefully he turned around. Raine was leaning against the closed candyfloss kiosk, smiling at him. She was wearing the same black leather beret perched on the back of her head that she had on the last time he saw her, when he had bundled her unconscious body into the rear of the van. She was dressed completely in black: black cargo pants and army shirt, shemagh tied loosely around her neck. On her feet were a pair of battered aviator boots.

'Hi Frankie. Have you missed me?'

Frankie looked up and down the pier, but the detective seemed to be alone. The only other pedestrians were an old couple and a lone fisherman.

'Interesting,' said Frankie, leaning back against the rail and placing his hands in his pockets. Although outwardly calm, inside he was staggered. How had she found him? What the fuck did she want? He felt the comforting shape of the butterfly knife in his pocket. Even though the woman was alone, he wasn't going to underestimate her. 'I was just thinking about you, and here you are. Too tough for a coat? You must be freezing.'

'Nah, mate. Thermal vest and long-johns. Warm as muffins.'

'What do you want, Raine?' He raised his eyebrows. 'Are you here for revenge? What happened with you and me was just business.'

'Putting me in hospital?' she raised her own eyebrows, but the smile never left her lips.

He shrugged. 'That was the job. I'm out of London now. Pastures new. How did you find me?'

He slowly opened the knife in his pocket, pulling back the handle and releasing the blade. He kept his features neutral. In his peripheral vision he saw the old couple shuffle off the pier, leaving only the fisherman, who seemed intent on reading the sea.

'It wasn't hard. You're a big fish in small circles, Frankie. You leave an impression. Didn't take long for someone to point me in the right direction. Although I would have thought trafficking was a little seedy, even for you.'

Frankie shrugged. 'At least I get to go to the seaside.'

'Funny.'

Frankie actually laughed. 'Leave it out, Raine. You're here for revenge.'

Raine spread her hands wide. 'If I took personally everything a criminal did to me, I'd never have time for anything else. I'm just here for information about what happened in London.'

Frankie weighed up the situation. She was lying, obviously. No way was she going to walk away without trying to take him down. But she could have just done it when he'd had his back to her. When she'd had the element of surprise.

'I don't know what I can tell you,' he said eventually. 'Green was a monster. He never told me anything about his business.'

'But you were a gun for hire, right? It wasn't just Green; you were working for others as well?'

Frankie nodded reluctantly.

'Don't worry, I only want to know about a specific thing. Or a specific person, really.'

'Who?'

'Heather Salim.'

'Never heard of her. Who is she?'

'Stop the bullshit. You know exactly who she is.'

Frankie shrugged. 'Really, I've no idea what—'

'Her parents hired me to find her, but when I did, she was supposedly murdered outside her office in Shepherd Market. Face blown off in a tragic drug-related case of mistaken identity and run over by a van that fled the scene.'

Frankie shook his head sadly, hand tight on the knife in his pocket. 'Well, these things happen. Those drug gangs are fucking animals.'

'Except it wasn't Heather who got shot. And it turns out the DNA of the dead woman was found in the back of your van.'

Frankie opened his mouth to speak, but nothing came out.

'Shall I tell you what I think? I think you were hired to switch out Heather, reasons unknown. I think that you got the body of a woman who looked like Heather, blew her face off with a shotgun so she couldn't be identified, then called Heather down to the street in front of her office so you could snatch her and dump the body in her place.'

'That's bollocks. The body would need to be identified. Collected or whatever. If what you say is true—'

'No, you're right,' nodded Raine. 'And her body *was* identified by her parents. The people who hired me to find her. That's why the police released it back into their care.'

'So what's the problem?'

'The problem, Frankie, is they cremated the body.'

Frankie spread his hands, palms out. Maybe there *was* a chance he could shake this.

'Sounds like—'

'Which, considering she was a Muslim, doesn't compute. Why would her very religious parents have her cremated when it's not part of their tradition?'

'Not my problem. I don't even know the girl.'

'Do you remember when you broke my arm with your hammer? It was just before your good buddy Bugzy tried to throttle me.'

'I'm bored with this. Tell me what you want or fuck off. I've got places to be.' Frankie glanced around. The fisherman had gone. There was only himself and the detective on the pier. If he could flip her over the rail, it wouldn't even look like murder.

'You said you already knew where I lived.'

'What?' He refocused on Raine, ready to take his chance.

'You don't remember? When you first attacked me, I asked you how you found me. You said you already knew where I lived.'

Frankie said nothing.

'Then later, when you'd scarpered and we found the DNA in your van, everything sort of clicked. 'Cos you see, the same time I tracked down Heather, my boat got broken into and my laptop stolen. The laptop that detailed where Heather worked.'

Frankie made a decision. There was no way he was getting out of this clean. She had figured it out, or enough to cause more trouble than he could cope with. He needed to shut her down.

'I think it was you who broke into my boat. You who planted that body and tried to snatch Heather. You who arranged for the body to be cremated.'

'You're out of your mind,' snarled Frankie.

'Nice business you've got here, Frankie?' Raine cut across him, a light smile flitting around her mouth. 'Selling tiny boats to desperate people? Been doing it long?'

The change of direction threw him. 'What do you mean?'

'Smart man like you, I bet you were in at the beginning. At the boom. And not just the boats. I bet you do a line in ID papers too.'

Frankie pulled the knife out of his pocket, all pretence gone. 'I should have killed you last time.'

The hand that clamped over his wrist was iron-hard. Frankie felt his bones breaking even as the knife dropped from his hand. He gasped as his arm was rotated and pulled behind his back. The fisherman was standing beside him, a grim look on his face. Except up close Frankie could see he was no fisherman. The broken nose and scarring around the eyes. The glint of gold in the mouth.

'Hey Frankie!'

Frankie whipped round just in time to see Raine's elbow as it smashed into his temple. After that, he didn't see anything at all.

'That's for killing my cat.'

* * *

Frankie woke to a world of pain. His wrist where the man had caught him was a ribbon of fire. Slowly, he opened his eyes.

'Hi,' said Raine, giving him a little finger wave. 'If you throw up on me I'll break your other wrist. I need you to answer some questions.'

Frankie coughed out a lump of phlegm. 'I'm not answering shit.'

Raine ignored him. 'I recently asked a friend of mine to chase up on Heather's parents, and do you know what? There was no trace of them.' Her eyes opened wide in mock shock. 'The address they gave was a shell house. A flat that, it turned out, had lots of people registered as living there. A scam house, Frankie. Fake. About as fake, in fact, as Mr and Mrs Salim. Who were they? Were they straight off a lorry or is there a network?'

'I need a doctor—'

'What did you offer them to pretend to be Heather's parents? A UK passport? New birth certificates? Help to get their relations over?'

Frankie spat on the floor. There were strands of dark blood laced through the yellow mucus. 'You're so clever, you tell me.'

'It doesn't really matter, does it? What matters is you used me to find her, and then you tried to snatch her and make it seem like she was dead. Why? Who were you working for?'

Frankie's face twisted into a snarl. 'You'll never see her again. That's if she's even alive. The people who are after her, you don't fuck with them.'

'Two minutes,' said Danny Brin, looking out of the dusty window. 'I can see the lights.'

'I fuck with whoever I want to, Frankie,' said Raine softly. 'You know that. Now who's after her?'

'They'd kill me if I told you.'

'They're going to kill you anyway,' she snapped back brutally. 'Kidnapping, trafficking and assault puts you in the same prison as Green. As far as he's concerned you threw him under the bus when you went AWOL. What do you think he's going to do with you in there?'

Frankie's face paled, the scar appearing almost silver in the failing light. 'You can't . . .'

'You killed my cat, Frankie. You tried to kill me. Of course I can.'

'They're closing the pier,' said Danny.

'Who are?' said Frankie. The urgency in Brin's voice was cutting through the fog of pain.

'The police,' said Raine. 'I called it in. You've only got a short time before they get here. Give me a name, Frankie, and I'll let you make a run for it. Give you a sporting chance. Do you know how to swim?'

He turned to Danny Brin, his eyes pleading. 'It's just business. Making a living. Not personal.'

A crackle of static reached them from outside. Distorted voices talking over personal intercoms.

'Nearly here,' said Brin.

Frankie closed his eyes, trying to see an escape route. There wasn't one. She wouldn't let him go. Why should she? He wouldn't, if he was in her boots. No. She'd be happy to see him banged up in max. But he'd survive. He might have to shank a few people, but he'd survive. He'd done it all his life.

He decided to give her the name because he knew she'd follow it up. Try to find Heather. And when she did, she'd be fucked. Dead before she'd even realised she'd stopped breathing. And at least that would be something. As soon as he gave her the name she'd be a dead girl walking.

He opened his eyes and smiled. And gave her the name.

CHAPTER 19

I think it's probably time to go to the next phase. The next level.

Everything's shaping up, although the police haven't gone public yet.

Melissa's still not headlines. Not new headlines, anyway.

No points for them. Do not pass go. Do not collect a dead body.

Still, there's beginning to be a bit of chatter. Things are slowly coming in.

On the Net.

Through the matrix.

That's the beauty of chatrooms.

Not fast, but the trickle has begun.

Like I said, time to ramp it up a notch.

First things first, though.

Burn Melissa.

CHAPTER 20

Hume and Echo were in the car, heading for Aquinas Street, when the notification came through on his mobile. Echo glanced at the unfolded device on the dash.

'It's active. Melissa's phone. It's been switched on again.'

'Where?' said Hume, peering at the phone. There was a new blue dot on the map.

'Close. It's crossing Waterloo Bridge.'

'Which direction?'

'South, towards the station.'

'That's only a couple of minutes away. Flip the lights!'

Echo accelerated, pulling out of the traffic and engaging the police lights in the unmarked car. In its car cradle, Echo's phone, mirroring Melissa's map app, showed the blue dot as it made its way across the bridge.

'Hurry,' said Hume. 'If we can get there before they leave the bridge then they'll have nowhere to go!'

Echo nodded, his eyes fixed to the road. The early morning commuter traffic was dense, but they could now see the bridge ahead. A minute later he turned left into Theatre Avenue, driving down and pulling in at the bollards separating the road from the pedestrian walkway.

'Lock it and leave the lights flashing,' said Hume, clambering out. 'Are they still crossing the river?'

'Nearly over.'

'Damn.' Hume broke into a run. When she reached the steps leading up to the bridge she scanned the pedestrians coming down, searching for anyone who looked suspicious. Echo stopped beside her, white breath pluming as he sucked in air.

'Blimey, you can put on a speed, can't you?'

'All the running I do,' she said, looking around. 'Where are they now?'

Echo squinted at his phone. 'Just passing us.'

Hume turned in a full circle. There were hundreds of people coming off the bridge and walking along the pedestrian way. Everybody was wrapped up against the cold in coats and hoodies. Just about all of them seemed to be holding a phone. 'Damn! Where now?'

'Back the way we came.'

'How accurate is it?'

Hume and Echo began following the blue dot, scanning the people ahead.

'Within ten metres.'

'Ring it.'

Echo nodded, swiping the app to one side of the screen and bringing up a dial box on the other. Hume scrutinised the people around her. A hooded figure ahead pulled out their phone and glanced at the screen.

'It just rings out,' said Echo. The hooded figure pocketed the phone.

'Ring it again.'

As Echo redialled, Hume concentrated on the person ahead.

'Ringing.'

The hooded figure pulled out their phone and pointed it back towards the bridge, taking a picture. Echo shook his head. 'Still ringing.'

Hume swore softly.

They followed the blue dot on Echo's phone, all the while ringing the number, but the roads were so congested with people that it was impossible to tell who was doing what.

'We can't do this all day,' muttered Hume. 'Either we cordon off the area, or we tell everyone to stop moving and search for the phone. Do we know what make Melissa's mobile is?'

'It's gone.'

'What's gone? The signal?'

'It just dropped. They must have turned the phone off.'

'Damn.' Hume stood on tiptoe, turning in circles, but it was useless. The swell of morning commuters, all with phones in their hands or audio sticks protruding from their ears, or tourists clicking for memories, meant that unless someone was noticeably acting furtive or running away, there was no chance. 'Nothing?' she asked Echo.

'Sorry. It's dead.'

'Right,' said Hume in clipped tones. 'Next time we throw a blanket over the whole area. Search everyone. Somebody's playing with us and I don't like to be played with.'

Echo followed behind as she headed back towards the car at a fast pace.

'Let's get to the house in Aquinas Street. I want to have another scout around. That carving in the tree bothers me. It's like bragging or something. Rubbing our face in it.'

It was only when Hume reached the car that she realised Echo was not with her. He had stopped a few feet away to read something on his phone.

'What is it?' asked Hume, staring at the concern on her sergeant's face. 'Has the signal come back?'

Silently he handed the phone over, still open in its tablet mode. On the screen was a post from Reddit, the social platform of communities, known for its toxicity. She quickly scanned the post. It was titled *Melissa Clarke Dead in Deadtown*.

'Shit,' muttered Hume.

Looks like she didn't do a runner after all LOL.

Below was the scene from Aquinas Street: Melissa getting her throat cut, looped in a two-second clip.

'Either somebody leaked it, or the killer has released it somewhere online,' said Echo quietly.

Below the post, the comments had already reached the hundreds.

Couldn't happen to a nicer bitch.

OMG her poor family.

Don't believe the lie: it's clearly a fake.

Agreed TBF she'd do anything for the clicks.

Hume closed the phone and handed it back to Echo. 'It won't be long until the mainstream news sites pick this up, and then all hell is going to break loose. I suppose it's too late to shut it down?'

'It's already on Bluesky and all over X,' said Echo. 'Not a chance.'

'Right,' she sighed. 'Let's head back to the office. Get in touch with media relations and set up a statement. I'll go and see the chief. On the bright side, he might dedicate some more staff. The press is going to want to know what we're doing.'

* * *

But by the time they neared the office things had gone from bad to worse. The websites of the heritage papers had already got hold of the story and were frothing at the mouth. Hume stared at the words, feeling her heart sink.

HALLOWEEN HELLHOUSE screamed one banner. *POLICE COMPLETELY IN THE DARK.*

CHAPTER 21

After she had handed over Ridgeway to the authorities, and they had confirmed her credentials with DI Conner, Raine met up with Brin again and they caught a return train to London. Within a couple of hours she was back in her boat, sitting at her desk.

She had never heard of the name Ridgeway had hissed at her. The look of satisfied malice in his eyes had convinced her that he wasn't lying; that he knew she'd track down the name and that it would put her in danger. Why else would he give it up?

Outside, she saw a woman walking her dog along the towpath. Her breath came out in unseasonal white puffs, hinting at the winter to come. Raine's boat didn't have a cosy wood burner like Jolene's. She never spent long enough there to warrant it. If she wasn't working, then she was sleeping. Filling up every waking moment with distractions so that she didn't have to stop and think about her own life.

She sipped coffee, unfolded her phone, and tapped in the name Ridgeway had given her.

Joseph Banner.

She got several top of the page hits, mainly on Facebook and LinkedIn. She spent a few minutes scatter-searching, following links down various rabbit holes. Nothing stood out.

Next, she ran the databases. The PND and a backdoor NCIC search. Although there were several criminals with the correct name, none rang any bells for her. Two were in their eighties, one was a teenager, and three were in jail. She did not think Ridgeway would give her the name of a convict. He expected her to chase the man down. In fact, she suspected, he thought the man would kill her. There had been that triumphant tilt of his head as he had been cuffed and bundled away. Like he had had the last laugh.

Raine stabbed at her phone in its stand. DI Conner answered on the second ring.

'Congratulations on your upcoming baby, Inspector!'

'Raine. How did you—?'

'Mary. She told me you were going to name her after me. You have my permission, but I expect an invite to the christening.'

'We're not going to call her Raine,' said the detective inspector firmly. 'I don't know where you got that idea.' There was a small pause before: 'But if you'd like to tell—'

'Joseph Banner. Mean anything to you?'

'Wasn't he the Incredible Hulk?'

'I think that was Bruce Banner. Any other ideas? Maybe someone not fictional? Or green? Preferably someone linked to drugs or trafficking? Or possibly prostitution?'

'It's not ringing any bells. I'll ask around and get back to you. Why, what's he done?'

'No idea. It's just a name that's cropped up regarding an old case.' Raine didn't mention which case. The DI knew she hadn't let go of finding Heather, but he, like everybody else, believed the woman was dead. 'It was a long shot, but I thought I'd ask.'

'Have you checked with DI Hume? She might have come across him in a murder enquiry.'

'The very next person on my list,' said Raine, giving her goodbyes and ending the call. But she didn't call Hume immediately. Instead, she gazed out of the window some more. She'd been a little thrown by her last meeting with Hume. Not only about what Mary had said, about wanting to spend more time with her: she understood that. Even felt the same, a little. Over the last year, their relationship had developed, woven and strengthened by a need to keep Clara alive. Her memory. Talking to Mary, sharing experiences and healing wounds, was a way of doing that. But it was also dangerous. As well as a way of coming together, it was a way of letting go. Accepting that Clara was in the past. It was selfish, but Raine didn't want to let go. Not of her memories. Not of her pain. Not of her anger.

And not of her love. Raine was terrified that if she shared Clara's memory with anyone it would somehow make her less. Make her leave. And Raine couldn't have that. Because without Clara she was nothing. Just an empty bag of skin and bones going through the motions of living.

She sighed, reached forward and tapped the screen. The call was answered after the first ring.

'DI Hume.'

'Mary! You know you sound more impressive each time I call. Very official. Have you been on some sort of course?'

'What do you want, Raine? I'm up to the gills in it here.'

'Why? What's happened?'

Hume gave a brief outline of the morning's events, culminating in the Halloween headline.

'Told you it would be a fuckstorm once the media got hold of it.'

'Why are you calling, anyway?' asked Hume. 'Has something happened with your Heather case?'

'Not sure. Have you ever heard of Joseph Banner?'

'Concerning what?'

'Anything, at this point, but pretty certain it would have to be London-based.'

There were a few seconds of dead air, and Raine could practically hear Hume's internal filing system whirring.

'Nothing comes to mind,' Hume said eventually. 'But it's a reasonably common name. He would have had to be linked to something major for it to trigger any alarms.'

'That's what I thought. Thanks anyway. Let me know if I can help with the Halloween thing.'

'I will, but at the moment I haven't got the budget.'

'Yeah, well that might change fast. The brass aren't going to want this one hanging about.' Raine was scrolling through the newsfeeds. 'Dead journo who wrote about vicious murders viciously murdered with the footage posted online. The hate jockeys are practically orgasming into their laptops as they post.'

'A beautiful image, Raine. Thank you.'

'Welcome. Later.' She leaned back in her chair and brooded. There must be some way in. Some angle she was missing. She thought back to everything she knew about Heather Salim. It wasn't much. All she had was a phone number that was never answered and a few pictures she had taken on surveillance when she'd been hired to find her. She opened her laptop and accessed the file on Heather. The images she had of the woman were sparse. A few outside the office where she worked. A couple as she was entering and leaving her rented flat in Catford. Raine had visited it after Heather's disappearance, but it had been cleared out. The only other shots she had were of the night Raine had rescued her from a sexual assault by a street gang.

Raine stared at the pictures on the screen. The young woman in the alley, hair covered by a hijab, face tight and frightened. The young men surrounding her. Corralling her. Cutting off her means of escape, their hard faces lit with evil intent. At the time Raine had thought it fortunate that the woman was being harassed. It had given her a reason to intervene. An excuse to interact with Heather. A way to get close without causing suspicion. She had pretended it was the gang members she was after. Had even got the leader arrested. But all the time it had been Heather she'd been trailing.

'Luke,' she said, recalling the name of the gang leader, zooming in on him as he manhandled the petrified Heather.

Even in the dark alley, he had been menacing. In his early twenties but street years older. When Raine had intervened, he had hit her and knocked her to the ground. Later, she had got him arrested for dealing, paying him back for the slap. She stared at his face on the screen. Her eyes unfocused for a second. Then she smiled.

The alley where they had attacked Heather was nowhere near their normal hunting ground, south of the river. Maybe they had been in the West End dealing, but if it was about drugs, they wouldn't have messed about with opportunistic rape.

'You were there on purpose,' she said to the image, almost affectionately. 'On business.'

Raine thought for a second, then fired off an email to her contact at police records, asking where Luke Parsons was currently being held. Then she tried to place herself mentally back in the alley. Tried to change her preconception of a sexual assault to . . . what?

While she waited for her contact to get back to her, she checked out all the online material regarding Melissa Clarke. As well as the original disappearance, there was a mushroom cloud of new information and speculation. Since the clip of Melissa's supposed murder had dropped, the internet had gone on a feeding frenzy. Pictures of Hume and Echo were tagged with assertions about police incompetence. Raine smiled grimly when she saw a copied Facebook post of Echo halfway up a tree waving a scarf.

The photo was tag-lined with: *WTF are we paying these people for?*

'Nice,' muttered Raine. She tapped out a message to Hume, asking her to ping over any info she had on the case.

Let me take a look, she typed. *Free of charge. Consider it an anniversary present.*

Then she shut down her computer, put another pod in the Nespresso machine and just let herself tick. Unconsciously, she held the fob cache containing Clara's ashes in her hand, her thumb gently stroking the black metal.

CHAPTER 22

Chief Inspector Rockall was not happy. He pointed to the image on his laptop, his face tight with anger.

'I mean why was he up a bloody tree, for God's sake! It makes us seem like bumbling idiots!'

'I sent him up,' said Hume, hiding her own anger, bubbling just beneath the surface. 'We were following a lead and, as it happened, we found a potentially important bit of evidence up there.'

'Yes, but the optics are terrible! How was this picture even taken? Wasn't there a cordon or something?'

'No body, no budget,' reminded Hume. 'If we actually had any staff working on this, then there would have been a very different turnout. Perhaps—'

'You still don't have anything,' interrupted the DCI. 'Not really. It's my understanding that it has not been possible to verify the veracity of the . . . the video clip?'

'No,' admitted Hume reluctantly. 'We have a mounting body of circumstantial evidence, but no actual corpse.'

'And why is that?' asked her superior. 'Any theories? Why would somebody kill this woman, then clean up the site as if nothing had ever happened?'

'The video clip was on a busted burner phone handed in anonymously. I don't think we were even meant to know about it.'

'I should bloody hope not!' said the Chief Inspector. 'If they, whoever they are, were actually goading us in some way.' He grimaced. 'That doesn't bear thinking about.'

'Yes, sir.'

'And the clip of Melissa Clarke being murdered that appeared on social media? Was that leaked by one of us?'

'It's a possibility, but unlikely. Far more plausible is that the killer leaked it themselves.'

'Why?'

Hume shrugged her shoulders, frustrated. 'I don't know, sir.'

'And what about this phone mapping business?' asked the DCI, scanning her report. 'Any ideas?'

Hume shook her head. 'There will be a reason. There always is. It's just a matter of finding the why.'

'Unless they're unhinged,' said her boss ominously.

Hume glanced at him. He looked tired. Beyond tired. Like he was being washed away inside. His face was sallow and seemed to hang looser than it had last time they had met. She softened her voice. 'No one unhinged could pull this off. Killing a person and removing the body, leaving no trace. Making fun of us in the media. Getting hold of that Facebook photo of Echo in the tree means they must be tracking us. Following the case and exploiting it for some reason. The whole thing requires a hinged mind, sir, however warped. Or minds,' she added, thoughtfully. 'Because there's quite a lot of activity for just one person.'

He sighed, nodding. 'Which, of course, is much worse. It means fewer mistakes. More planning. I'm going to recall DC Jonas and have him rejoin your team.'

'Really?' said Hume, perking up. 'Thank you, sir. Echo has been stretched. There are so many data points on this case that—'

'But I expect a resolution, Mary. We are already compromised in the public's eye. Much more of this . . .' he pointed at the screen showing a triumphant Echo waving the scarf, 'and our position will be unsalvageable. The Commissioner is already thinking of making more cuts . . .'

'Sir,' said Hume.

* * *

'We need to take that video apart,' said Hume, as soon as she arrived back at her office.

Echo looked up from his tablet.

'Prove that it is either real or mocked up,' she continued, throwing herself into her seat. Melissa Clarke stared out at her from the smart board. Hume thought she had an accusatory expression on her face. 'Until we do that, we can't progress. If it's a fake, we need to investigate an entirely different line of enquiry. Find out how it was staged. What kind of—'

'That may not be necessary,' said Echo, handing her his tablet. 'This came in while you were having your meeting.'

Hume raised an eyebrow, taking the device. Echo's voice was serious, his face tense.

'What is it?'

'Another social media clip. A screenshot of a video playing on a computer.'

'A screenshot—?'

'It means there's no metadata of the video itself.'

'I'll take your word for it. What does it show?'

'Here's the post.'

Hume read the short message.

All over the socials. Somebody's burning their bridges. What are the police even doing to stop this? Not even trying. No points. Do not pass go. It seems like the press is right; They're just bumbling about in the dark.

'Well, that's not very nice. We're doing our best.'

Hume clicked on the still image below the message. A scene opened in what appeared to be a basement. It was dark, with bare brick walls. The only light came from a furnace of some kind. The door to the furnace was open, the gas flames casting a blue tint to the image.

'What is that?' asked Hume, squinting. 'Doesn't look like a domestic furnace. A hospital? Warehouse? It looks industrial.'

'I don't think so,' said Echo. 'See the tag on the front?'

Hume peered closer. There was a square plate in the bottom left of the face of the incinerator. 'I can't read it. What does it say?'

'It's the manufacturer's ID. DFW Incinerator 100. I looked them up.'

'Right,' said Hume. 'Good. And who do they supply to? Can we get addresses?'

A figure in a baggy hoodie appeared on screen, pushing a gurney. On the trolley was the body of Melissa Clarke, clearly dead. She was still wearing the same clothes as in the last video, in Aquinas Street. The ribbons of blood were dry now. They didn't glisten in the light from the furnace as they would if they were fresh.

'Jesus,' Hume whispered.

'The company doesn't supply warehouses,' said Echo. 'In fact, their clientele is super specific.'

'Yes? Who are their clientele?'

'Dead people. They supply incinerators for crematoriums. That's what you're looking at. A furnace for cremating human remains.'

Hume blinked at him, then focused again on the tablet. The hooded figure was pushing the body of Melissa towards the open door of the incinerator. The screen went black just as she reached the furnace. Hume stared at the blank screen for a moment, then wordlessly handed the tablet back to Echo.

'What do you think?' asked Echo.

Hume closed her eyes for a moment, trying to pull everything together. It was too much. The house in Aquinas

Street. The scarf in the tree. The seemingly random appearances of Melissa's phone on the location app. Now this. There didn't seem to be any logic to it.

Her phone buzzed: a message from Raine, asking her to send through any information she had on the case. Sharing information with Raine could get her in trouble, even if the detective was technically still with the force, albeit mothballed and inactive. To all intents and purposes, she was a civilian. If anybody got wind of her using an outside source without authorisation, there would be consequences. On the other hand, the cutbacks and lack of staff meant this investigation was severely hampered. A different perspective might make sense of the seemingly random threads of the case.

Hume passed her phone to Echo. 'Get it all to her. I'll fix it with the boss.'

'*Consider it an anniversary present*,' read Echo. 'I didn't know it was yours and Robert's anniversary.'

Hume shook her head. 'No. She's talking about the anniversary of Clara's death.'

'Oh, right,' said Echo. He knew Raine had been married to Hume's daughter. That it had been a difficult relationship since Clara had died. Probably before she had died. He also knew that Raine carried a cache of her wife's ashes around with her, but that was as far as his knowledge went. He didn't know how she died. 'I'm sorry.'

'Nothing to be sorry for. It's on Friday. Her anniversary. We're going out for a meal. Robert thinks I should invite Raine.'

'Right,' said Echo again. He didn't know what else to say.

'Just send her the stuff,' sighed Hume. 'And find out where that incinerator is.'

CHAPTER 23

The next few days were frustrating. Hume felt she was wading through a blizzard of information that was blinding her to the facts that would move the case on. Echo had traced the leak of the video clip of Melissa getting her throat cut to a puppet TikTok account — an account with a fake ID — that had then been shared with a large selection of conspiracy blog sites. The account had only been used for the one post and had since been deleted. Tracing the owner of the Facebook account that had posted Echo climbing the tree had been harder as it was made from a shadow profile.

'What's a shadow profile?' Hume had asked.

'It's a Facebook account made from data used without a person's knowledge. Usually, the data is scraped from other Facebook accounts. It's a way of having an account anonymously, without it being obviously stolen or fraudulent.'

'Is that legal?' Hume asked.

'Facebook themselves do it all the time. Create accounts for people without their consent.'

'Jesus. What a world we live in. How did you find it?'

'I didn't: the account holder came forward. Beatrix Stevens. The same woman you were talking to when I was retrieving the scarf from the tree.'

'Being lectured to, more like. And you're telling me that little old lady set up a shadow account?'

'Normal account from a shadow profile, but yes, seems like it. We'll be able to ask her tomorrow. We have a breakfast appointment with her at 8 a.m.'

'Eight? That's very early.'

'It's the only time she could fit us in, apparently.'

'Right. Well, she'd better supply us with a nice cup of tea at that time, then. What else?'

'Melissa's phone made another appearance, but there were no officers near enough to get a sighting before the signal dropped out.' Echo swiped the location onto a map of the capital and displayed it on the board along with the two earlier digital sightings. 'Also, the footage from Aquinas Street has finally come through.'

'Which footage?'

'From the property across the street.'

Echo sent the video file to the smart board, and Hume watched as the door camera stream showed two people entering and leaving the property. The time stamp confirmed it to be earlier on the same day Hume had been there, but neither of the two were Melissa. The images didn't show their faces, but they were completely the wrong build. One was tall and skinny and the other short. Both wore hoodies pulled down low and buffs pulled up high to cover their faces.

'Who are they?' Hume wondered aloud.

Later, as they ate steaming beef rendang with noodles, picked up from a cafe on Gerrard Street, they viewed the footage again.

'They move like teenagers.' Hume stabbed at the cardboard carton angrily, managing to spear a wafer of beef. 'All angles and elbows. And the way they interact, it's like they're heading to a party rather than a . . . whatever this is.'

She and Echo watched as the two figures looked around. One of them seemed to be filming the scene on their phone.

'Definitely teenagers,' muttered Hume. There was no audio with the images, but the way they were looking around and nudging each other did not suggest a dark deed. More of an adventure.

'The property wasn't broken into,' said Echo. 'So they don't jimmy the lock.'

The detectives watched closely as the two figures approached the door.

'Which suggests either the door wasn't locked in the first place, or they had a key.' She munched thoughtfully, watching the scene unfold. After a few moments, the door opened and they disappeared inside. She noted the time stamp. 'They spend fifteen minutes there. They must have seen the body. Why didn't they call the police?'

'And why are they even there, whoever they are?' added Echo. 'We can track them leaving for a few streets via CCTV, but after that . . .' He shrugged. 'The walkways and underpasses around London Bridge are a maze. Plus all the commuter traffic. We lose them.'

'But their prints were on the tree in Chelsea, which puts them at two of the crime scenes.'

'Potential crime scenes. We still have no body.'

Hume pointed her chopsticks at him. 'Correct. Which brings me to my next question. How are we getting on with tracking down the crematorium furnace?'

'There's only a dozen crematoria in London,' said Echo between mouthfuls. 'And I've visited every one of them.' He gave an involuntary shiver. 'Knowing that bodies were being incinerated somewhere in the building gave me the creeps.'

'Isn't cremation popular in the Maori community?' asked Hume, interested.

'Not really. It's not banned or anything, just not common. The only time it's recommended is if you die in an enemy's territory.'

'Why?'

Echo smiled. 'So that your bones can't be captured and used against you.'

Hume stared at him. 'You're kidding.'

'Nope.'

'What, like as a club or something?'

Echo winced. 'It's more metaphysical than that.'

'Of course it is.' They ate in silence for several moments before Hume continued:

'Well I don't suppose it will come up. It's not like you'll ever be cremated, is it? The vampire dentist will have turned you into a dried-up husk long before that.'

Echo grimaced. 'Not funny.'

'Or Bitz might have uploaded you onto some personal gaming platform for her pleasure.'

'Now that sounds more like it.' said Echo, grinning. 'What about you? Maybe Robert will turn you into one of his culinary experiments.'

He dodged the ball of paper Hume threw at him.

'How's it going with Bitz, anyway?'

'Excellent. My mother doesn't understand her.'

'Thank God I'm not the only one.' Hume paused, then said: 'Should I be saying "they", by the way? I wasn't sure about Bitz's pronouns.'

'Good to check, but she's happy with *she*.'

'I thought she was non-binary.'

Echo nodded. 'Or quantum, as she likes to put it. As far as she's concerned gender is a user interface, with her body having heritage female physiognomy.'

Hume gave him a worried stare. 'Am I supposed to know what that means?'

'She thinks addressing people by their preferred pronouns is a matter of respect and acceptance, but she's easy with whatever you want. She doesn't think any of it really applies to her, so she's impossible to misgender.' He shrugged. 'She's Bitz.'

'Right. I'm glad we've sorted that out,' said Hume, feeling like she'd skipped a lesson in body politics and would never catch up. 'Tell me about the crematoria.'

'Like I said, I've visited them all. Checked out their furnaces. There's no match to the video.'

'So that means what? That we're going to have to expand it to the rest of the UK? How many crematoria will that be?'

'Actually, I don't think we need to go there yet.'

'Why?' Hume was suddenly alert, picking up on something in his voice. 'Is this one of those times where you hold information back until the end? Because you know I don't—'

'Nothing like that. It's just that at the last crematorium, the manager said something that got me on to a different path.'

'What?'

'He said that the incinerator was one of the smallest ones he'd seen.'

'So?'

'So I did some research. Did you know that they make furnaces just for pets?'

Hume paused, chopsticks in mid-air. 'For pets?'

'Well, not just pets. But for small animals; used by vets and such. But pet cremations are a growing market, apparently.'

Hume had a flashback of Raine emptying the ashes of her cat, Melania, into the Regent's Canal. She shook her head to dislodge the image. 'Okay, so what have you found?'

'Hard to find a complete list. Some are attached to veterinary practices. Others are privately run, complete with their own gardens of rest. Then there are mobile services. Some of those are not registered as pet cremation. It's going to take me a while to chase them all down. I've asked the furnace company for a list of businesses they've sold to, but it could be a second-hand product.'

Hume raised her carton of beef rendang. 'Good work. Sounds like we might actually have a lead.'

'I've sent a cropped photo of the furnace and wall to as many of the businesses as I could scrape off the Net. Hopefully we'll hear something soon.'

Hume nodded. 'Fingers crossed. What about Melissa's mother? Any sign of the partner — ex-partner?'

'Nothing yet, and I'm still trying to track down the so-called old flame from the newspaper article.'

'Okay, well keep digging.' Hume stood, putting on her coat. 'That's it for tonight. I'm shattered. Don't stay here too late. We have that interview with the Chelsea woman, Beatrix Stevens, in the morning.'

* * *

A couple of hours later Echo sat on his nano-balcony, gazing out over Shoreditch. Across the river, he could see fireworks above Rotherhithe and Deptford. It reminded him of footage he had watched on the news: war videos from besieged desert towns. Rockets and tracer fire above a burning city. Although the night was unseasonably cold, he stayed out, watching the spectacle, until his bones started to ache in the bitter air.

Back inside, Echo shut the sliding glass door and slouched onto his bed. He grabbed a beer from the mini-fridge and reached for his tablet. Opening up a map of London, he placed a digital marker on each of the areas where Melissa's mobile had reappeared. Unfolding his phone, he typed the names of the streets into Google, trying to find a connection. Nothing sprang out. He punched in all the prominent buildings. Pubs. Restaurants. Theatres. Anything that might have a history he could search. There had to be a reason the person, whoever they were, had visited the locations.

He took a swig of his beer, tapping the neck of the bottle against his lip.

He added the three possible crime scenes. Aquinas Street, the tree in Chelsea and Melissa Clarke's flat. He rotated the map, examining the points from all angles, trying to see the pattern. He knew there must be one. There was always a reason for things, even if the reasoning was flawed. There was a reason for everything. Nothing was random. Even random wasn't random, merely the breaking down of short-term predictability as the possibilities increased. All that was required were enough data points and the reason would reveal itself.

Bitz came crashing into his room, startling him out of his reverie. The door banged off the wall, hitting the indent she'd caused by doing the same thing dozens of times before. 'Knock knock!'

Echo smiled. She was dressed in cut-off, faded dungarees with the bib and straps hanging down. 'You have no conception of personal space, do you?'

'Of course I do,' she said, flopping down on the bed and giving him a peck on the cheek. 'And I knew you'd want me to be in yours. Do you fancy a game of something? I've been coding five hours straight and need to work off some energy before I explode.'

Bitz was wearing an old green army tee that declared:

I'm not in
leave a message

'Or maybe a dance-off?' she suggested. In the basement of their building was a games area containing a state-of-the-art dance step machine.

'I'd love to, but my brain is fried. I need to get some sleep and reboot.'

'So what's frying your brain?' asked Bitz, eyebrow raised. Echo saw that there were reverse tramlines cut into it. Not gang-style, more barcode.

'My current case. I can't really go into details.'

'So how about giving me an overview, then? No specifics. It would be good for my brain to have somebody else's problem in it.'

'So I'd be doing me a favour?'

'Exactly.'

Echo made certain there was no sensitive information on the tablet that could compromise the investigation, then swivelled it round to show Bitz.

'Map of London,' she said, reaching across him into the mini-fridge and pulling out a coke. 'Solved.'

'If you're wired from coding, should you really be drinking that?' he enquired, his own eyebrows raising as she cracked the ring pull.

'Absolutely. What are the location markers for?'

'That's the problem. We've been trying to track a phone. Whenever it's switched on, it plots its route to follow in real time.' He pointed at the flags on the screen. 'These are the locations where it has shown up.'

'Why?'

'Why what?'

'Why does it have its location broadcast?'

'Ah, right. It was linked to another phone. The two phones belonged to work partners. The location sharing was so each of them knew where the other was. But this phone,' he tapped the screen, 'is only being switched on periodically. We've tried to find it. We sent officers to the area, but never caught up with it. It doesn't make it easier that we don't know what the user looks like.'

'Did you try ringing it?'

'Of course, but hardly anybody has their ringer on these days.'

'If you know the number you can force it to ring,' said Bitz. 'Even if it's on silent.'

Echo nodded. 'Tried that too, but no joy.'

'So maybe it's not really there,' Bitz said brightly.

Echo looked at her uncertainly. 'What do you mean?'

'Maybe somebody spoofed it.'

Echo nodded. Geospoofing. The use of software to make an IP address or phone register in one location when it was really in another, completely different area. 'But it isn't stationary. It moves.'

'You can do that these days,' said Bitz. 'It's not just used to mask your location for cheaper Netflix or whatever. It's massive in the gaming industry. You can buy spoofed phones that geo-jump to order.'

'Okay. But what would be the point here? Why make a false route that leads nowhere?'

'Why switch your device on at all if you know you can be tracked?' said Bitz reasonably.

'Right.' Echo swigged the last of his beer and pocketed his phone. 'My brain's melting. Let's go and race.'

Bitz's face lit up. 'Cars?'

'How about skis?' The building's arcade room had recently acquired a downhill ski simulator. Contestants could race against each other on a choice of Alpine slopes, their progress mapped on giant screens in front of them.

Bitz nodded her head enthusiastically. 'Brilliant. It's got a cool Easter egg I can show you.'

For the next hour, Echo forgot all about work, losing himself in the enjoyment of the game and being with Bitz. After she'd beaten him for the sixth time, he held up his hands. 'Enough. How come you're so good at virtual skiing? Have you even done it in the real world?'

'As far as my brain goes, this is the real world.'

'Fair enough.' Echo drained the bottle of Red Stripe. 'I need to get to bed.' He started to step off the game platform, then paused. 'Where's this Easter egg you were going to show me?'

Bitz grinned, the light glinting off her lip rings. 'We'll need to play one more game.'

'Bitz,' began Echo. 'I'm tired—'

'No, really. It's at the end of the run. We'll need to play the slope and then you let me go in front.'

'Like that will be a change,' he said. He climbed back onto the platform and slotted his feet into the skis. The game began and they glided down the virtual slope on the screen in front of them, dodging trees and boulders until they came to the final run.

'Now tuck in behind,' said Bitz. 'And follow me.'

Just as the finishing line came into view, Bitz pulled a hard right, skiing between two buildings. Echo followed, the game's haptics making his skis vibrate. Ahead of him Bitz crashed through a fence onto an iced-over lake. Her skis immediately turned into ice skates, and he watched as she began to glide over the ice.

'Cool or what?' she said excitedly.

Echo skied through the broken fence and onto the ice. Bitz pressed a button on the console, changing the perspective. The screen now showed an overshot of their two avatars skating on the lake. Silver lines glowed, revealing the routes their skates had taken.

'Watch this,' Bitz said breathlessly. She bent her legs, changing direction. On the screen she began to skate in a circle. 'Once you get the hang of it, you can write your name on the ice!'

The joy in her voice was infectious. Echo twisted, causing the figure on the frozen pond to turn. He watched as Bitz scribed a perfect B. His own attempt at an E looked more like a scribble.

'Excellent first attempt!' Bitz shoulder-bumped him.

They skated on for another few minutes before Echo stepped back. 'I really do need to hit the sack.'

Once they'd said their goodnights Echo returned to his flat feeling relaxed and happy. Wherever his relationship with Bitz went would be fine. He was just grateful he had her in his life. As he climbed into bed, he thought of her skating her initial and smiled. He turned off his light and rolled over.

Then he rolled back and turned the light back on. 'No way!' he muttered, sitting up and grabbing his tablet. He swiped back to the map of London and pulled up the locations where Melissa's mobile had been activated. This time, rather than just showing the coordinates with a flag, he expanded one of the journeys, the route around the pub in Soho, and let it play out at five times the normal speed. He watched as the flag moved along Old Compton Street and into Greek Street, circling the Coach and Horses. He set it on repeat, the journey beginning again as soon as it ended. Then he split the screen, copying the map app, removing everything but the flag, mapping out its virtual journey with no background. With a stylus he followed the cursor, creating a visible line showing the mobile's route.

'Like drawing letters on ice with the blade of a skate,' he whispered. He rotated his drawing ninety degrees and stared at what he had drawn.

Quickly, he pulled over the two other mobile routes and repeated the process. He stared amazed as the digital journeys revealed a second and third letter.

eod

He stared at what he had drawn, following the routes, then added the initial letters in the other three key locations he had notated earlier.

Aquinas Street, where Melissa had been murdered.
Wilbraham Place, where the leaves may have come from.
Drake House, Melissa's home address.
He now had E O D A W D.

He stared into space for a moment, then grabbed his phone and went back through his notes from the investigation. After a moment's searching, he found what he was looking for. The street where Oliver Bell supposedly parked his van: Tressillian Road.

He added the T.
E O D A W D T.

The sequence of letters rearranged themselves in his head, and even as he typed them in a different order on the screen of his tablet, he felt the chills slither down his back.

deadtow

All that was missing was the final N.

CHAPTER 24

Luke Parsons didn't look like the cocky roadman who had assaulted Heather Salim. He looked beaten down. His hair was greasy and his skin sallow. When he entered the interview room of the security facility, his wary gaze flicked around the small space, searching for danger. It settled on Raine, sitting at the table.

'Hi, Luke,' she said brightly. 'Good to see you. Take a seat.'

Luke just stood there, confusion and resentment causing his muscles to writhe, snake-like, under his skin, his jaw tight with the pressure. The guard held onto his elbow and guided him to the seat on the other side of the table. His cuffed hands were secured to a metal restraint bolted into its surface. Raine smiled and nodded at the guard. 'Cheers, Michael. I'll be fine from here.'

'Fifteen minutes,' he said, leaving the room.

Raine stared at the young man, a gentle smile on her face, her head cocked slightly as if she was watching a vaguely amusing animal. There was a digital clock on the wall. When two minutes had passed, Luke muttered, 'What you doing here?'

'You remember me?' said Raine. 'You know who I am?'

'You're the one who put me here.' He shook his cuffed hands. 'Got me chained up. Can't remember your name, though.' He leaned back and stared at the ceiling.

Raine banged her hand on the table, the loud sound causing Luke to jump slightly. 'It's Raine,' she said. 'Like the weather only with an "e" on the end, and I don't believe you.' The grin she offered was full of mischief. 'Not after all the good times we had together. I'm certain my name would have wedged in your brain like a poker.'

Luke nodded slowly. 'Raine. Yeah. Whatever.'

She was right. He remembered her. How could he not? She'd fooled him in the alley where he and his boys had been messing with the Muslim woman. Then she'd sucker-punched him later and stolen the drugs he'd been transporting for the Nightingale crew. Finally, she'd set him up and got him arrested on an assault and restraint charge along with everything else. Of course he remembered her.

'How come you're still on remand, anyway?' asked Raine. 'I thought that only lasted up to six months. You've been here what, a year? I thought you'd be all snuggled up in big-boy prison.'

'Backlog, innit,' drawled Luke, seemingly bored now. 'Why are you here?'

'I just wanted to catch up on old times, Luke. How's Blade, by the way? Has he forgiven you for losing all his drugs?'

'I didn't lose them. You stole them from me.'

Raine made a see-saw action with her hand. 'You say potato, I say who cares?' She gazed at Luke, concern on her face. 'You're looking older, Luke. Tired. Maybe a little bit tense. Are you being picked on in here?'

Luke didn't answer. The fact was, he barely slept at all. Raine was right. Blade, the head of the postcode gang from the Nightingale estate, had put a price on his head. He'd narrowly avoided being shanked with a blade made from a sharpened toothbrush handle just a few days ago. Before that he had barely dodged a burnbomb — a plastic bag full of boiling water mixed with liquid detergent — thrown at his face. He'd managed to raise an arm, but he hadn't escaped unharmed. The soapy liquid had stuck to the skin, meaning the burn couldn't immediately be cooled. His skin had literally melted. Burn marks now streaked his face and neck. He'd taken to staying in his cell, but he knew it was only a matter of time. If not on remand, then for certain when he went to the nick proper.

'You know, I checked you out, Luke. When I decided to come and see you.'

Luke gave her the street stare, disdain mixed with boredom all wrapped up in a fuck-you hardness, but inside he was scared. Before Raine had atom-bombed his life, he had been almost ready to move on. Leave London. Escape the trajectory laid out for him since he was a baby. Not that his story was much different to any of the others on his estate, but he had been a quick learner. Had made himself useful to the local gangs. Got a name as a reliable courier. Got himself some protection.

He'd built a reputation as a reliable go-between. A safe zone that could deliver money, drugs, messages — anything. But Luke wasn't stupid; he wasn't going to be in it for life. As soon as he'd stashed enough coin, he was going to sack London, move out and open a club somewhere. Maybe even go to college.

'Very scary, Luke,' smiled Raine, completely unfazed by the hard-man stare. 'Shame I'm not impressed by the gangboy posture. Like I said, I've been reading up on you.' She leaned forward on her elbows and widened her eyes.

Luke held her gaze, but it wasn't easy. There was something about the woman's eyes that was disconcerting. There was a hint of purple in the grey iris. A shadow of something that made the skin on the back of his neck want to contract. 'Why are you here, Detective?' He gave the last word a spin, putting as much derision into it as he could.

'I'm here to give you a redemption arc,' said Raine simply. 'You're still on remand. Which means your case hasn't come before a judge, yet. I can get your sentence reduced, Luke. Speak on your behalf about your choices.'

'And why would you do that?' scoffed Luke. 'You're the one who put me in here.'

'No. *You're* the one who put you in here.' Raine paused. 'Did you know I used to be a police officer? That's why they are letting me see you. This is strictly off the record. A favour. Michael won't be writing down this visit. I'm not here in any official capacity. But make no mistake, Luke. I can help you. If you help me.'

'I don't believe you.'

'I can't get you off. You were caught with a bucket of drugs and resisted arrest. You're going down for sure.' Raine leaned forward a little more. If Luke's hands weren't tethered to the table, he could have touched her. 'The question is: where, and for how long?'

Luke blinked. Raine's gaze was so intense he felt nailed to the seat. He couldn't believe he hadn't seen it in the alley all that time ago. If he had, he would have run a mile.

'Hard time is never good time, Luke. I could say I could get you to a low-security prison but I'd be lying. And it wouldn't matter anyway. Blade could get you there as well as anywhere. Might take longer, but he'd get you.'

'Wants to get you more,' said Luke, suddenly grinning. With the weight loss, his head looked like a skull waiting to break out. 'You snapped his arm and made him talk. Must have done, to set me up.'

'And that, my friend, is what I have to offer.'

'What?' said Luke, confused.

'Remember how I fooled you? Got you to leave Heather and run?'

'Who's Heather?'

'Stop fucking about. The woman in the alley you were going to rape.'

Luke made a point of scanning the room, showing Raine that he knew they were being recorded. Bound to be. 'I never raped no one.'

'Only because I was there to stop you. Remember how I did that?'

Luke nodded slowly. 'Said you were recording on a camcorder. So I smashed it.'

'You still owe me for that,' said Raine. 'Good memory. Worked, though, didn't it? You fell for the line.'

'Why are you bothering to go back over all this?'

Raine reached into her jacket pocket. Luke tensed, then relaxed when she pulled out her phone. She unfolded it halfway, so it acted as its own stand. 'This is the recording I made when Blade attacked me.'

Luke listened in silence. Heard Blade threaten her with a knife. Heard Raine retaliate. Heard the wet snap as Blade's wrist broke. Heard Raine tell him to set Luke up. Heard her thanking him.

'How long do you think Blade would last if this got out, I wonder?' mused Raine. 'That he had ratted on someone? That he let a woman give him a beating and then spilt his guts? That straight after going into custody his gang-house was raided? Almost as if someone had told the feds what was there.'

Luke's eyes went from the phone to her face. 'You telling me he sold out his crew?'

She nodded at the device sitting on the table. 'Certainly could be seen that way.' As it happened, Blade hadn't done any such thing. It was Raine who had phoned the police and suggested the raid, but Luke didn't need to know that. 'If this recording were to get out, then I imagine you would be the least of Blade's problems.'

Luke licked his lips, fully engaged. 'How can I trust you? For all I know you'll just screw me over.'

'No reason for you to trust me, but I'm your best hope, Luke. If you don't do something — if you don't take control — then Blade, or someone like Blade, will kill you.' She gazed at him, expressionless, for several moments, then gave a small nod. 'Like I say, you're on a redemption arc. This is your first step.'

A full minute went by.

'What do you want to know?' he said, finally.

Raine flashed a brilliant smile. 'Excellent! I want you to tell me a story. Do you like stories?'

'What you even talking about? What story?'

'The stories that make up our lives, Luke. That night, for example. When I first saw you. The story I told Heather was that I was just passing by. That I was in the right place at the right time to rescue her from you and your rape-boys. The truth was that I was following her. You see? The narrative I built for Heather convinced her of a story, but it was only that. A story.'

'So you lied to take advantage.' Luke gave a dismissive hiss between his teeth.

'Yes. But then I also told *myself* a story. I told myself that I saw Heather being harassed by a bunch of road-drones out on the prowl, and it was a golden opportunity. All I had to do was save her from this random assault and I would have her trust. Another narrative, you see?'

'What's all this got to do with helping me?'

'Nearly there,' promised Raine. 'You see, I was so blinded by the narrative I'd built that I never considered another. A third story. It was only when I reviewed the footage that it made sense.'

'What made sense?'

Raine smiled. It was probably the scariest thing Luke had ever seen.

'Who's Joseph Banner?'

As she spoke the name, Luke seemed to collapse in on himself, like he'd been punched.

CHAPTER 25

Echo's phone vibrated in his pocket.

'Hi, guv,' he said, answering the call. 'Bloody cold today.'

The pre-dawn frost had yet to lift, turning the London pavements into icy death-traps. Echo had already slipped over several times.

'Absolutely bloody freezing. Are you okay?' asked Hume, her voice concerned. 'You didn't say much in your message, just that you couldn't meet me to interview Beatrix Stevens. What's the problem?'

'Yes, sorry. I think I worked something out last night. It might be nothing but I thought I'd better check it out straight away.'

Echo told her about the geospoofing possibility of Melissa's phone tracking. How the routes formed letters. As she listened, she watched her breath crystallise in front of her; white clouds of cooling vapour in the grey light.

'That's . . . bizarre,' she said, when Echo had finished. 'And when you added in the three other locations? Melissa's flat and such?'

'It spelled Deadtown, yes. Or very nearly. We're still missing the "n".'

'Right. And you think you know where that is?'

'No, but I think I know what it is.'

'The site of the furnace where Melissa's body was burned,' said Hume, catching his thought process. 'The pet crematorium.'

'Yes. I've messaged Jonas to narrow his search to only those beginning with N. Or with streets beginning with N.'

'And large buildings. That basement looked sizable.'

'That makes sense. I'll pass it on.'

'Really good work, Echo.' Hume stamped her feet, trying to create some feeling in them. 'It doesn't explain why whoever killed her is doing this, but it shows that it's linked to the podcast somehow.'

'Which is why I'm going to see Oliver Bell,' said Echo. 'I'm nearly at Tressillian Road now.'

'You're not going alone, are you?' said Hume, alarmed.

'No. I've arranged to meet the PC who works in that area. We're going to check out Oliver's van. Depending on how he is, or what we find, I'll take it from there. I think you were right. He has more questions to answer.'

'Okay.' Hume had an image of Oliver's van being something out of *Mission Impossible*, stuffed full of high-surveillance gadgetry. 'Well, be careful. You don't know what you'll find.'

'Probably just him under a hundred duvets and a hot water bottle,' said Echo, shivering. 'Seriously, how do people live in vans when it's this cold?'

'I think they have wood burners,' said Hume.

'Like I said: boats on wheels. Gotta go, boss. I can see the constable up ahead now. I'll let you know what I find.'

'Excellent. I'm going to go into a nice warm flat to drink tea with a tiny woman, but I'll be thinking of you.'

Hume ended the call and walked up the steps to the blue door of Beatrix's building. The smart mansion block was typical of the area. Late Victorian, with generous bay windows and a red brick front pitted by a century of polluted air. From acid rain to a million coal fires to the fumes of London traffic. Beside the door was a panel with push bells. Hume scanned down the labels until she found B Stevens. She pressed the button and turned back to the street. The constable who had driven her there gave her an enquiring look.

'No need for you to come in,' said Hume. 'But wait here for me please.'

'Ma'am,' he said, as the intercom behind her squawked.

'Yes, what is it?' Even through the tinny intercom the voice was recognisable to Hume as belonging to the woman who had harangued her beneath the tree a few days ago. 'Are you selling something? Because I don't want it.'

'Mrs Stevens? Beatrix?'

'How do you know my name?' She sounded suspicious.

Hume sighed inwardly. 'It's Detective Hume, Mrs Stevens. We spoke on the phone yesterday.'

'The policewoman?'

'The detective, yes. You invited me to meet you today. Could you buzz me in, please?'

'Hang on a minute. I can't hear a bloody thing through this machine. I'll buzz you in.'

Hume stared at the intercom for a second, then turned and looked at her driver. He was grinning.

'If I'm not out in half an hour, call for reinforcements,' she told him, scowling.

The buzzer sounded, and the door unlocked with a click. With a sense of doom, Hume entered the building.

'I'm up here!' shouted a voice above her.

Facing Hume, in a tastefully decorated entrance hall with parquet flooring, was a wide, curving staircase. She looked up to see the head of Beatrix peering out over the first-floor bannisters.

'Take your shoes off and come up. I'll leave the door open.'

'Mrs Stevens. I don't think I—'

The head disappeared. Glancing round the hallway, Hume noticed a set of open shelves by the front door containing various items of footwear. All of them expensive. Hume glared at them a moment, then turned back to the beautifully polished floor and stairs.

'Bollocks.' She untied her brogues, slipped them off and put them carefully on the shelf next to a pair of prim court shoes. 'Wouldn't be surprised if I slipped on this bloody floor and broke my neck,' she muttered, before carefully ascending the stairs. There were four flats on the top floor, but only one with an open door. Hume knocked on it. 'Mrs Stevens?'

'Come in, come in! I haven't got all day!'

Hume entered, finding herself in exactly the sort of flat she'd imagined. High ceilinged, with long heavy curtains framing the massive windows, and tasteful prints on the wall. The furniture was wooden and antique. It looked less like someone lived there, and more like a film set from a period drama. Beatrix, who was dressed in a floor-length deep red paisley dressing gown, was pouring tea into two china cups on the table by the window. Given her size and shape, her outstretched arm and the fact that the dressing gown hid her legs, Hume thought she resembled a Regency Dalek.

Beatrix caught her looking and barked a laugh. 'I know! It's a bloody travesty, isn't it? Comfy, though.'

Hume blinked. 'Excuse me?'

'You're excused,' said the woman breezily, sitting down in one of the high-backed chairs by the table. 'Come and have some tea.'

Hume approached cautiously. Beatrix's dressing gown was open, revealing a pair of grubby sweatpants and a vest.

'If I thought I could get away with it I'd gut the entire place. It's an absolute bugger to heat. Plus a nightmare to recycle anything. And don't get me started on the neighbours. A bunch of stuck-up rich cronies who think that environmental catastrophes only happen to poor people. Milk?'

'Er . . .' began Hume.

'Well, not milk, because who wants to enslave animals? But you know what I mean. Plant milk.' Beatrix looked at Hume, milk jug poised. The sleeves of the dressing gown had ridden up and Hume noticed that the ancient woman's arms were corded with stringy muscle.

'Um, yes, please.'

Beatrix nodded and poured. 'Chin chin.' She picked up her cup and took a slurp.

'Thank you for coming forward. We were having trouble tracing you.'

'That would be because of the false account,' said Beatrix, beaming. 'On Facebook. Fakebook, I call it. Half the profiles on there are for chips. It's just a trap to steal your personal information and sell you something. Bastards.'

Hume guessed that the woman was in her seventies, but well-preserved. Her hair was white and tied back in a neat ponytail. Her eyes sparkled with a light undimmed by age. Somehow she fitted perfectly into her environment, yet at the same time clashed with it.

Hume took stock of the room. As well as the faded opulence, she saw that there were several oddities. A framed print of the CND symbol was leaning against the wall, and there was a biography of Greta Thunberg, spine broken, on the sofa under the bookshelf. She thought back to their last meeting. When Beatrix had called her a stormtrooper and mentioned the state of the environment.

'Right,' said Hume quietly, reaching for the tea.

Beatrix raised an enquiring eyebrow.

'I'm going to guess Greenpeace,' said Hume. 'Or maybe Amnesty?'

'Greenpeace,' said Beatrix, holding up her cup in mock salute. 'Have you any idea just how little topsoil we have left, Inspector? Almost none. And don't talk to me about the fish. The amount of mercury in a salmon, you could use the bloody thing as a thermometer!'

'I don't think they use mercury in thermometers anymore,' said Hume mildly.

'That's because it's all in the fish,' said the woman with some satisfaction.

'Mrs Stevens,' began Hume.

'Not married,' said Beatrix.

'Apologies. Miss.'

'I'd rather you didn't. Just Beatrix, please. Would you like a crumpet?'

'No thank you, Beatrix,' said Hume, hoping to keep a grip on the interview. 'Could you tell me why you posted a picture of my sergeant up the tree?'

Beatrix paused, tapping the side of her cup before answering.

'Did you know that London has almost nine million trees, Detective?'

'No, I didn't.'

'It's the world's largest urban forest. That's one tree for every person in the capital. The biological benefits are boundless. Not just wildlife and photosynthesis and air moisture, but also the canopy. Creating different temperature environments. Giving shade.'

'I'm not sure what—'

'And that's not even touching on the sociological benefits! The gift to our mental well-being. It's been proven that two hours a day in the company of a tree will make you a happier person.'

'I don't doubt it,' said Hume, thinking that the woman probably had friends who were trees. 'But that doesn't explain why you took a picture of my sergeant up one.'

'I thought you were vandals,' said Beatrix. 'Or one of those bastards from the council doing a survey. Getting ready to hack some more of our green lungs away.'

'Ah,' said Hume, nodding. 'I see. You thought we were doing a removal survey.'

'It's happening all over London. Especially in the more deprived areas. Digging up the trees. Concreting over the parks. Filling the air with particulates. The air is so bad in London that the toxin levels are illegal. Can you believe that? We've got all these trees but our air is illegal! Imagine what it'll be like when there aren't any trees.'

'How did you come to be living here, Beatrix?' asked Hume. Having solved the reason for the woman taking Echo's photograph, Hume was still intrigued. 'It seems a long way from Greenpeace.'

'Teenage rebellion,' said Beatrix. 'I blame it on Hendrix.'

'I'm sorry?'

'Jimi Hendrix. The guitarist. When I left school I went to work at the Royal Academy of Arts, just off Piccadilly. My parents didn't hold with women going to university. That was in 1969.'

'Right.'

'I used to walk up to Grosvenor Square to eat my lunch. I loved the trees there. I liked to sit under the branches in the summer and watch the people walking about. You used to get all sorts there, what with it being between Mayfair and Soho.'

'I bet.'

'Anyway, one day there was a man playing guitar. He had a few friends with him and they were smoking weed.'

'Jimi Hendrix?' Hume guessed.

Beatrix nodded happily. 'I hadn't a clue who he was. Just this beautiful man with hair like the tree I was sitting under, smoking and playing guitar.'

'Wow,' said Hume. 'That must have been amazing.'

'It was. He saw me watching and invited me over. Then back to his flat in Brook Street. I stayed there for two days. When I went home my parents disowned me.'

Hume desperately wanted to know what Beatrix got up to in Jimi Hendrix's flat, but couldn't quite compose the question.

'That must have been hard,' she said instead.

'Not really. I was never happy here. Being kicked out was the best thing that could have happened to me. I joined the environmental scene that had grown up out of the hippy movement. Went on marches and sit-ins. Eventually I found my way to Greenpeace.' She shrugged again. 'Went round the world having a great adventure. When my parents died, they left me this.' She looked about her, shaking her head slightly. 'I never believed I'd end up back here but . . . well, there's only so many years you can live in a tent before the bones rebel.'

Hume nodded, finishing her tea. If she hurried, she might be able to join Echo at Oliver's van. 'Well, thank you again for seeing me. Did you get many people viewing the photograph? The only copy we saw had the metadata scrubbed. By that I mean—'

'I know what metadata is, Detective,' said Beatrix, her tone amused. 'You don't live half your life in the counter-culture without understanding how technology spies on you. Hence the Facebook account not being in my name.'

Hume nodded again, thinking that back in the day this woman must have been formidable.

'And yes, there were quite a few. The tree is quite famous, you know.'

'So I understand,' said Hume, standing. 'Well, if you think of anything that might be—'

'But not as many as the others,' said Beatrix. 'Are you sure you wouldn't like a crumpet?'

'What others?' asked Hume.

'The other people I photographed climbing the tree,' said Beatrix. 'Those posts got hundreds of views.'

Hume slowly lowered herself back into the seat. 'You mean somebody else climbed that tree?'

'At least half a dozen,' said Beatrix. 'Did you know it's one of the few mature examples in London? I practically wept when vandals cut off those branches.'

Hume felt the whisper of electricity on the back of her neck as she studied the compact woman in front of her. 'Ms Stevens. Sorry, Beatrix. Do you mind starting at the beginning? When was the first time you noticed someone climbing the tree in Wilbraham Place?'

CHAPTER 26

Echo felt the wrongness as soon as he approached Oliver's van. Most of the vehicles parked along the road were stealth vans — vans that looked like normal delivery vans — disguising their after-sales purpose by not adding any windows to the rear, but rather putting skylights in the roof. A few were off-grid homes, complete with flues indicating a wood burner of some sort. But they all looked either lived-in or in some other way like they belonged. Like they were cared for. Using a van as a home required maintenance and attention.

Oliver's looked like it had been beaten up and left to die.

There were scratches down the dirty green paintwork. One of the tyres was flat.

'Sir?' whispered the uniformed officer next to him. Echo turned, and the woman nodded her head, indicating a puddle under the sliding side door.

Echo bent forward. The liquid was rusty brown in the brittle light and somehow appeared thick. He was in no doubt that it was blood.

He stepped back and studied the van. There was no condensation on the glass or metal like its neighbours. Nothing to indicate warmth inside. Echo noted the scarred windscreen and the pool of viscous liquid beneath, and felt the residual whisper of violence that hung around the vehicle like mist.

The sound of a sliding door nearby caught his attention. Two vans down, the occupant of a gunmetal grey Mercedes Sprinter had just stepped out. She was dressed in patchwork baggy grey fisherman trousers, a shapeless blue jumper and a black beanie hat.

'Wait here,' said Echo quietly to the constable. He walked over to the woman and showed her his warrant card.

'Good morning,' he said, smiling. 'Nice abode.' He nodded at the open door behind her. The inside of her van had been converted into a cosy living space. It had clearly been done lovingly. The interior walls were lined with stained maple wood and there was a small kitchen area, complete with a tiny Everest stove. On top of the stove, a pot of coffee was gently percolating.

'Cheers, love.' The woman's accent was Welsh; soft and warm. 'Do you and your friend fancy a brew? It's a cold one today.'

'Thanks, but we're fine. How long have you been here, Miss . . . ?' He raised his eyebrows.

'Anwen, pleased to meet you.' She reached out a hand to shake. 'Mr . . . ?'

'Etera,' said Echo, surprising himself.

'It's not illegal, Etera. Living in a van. I have a right.'

'I agree. I think it's quite cool. It looks lovely. Bigger than my apartment.'

The woman, who had tensed a little, relaxed. 'Well it may *look* lovely, but it's hard work, cariad. I have to lug everything down to the laundrette once a week.'

'How do you shower and stuff?' he asked.

'Gym membership on rotation. Lots of free trials in London, isn't it?'

'Of course.' Echo briefly scanned the line of vans. 'Tell me, Anwen, do you all know each other? Is it a little community here?'

Anwen stepped back into her van to get the coffee. 'Sure you won't have one?' When Echo shook his head, she continued, 'Well, I know Eric three down. He's been here a few months. Split from his missus. She took the house. Then there's Lottie and her little girl. They live in the Transit. Not too social, them, but nice enough.'

'What about Oliver?' he asked.

Anwen came back out with a steaming mug of coffee. 'Who?'

'The guy who lives there.' Echo pointed at the van next to the uniformed officer, who nodded.

'Freddy?'

'Ah, maybe I was given the wrong intel. I thought a man called Oliver lives there.'

'Well, he introduced himself to me as Freddy. I never liked him, though.'

'Why not?'

'Dirty. Left rubbish out.' Anwen wrinkled her nose. 'One thing you learn quickly is if you live in a van, you need to be clean.'

She leaned in candidly. Echo got a hint of cinnamon and tiger balm.

'Rats,' she whispered. 'Leave any rubbish out and Mr Rat comes calling. And let me tell you, London rats are like bloody mutants. Scare the crap out of you.'

Echo believed it. 'You said, "liked". Is he no longer around?'

'Haven't seen him for a while,' said Anwen. 'And his van looks unoccupied. Wouldn't surprise me if he's done a runner. Happens. It's not for everyone.'

'But wouldn't he still own the van?'

'If he owned it originally. Lots of grey areas. You don't enquire, isn't it? He might have sold it. A few strangers were coming to look around it. Only outside, mind. Photograph it with their phones. He was a bit creepy, Freddy, so I tended to mind my own.'

'Creepy how?'

'One of those men with yo-yo eyes.'

'What do you mean?'

'Always looking from your face to your tits when he talks to you.'

'Ah.'

'Some men are like that. Cock lodged in their brains.'

Echo shook off the image. 'But you haven't seen Freddy for a while?'

'No.'

'Thanks for your help, Anwen.'

'Who is he, then? What did he do?'

'Not entirely sure,' said Echo truthfully. 'Does your vehicle work? I mean, can you drive it?'

'Fully serviced,' said Anwen proudly. 'I often go out to the coast on a weekend. Clear the lungs. Why?'

'Because I might need your spot.'

'My spot? What for?'

'For the forensics van.'

He walked back to the constable, who seemed to be turning a little blue.

Echo knocked on the van. 'Mr Bell? Oliver?'

There was no movement from within.

'Freddy?' Echo tried, knocking louder.

'There's defo no one in there,' said the uniform. 'At least, no one alive.'

Echo gazed down at the muddy puddle of brown liquid below the vehicle. Little stalactites of the same semi-frozen liquid hung from the bottom of the van door mechanism. 'Shit,' he muttered. He put on a pair of nitrile gloves and tried the handle. There was a loud click as the lock disengaged and the door opened a crack. The tiny stalactites fell to the ground. Echo slid the door a few inches, enough to see inside without exposing the interior to Anwen, who was peering interestedly over at them. The inside was nothing like the woman's cosy home. It was more like a squat. Old take-out cartons were on the floor, and a mattress sat directly on the deck with a grubby sleeping bag. On top of that was Oliver Bell, clearly dead. His eyes stared past Echo into the cold day. He was lying on his back, head off the mattress, with his arms outstretched. There was a deep, vertical slash on both arms from his wrist to the crook of his elbow. The cuts were so deep that the flesh had separated, exposing the fat and severed veins beneath.

'There's no way he did that to himself,' whispered the constable behind him.

Echo agreed. 'Call it in,' he said quietly, closing the door. 'But quietly. I don't want anybody to leave. We'll need a cordon and a forensics team.'

The uniform nodded and began talking into her radio. Echo turned back to Anwen, hitched a smile on his face and walked towards her.

CHAPTER 27

It's all beginning to happen now.

    About time. I've practically had to lead them by the nose.

    Still, it will be worth it in the end.

    Now they've found Oliver's corpse it shouldn't take them long to find Melissa's.

    I wonder if they'll think he killed her?

    Fingers crossed.

CHAPTER 28

'Fuck!' said Luke, staring at Raine. He rocked like she'd just slapped him.

Raine nodded. 'I thought so, but I wasn't a hundred per cent sure. What was in the bag?'

'What?' Luke was breathing hard, his eyes slightly dazed. 'What bag?'

'The bag you took off Heather's shoulder. When I reviewed the footage it was so obvious. I felt like a total idiot for missing it.'

'The footage?'

'Stop stalling, Luke. From the video cam I was wearing. It recorded everything. And watching it again I picked up on a couple of things. I apologise. It was very sloppy of me. I'd been hired to find Heather. When I saw you and your little gang there, I thought it was Christmas. The perfect excuse to rescue her and get into her good books. It never even crossed my mind that you were there to do anything other than your own mischief.'

'Look, I don't know what you think you know, but that was it.' Luke's voice was tight, with a strand of desperation snaking around it. 'Me and my crew were out on the prowl, okay? We was just going to rob her but—'

'Doesn't wash. Like I said, I watched the footage again. You took something from her bag.'

'I don't remember anything,' said Luke sullenly.

'And then there was where the bag came from. Really, I'm some rubbish detective. It never even clicked at the time. It's always the small details, isn't it?'

'I don't know nothing.'

'She said her sister gave it to her. That's why she didn't want you to take it.'

'So?'

'So, where's the sister?'

He stared at her silently as the seconds ticked by.

'Come on, Luke,' said Raine softly. 'Who's Joseph Banner? I've tried finding him online but didn't get any hits. I've also asked a few cops I know but again, nothing pops. The only person who seems to recognise the name is you. So, did Banner ask you to steal something from Heather? Is that why you were there?'

'No.'

'You didn't take something from her bag?'

Luke shook his head. 'I want you to leave.'

Raine ignored him. Her eyes unfocused for a moment, then she smiled at him. 'You didn't take something *from* her bag; you put something *into* her bag. What was it, a tracker?'

Luke didn't answer. He didn't have to. The answer was clear in his face.

'Did he need to track her? Banner, I mean.' Raine mused. 'But why would that be? If he was posing as Heather's parents, using me to find her, how come you were already there? How come he needed to track her?'

Luke sat in silence.

'Somebody broke into my boat after I told Heather's fake parents I'd found her,' said Raine, her brain ticking through her memories. 'Stole my laptop with all my surveillance details on it. After that Heather was supposedly shot. There was an autopsy, but then the body was cremated.'

'Stop,' said Luke.

Raine ignored him. 'But then I got a text from her. Or at least from her phone. And I tracked my stolen laptop to a building used for housing immigrants waiting for processing.'

'If you try to find her he'll kill you.'

'Don't care,' said Raine, shaking her head. 'What am I missing, Luke? Were there two groups trying to find Heather? Why did he need the tracker?' She leaned forward. 'Who is he, Luke?'

Luke closed his eyes, breathing hard.

'You're hyperventilating. Breathe through your nose.'

Luke took a deep breath and held it, then let the air slowly out through his nose.

'Now look at me.'

Luke opened his eyes and looked at her. She was perfectly still. Medium height. Not physically imposing in any way. But there was something about her. Something . . . wrong. As if she wasn't quite in focus. Wasn't quite there.

'That night, after you and your buddies had legged it, I took Heather to a cafe. She was scared and shaken up, but now I think about it, nowhere near as much as she should have been. I mean, she'd just escaped being robbed and raped. She should have been a wreck. But she wasn't. Why was that, do you think?'

'How should I know?'

'And she was evasive when I mentioned the police. Didn't want to make a statement. Like maybe she had something to hide.'

'Not everybody likes the police.'

'Agreed. But then she asked me something odd. It never clicked at the time, but it's ringing bells the size of Big Ben now. She asked me if I really believed most people were good. Like she knew better. Like that wasn't the case in her life.'

Raine's eyes spiked him to his seat. He felt like he was being peeled open.

'Tell me, Luke. If you don't tell me I can't help you.'

'Yes,' he said finally, his tone flat and defeated. 'It was a tracker. Banner knew where she'd be and told me. Gave me the tile to put in her bag.'

'Do you mean a tracking disc?'

'Yeah.'

'But I was already following her. Why did he—'

'I didn't know any of that. I just had the job and that was it. When you turned up, it was a total headfuck. No one was meant to be there.'

'But you did the job, right? You put the tile in the bag.'

'Yeah.'

'And then I was taken off the job. Because they had what they wanted.' Raine's gaze turned distant. 'They used me so they would know where to find her. They played me.'

'Banner plays everyone.'

CHAPTER 29

The first thing Hume did when she left Beatrix Stevens was phone Jonas. 'You need to go back further. Not just a few days before the incident. A week. Maybe two.' She strode out of the house and down the steps to her car.

'Boss,' said Jonas, relief in his voice. 'I've been trying—'

'Even three. I've just come out of a meeting with the woman who photographed Echo up the tree.'

'That's why your phone was off? My calls were just flipping to voicemail.'

'Well, I'm here now. Anyhow, apart from learning that she may or may not have lost her virginity to Jimi Hendrix, she also told me Echo wasn't the first.'

'Jimi Hendrix? The first what? Boss, I've—'

'The first person she'd photographed,' said Hume impatiently. 'Pay attention, Detective Constable. Up the tree. That's why she was so het up when she saw DS Echo. Other people had already been up there.'

'Why would she be bothered?'

'She's an original environmentalist. Like from the sixties. She moved back into the area when her mother died. Probably been living up a tree before that. Plus she has crumpets for breakfast, which is just weird. When she saw people desecrating the Catalina Ironwood—'

'Desecrating?'

'Her words. Carving into it. She saw them with a knife. Took photos. She said she'd sent them to us weeks ago. Not us, us. But the police.'

'Right.'

'Exactly. They would have just been filed. Or binned. Some kids climbing a tree wouldn't have even registered.'

'Kids? Like children?'

Hume nodded at her driver and the car started moving. 'No. Like teenagers. Or maybe early twenties. Beatrix wasn't sure. She's probably in her seventies. Almost everyone might seem like a kid to her. She's going to dig out the photos and send them to us. The thing is, it was weeks ago, like I said. So—'

'So it might be weeks ago for the house on Aquinas Street as well,' said Jonas, catching up.

'Exactly. So we need to go back to the owner of the door footage and ask if they have kept the feed from further back. Cross-reference with Beatrix.' She paused, the start of her conversation with Jonas registering at last. 'Hang on. You've been trying to reach me? Why, what's wrong?'

'I've found the crematorium.' The DC's voice was fizzing with excitement.

'Really?' said Hume. 'That's great!'

'It was Echo who nabbed it. Narrowing the search parameters to establishments beginning with N. It cut down on the information pool.'

'So where is it?'

'Southwark.'

'That doesn't begin with "N".'

'It's a disused abattoir. Not a crematorium at all. That's another reason it's taken so long. The place is abandoned, but the furnace has been used on an ad hoc basis. Usually for roadkill. Local pets. It's not an official site.'

'Is that legal?'

'The actual cremation is. Animal remains are considered waste. The abattoir was called Nailman's. It's on an old industrial estate.'

'Brilliant work, Jonas. Let Echo know and get a team there.'

'Already done.'

'Great. I'm on my way. You chase up the door cam.'

'Will do. And boss?'

'Yes?'

'Who's Jimi Hendrix?'

Hume paused and stared at the phone, before putting it back to her ear.

'Are you kidding?'

'No. Who is he?'

'How old are you, Jonas?'

'Twenty-five, boss.'

'Who's your favourite singer?'

'Probably Taylor Swift. She's brilliant.'

Hume closed her eyes. 'Just let Echo know I'm on my way.'

Her phone buzzed, indicating another incoming call. She checked the ident. 'Never mind. That's him now. Let me know if you find anything with the door cam.'

She swapped the calls. 'Echo, please tell me you've heard of Jimi Hendrix.'

'He's dead, guv.'

'Well of course he's dead. He—'

'No. Oliver Bell. He's been murdered. In his van.'

'What?' said Hume, the gears of her brain mashing. 'When?'

'Unknown. Maybe yesterday. Perhaps the day before. Forensics are on their way. It's . . . brutal, boss.'

'In his van? Didn't somebody hear something?'

'Apparently not. I've got a DC taking statements but nothing so far.'

Hume clicked her teeth together in thought. 'Right. Did Jonas send you a message?'

'About the furnace? Yes. Good news.'

'Great. I'll go and check out the abattoir. You stay there. See what you can find. We don't need more questions; we need answers.'

'Guv.'

Hume ended the call and gave the address Jonas had shared with her to the driver. As the car sped through central London, Hume thought about Oliver. He had been bolshy and evasive, but Hume hadn't got the impression he had been into anything criminal. Nothing that could explain his murder.

Which probably meant it either had something to do with what he knew, or what he had found out as a journalist.

Or, Hume considered, what he might have been unwittingly party to with the *Deadtown* podcast. Something Melissa had been working on before she was murdered.

Thoughts of Melissa brought her back to the present. She wondered what she was going to find at the old abattoir. The video clip suggested Melissa's body had been about to be incinerated. Turned to dust. In a way, Hume hoped that was what they were going to find.

Ashes.

The thought that she might have to sift through burnt remains, and all the smells that accompanied charred flesh, made her feel nauseous. She had attended such things before. Arsons gone wrong. Explosions. Car crashes. It was always hard, and the stench seemed to permeate right through to the bones.

Hume was shaken out of her thoughts as the car turned off the road and onto the disused industrial estate. Skeletons of buildings seemed to grow out of the brittle ground. Small pools of oily water suggested deep pits where manhole covers might have been, long since stolen and sold for scrap. The whole estate reeked of decay and disuse. As the car carefully navigated the overgrown tarmac, Hume stared into the broken windows of dead factories. The darkness beyond the jagged shards of glass promised nothing and offered less.

'Jesus,' she muttered. 'What a place to finish up.' Already dead and then brought to this unloved part of London to be incinerated was beyond depressing.

As the disused abattoir came into view, she saw an officer standing guard at the entrance. Hume took a deep breath, quashing all thoughts of morbidity and focusing on the job at hand. By the time she opened the car door, she was all business.

'Ma'am,' said the uniformed officer, offering his hand to help her out. She looked at it, and then at him.

'It's slippy, ma'am. The ground must have been saturated with oil at some time. . .' His voice petered out as he saw her expression.

'I see. And you've offered your hand to every officer who has arrived, yes?'

When the man didn't reply, Hume nodded. 'Please set up a cordon, Constable. This is a potential crime scene and I don't want it compromised.'

'Yes, ma'am,' he said meekly.

'And don't call me "ma'am". It makes me sound like I'm in an episode of *The Crown*. Call me boss, guv or sir.'

'Er, yes, boss. This way.'

He led her around the side of the building to a door guarded by another uniformed officer, who took her inside.

The cellar appeared much like it had in the video: bare brick wall and dim lighting. Situated at the rear of the space was the furnace, cold and inert. Surreptitiously, Hume took a small sniff but detected no odour of burning flesh. Just the autumn smells of fire and age.

'And this is exactly how we found it? Nothing moved?'

'No, guv,' the constable said, his voice quiet. 'We were told to wait for you. And since we've arrived nobody has been down here. The forensic team is twenty minutes away.'

Hume focused on the furnace. Its door was closed, and there was no viewing window. Anything could be inside it. She slipped on a pair of nitrile gloves. 'And is anybody on site? Somebody who can tell us when it was last used?'

'Yes, there was a neighbourhood clean-up group having a meeting when we arrived.'

'Which neighbourhood?'

'Just local. There's been a lot of theft on the estate. Most of the metal was scavenged when the place was shut down. This round is old pallets. Internal doors from the industrial units. Anything that can burn, basically.'

'Burn?'

'For the bonfires. The kids use this place for recreational fires and stuff. Fireworks.' He shrugged. 'The group upstairs had met to discuss what to do about it.'

Hume nodded. 'What about down here? When was the last cremation?'

The constable shuddered. 'Gives me the creeps, guv. Thinking of bodies being burned down here. I mean, it's a cellar. Like something from a horror show.' He glanced at the furnace door, closed, with no clue as to what might lie behind it.

'The last cremation,' Hume prompted. 'When was it?'

The constable referred to his notebook. 'A stray dog a couple of weeks ago. It had got trapped in some security wire. They burned the body to stop scavenger animals from sniffing about. Foxes and such.'

'Shouldn't the council take care of that sort of thing?'

'Absolutely.'

Hume nodded. There was no money.

'Same old. And since then?'

'Nothing. The internal door is deadbolted, and the external padlocked. We had to get the key to gain access.'

Hume studied the floor. It was clean. There were no footprints on the scarred flagstones. No drag marks indicating where a body might have been pulled. No wheel tracks where a trolley bearing a body would have travelled. Nevertheless, she put on a pair of overshoes before approaching the incinerator. She still couldn't smell anything.

Taking a shallow breath, she used a finger to slide the bolt and open the door of the furnace. It swung back to reveal the interior. The constable helpfully switched on his torch app.

The walls of the interior were scorched metal, with small holes which Hume assumed allowed the gas burners entry. The bed of the oven was a slotted grate. Ashes were coating it, but no body. No charred remains. Hume let out a relieved sigh. She leant closer. The interior stretched back several feet and was perhaps three feet wide. Enough, at a squeeze, to fit a body if it had been scrunched in.

She stood back up and looked again at the front of the incinerator. Beneath the door aperture was another, slot-like panel.

'That's where all the ashes will be,' said the constable next to her.

'How do you know?'

'Grew up in the country. We used to have a coal fire. Once the coal is burned through, the ashes fall between the slats of the grate to a tray beneath. Easy to empty that way.'

'Right,' said Hume. The panel had a latch and handle. Hume undid the latch. 'Grab the handle and slide it out, then. Let's see what we've got.'

Taking a firm grasp, the constable slowly pulled back on the panel. It was attached to a collection tray. Hume watched as it slid out. It was filled with ashes.

'Stop.'

The constable stopped. The tray was sticking out a couple of feet. The two police officers stared down into the fine grey granules that resided.

'Bloody hell,' whispered the constable.

'We're going to need SOCO down here. Tape everything off and start taking statements. I need timelines of anyone who has anything to do with this building.'

'Do you think . . . ?' The officer beside her hadn't moved.

'I don't think anything. Not until the scene's been catalogued. Now get to it.'

'Guv.'

The constable took one last look, then turned to carry out her orders. Hume stayed still, staring down into the ash collection tray. What was visible was approximately half full.

Perhaps a couple of inches thick with ash. Hume had no idea how much of the stuff a human body generated. It looked far more than would fit in the urns people were given after a cremation.

And of course, Hume thought, focusing on the piece of a finger that lay half hidden among the grey ash, you wouldn't get that in an urn.

Hume couldn't tell which finger it was. It was slender, just a small section, blackened from the heat. The nail had burned off, or perhaps melted away, Hume thought ghoulishly. The finger stopped at the knuckle, wisps of burnt sinew and coagulated bubbles of boiled fat forming a grisly stub. It was impossible even to tell whether the finger came from a male or female body, but DNA would be able to confirm.

Not that Hume needed DNA conformation. She was already sure she was looking at the remains of Melissa Clarke.

CHAPTER 30

Echo sipped the tea, scalding his lips as he drank. He watched as the SOCOs removed the inside of Oliver's, AKA Freddy's, van piece by piece. Normally he would wait for Hume to arrive so that she could imprint the scene in her head, but there was no way she was going to be able to get away from the old abattoir housing the cremation furnace . . .

'I can't believe it,' said Anwen beside him, sipping her tea. 'I know I said he was a bit creepy, but . . .'

She didn't finish her sentence; she didn't need to. Echo understood. The comments she had made earlier had turned into guilt, as she realised she had spoken ill of the dead.

'There was nothing you could have done,' assured Echo.

'Heart attack, was it?'

Echo thought of the marks around his neck, indicating strangulation. Whoever had ripped open his wrists must have first rendered him unconscious. 'No, not a heart attack.' He wrapped his hands around the hot cup, warming them. 'You're certain you hadn't seen him out and about over the last few days?'

'No. Like I said, we thought he'd maybe moved on. Especially when those kids came and photographed the van. Thought he'd put it up for sale, we did.'

'Kids?'

Anwen smiled. 'Well, youths then. In their twenties. That's the usual demographic for London vanners.'

'I understand. You said "we"? Who do you mean exactly?'

She raised one hand to indicate the street. 'Us. The people who live here. We're not all close, but we see each other. Inevitable, isn't it?'

Echo had images of fires and guitars and wine but realised it couldn't be like that. These people weren't modern-day hippies living a bohemian life. Van dwelling in London would be hard. Cold and dangerous and hostile. One wrong move, one bad parking choice or breakdown and you would be in a world of trouble. There was no safety net at ground zero.

'Where?' he asked. 'Where do you see each other?'

'Well, there's the standpipe at the garage down the hill. So long as we buy enough groceries, the manager lets us fill up with water. Use the facilities. I used to see Freddy there sometimes.'

Echo made a mental note to visit the garage.

'There's a shower there, too, if you're willing to pay. Hardly anyone uses it, though. Cheaper to use the swimming pool showers.'

'Why would there be showers at the petrol station?' asked Echo.

'Lorry drivers, cariad. There's a few stations around London that still cater for them.'

'Right. Anywhere else?'

Anwen nodded. 'There's the work hubs. Office space you rent by the hour. Good for charging phones and laptops. Lots of us are freelancers. We can work from the vans, but sometimes you need to have a professional environment. For meetings and video calls and such.'

'It sounds complicated.'

Anwen smiled. 'It may require a little bit of planning, but it's worth it. Every morning brings something new. It's not for everyone, and it's not for ever. But if you want to work in London, it's an option.'

'So who *was* friendly with Freddy?'

Anwen frowned in thought. 'Nobody. He didn't mingle. He had a woman who used to visit him, a girlfriend I think, but other than that . . .' she shrugged. 'He kept himself to himself.'

Echo unfolded his phone and pulled up a headshot of Melissa Clarke. 'Is this the woman?'

Anwen peered at it. 'No. The woman who visited was fairer. She had a ponytail and her glasses were round, you know?'

Echo nodded. 'And did you catch her name?'

'Sorry. I only really noticed her at all because of her cardigan.'

'I'm sorry?'

She smiled. 'I like cardigans. Hers was long. Hand-knitted with the sleeves hanging over the fingers. Expensive.' She lifted her hands, showing the fingertips poking out of her own cardigan. 'That and the Lennon glasses is a look I like.'

'Well, thank you for your time, Anwen. I'll get the detective to take down your details in case anything else comes to mind.'

'No problem.'

Echo started to walk away.

'I keep my passport in my gas tank.'

Echo turned. 'Excuse me?'

'In my gas tank. That's my hidey-hole. Most everybody has one.'

Echo glanced at the van's petrol cap. 'Really?'

She laughed. With her soft accent it sounded to Echo like pebbles gently turning in the sea. 'Not that kind of gas. Here.' She pointed inside, at the Everest gas stove. Echo saw that beneath it were two squat gas cylinders.

'Ah. I see.'

'One of them's a dummy. It's just connected for the show of it. The bottom screws off.'

'And you keep your passport there?'

She laughed. 'We all get broken into at some point. Laptops. Bikes. Phones. Those things you can replace in a day. But passports. Bank cards. Jewellery.' She shrugged.

'Where else?' asked Echo, sizing up her living quarters. 'Where else is a good hideaway?'

Anwen raised her eyebrows. 'You're not thinking of doing a drug search, are you?'

'No, I'm more interested in where someone might stash a phone. Or wallet.' *Or maybe a flash drive*, he thought.

'Well, the headrests are always good,' said Anwen. 'Plenty of room in those. Spare wheel. Safe box in the engine compartment. Same behind the number plate. There are lots of nooks and crannies in a van.'

Echo looked over at the SOCO team who were systematically going through the interior of Oliver's van, then shifted his gaze to the front of the vehicle. Whoever had killed Oliver could easily have searched the interior, but to pop the hood and search the engine space . . . or unscrew a numberplate? That would attract attention.

Echo thanked Anwen and moved back towards Oliver's van.

CHAPTER 31

As Raine was about to step onto her boat, she caught sight of Jolene hurrying over. The woman seemed tense, her fingers twisting the front of her cardigan into knots.

'Hi, Jolene. Is everything all right? How's Libby?'

The smile that spread across Jolene's face seemed to light up the cold grey morning. 'Mr Brin is great. Libby's really taken a shine to him.'

'That's fantastic, Jolene. I'm glad. Danny knows his stuff. He's survived the bouncer circuit for years. There's not much he hasn't seen and dealt with.'

'Well, all I can say is that Libby seems more herself than I've seen her since . . . since it happened.'

'I'm sure it will just continue to improve. She's a strong woman. Like her great aunt.'

Jolene nodded. No false modesty. 'Any news about the dentist?' she asked hopefully. 'Only Libby won't smile because of . . . you know. Too self-conscious.'

'Understandable. Give me a couple of hours and I'll chase it up for you. You'd better get back in. It's freezing.'

Raine turned, ready to board her vessel.

'Actually, that wasn't why I came out. Well, not just that. I wanted to see you.'

Raine put a foot on her boat, eyebrows raised. 'Yeah?'

'I know you're a very private person.'

'Okay,' said Raine, unsure what the woman was getting at.

'I mean, you don't get a lot of visitors. Guests. Just that woman and her colleague.'

'Mary and Etera.' Raine nodded, her face neutral. 'Why are you asking?'

'And then that man a few months ago. The one who pretended to be your brother.'

Raine nodded again. Frankie Ridgeway had tracked her down, telling her neighbour that he was related. Raine had asked Jolene to alert her if she had any more unexpected visitors. But he couldn't have come round again because he was in jail. She had seen to that. 'So who was it this time?'

'Students,' said Jolene. 'Or at least that's what they said they were. They seemed very nice. But I didn't know that when I saw them on my security camera. That's why I came out to check. Libby . . .'

'You thought they were searching for Libby? They were part of what happened to her?'

'Yes, but they weren't like that. They were polite.'

Raine didn't explain to Jolene that polite, nice young people could be gang members, too. That thuggery being the sole province of the postcode estates and hard men and women covered in scars was a myth. There was too much money involved. Some of the most dangerous individuals Raine had dealt with were nice, clean-cut young people.

'Did they say what they wanted?' Raine kept her voice light.

'No. They just asked if you were the detective who shut down that trafficking gang.'

Raine nodded again. It was one of the reasons she had moved her boat from the Regent's Canal to Little Venice. It had been targeted. 'And what did you say?'

Jolene smiled, pointing at her garb. 'I played the dotty old lady card. Said I didn't think so.'

Raine grinned. 'You cardiganed them: nice. You know that in my business I can't advertise where I live.'

'I told them that I thought you had something to do with Pilates.'

'What have I done to make you hate me so much?' smiled Raine. Jolene smiled back.

'I don't think they believed me. They said they were writing a project on female detectives. Something to do with patriarchal structures of the city, creating phallocentric crimes.'

'Erection detection,' said Raine.

'Sorry?'

'Nothing. Did they say anything else?'

'No. They just kind of sniggered and took some pictures of your boat.'

'Did they?' said Raine thoughtfully.

'I told them not to. That it was disrespectful; someone's home. They apologised and left.'

'Would you recognise them again. If I had some photos?'

'Well, yes. They're recorded on my camera.'

'Are they? Do you think you could get me the footage?'

'Yes, of course.'

Raine smiled. 'Don't worry, Jolene. You did the right thing.'

The old woman relaxed, relief clear on her face.

'Gotta boogie, Jolene. I'll catch you later.'

Raine began to step onto her boat, but something caught her eye. She squatted to get a closer view. 'Deadtown' had been carved into the wood by the boarding step. The paleness of the exposed plank where the varnish had been removed was what had drawn her gaze. She ran her fingers over the word.

'What is it?' asked Jolene.

Raine stood and smiled at her. 'Nothing. You go back to Libby. I'll catch you later.'

She watched Jolene until she was safe back on her own boat, then descended into the cabin. She stood by the door, scanning the space. Nothing had changed; nothing had been moved or taken. Raine sat down at her desk and gazed out of the window. After several minutes she opened her phone and checked her house app. The batteries that powered the boat's electric engines were fully charged and all systems were showing green. She swiped the app away and saw that Jolene had sent through the footage. It clearly showed the faces of the young people and Jolene coming out to talk to them. Just as Jolene had said, they looked friendly and approachable. Not like gangsters, more like students. Raine pulled the timer bar back to the beginning and watched as one of them knelt down in front of the cabin, presumably to carve the words into her boat. After a few minutes, Raine called Mary Hume.

CHAPTER 32

'You found it in the engine?'

'Not in the engine itself. A metal box in the engine compartment,' Echo clarified. 'You need to open the bonnet from inside the vehicle to access it. It was magnetically attached to the chassis under the exhaust manifold, like a door key safe. Impossible to see unless you knew it was there.'

'And what made you check the engine compartment?'

'One of the other van residents. She mentioned they often have storage hideaways for their valuables. Lots of break-ins.'

'I can imagine.'

'If you keep it under the bonnet, even if the van is robbed, the chances are they won't search the engine compartment.'

'Makes sense.' Hume noted the photograph displaying the contents of the safe. Echo had swiped it onto the smart board.

'As well as an external hard drive, there was close to a thousand pounds in cash.' He looked at Hume inquiringly. 'What do you think? Rainy-day money?'

'Runaway money, I imagine. And that he didn't store it at Melissa's flat is interesting. Maybe he didn't trust her.'

'Or didn't trust her friends or associates.'

'Did we get anything back from the CCTV outside her flat?'

'No. We got the feed, but it doesn't show anything close to an abduction, even disguised. Nobody leaves the premises holding somebody else up as if they were drunk or ill. No large groups you could hide a removal in. Nobody pushing a massive suitcase that could conceal a body.'

Hume eyeballed him. 'Massive suitcase that could conceal a body? Are you serious?'

Echo nodded, deadpan. 'Or a trunk on wheels.'

'Been watching your Bond box set again, have you? What about other exits?'

'There's a rear entrance, but no CCTV. We've checked door feeds where they exist but there's lots of gaps. It's possible she could have been bundled out that way.'

'Well, if she wasn't taken via the front door, it's the only way.' Hume turned and pondered the murder board display. 'Tell me where we're at.'

'Frankly, it's a mess. We've got so many data points we can't see the wood for the trees, no pun intended.'

'None taken. Let's strip it back. How many sites do we have?'

Echo counted them off. 'Melissa's flat in Aquinas Street. Wilbraham Place with the tree, and the abattoir.'

Echo cleared the board and split it into four columns, each headed with the possible crime site.

'And we've got "Deadtown" being spelled out across London by a ghost phone,' said Hume.

'Geospoof,' nodded Echo. 'Which could work in three ways. Either someone did the actual route using Melissa's phone and then delayed it appearing on the shared map app. Or the same route was done in a different area entirely and copied over onto the map.'

'Like they could have gone the same route but a few streets over?'

'Exactly.'

'What's the third option?'

'That the phone was never there. That the entire route, all of them, were done digitally. Mapped out on a computer and posted as Melissa's phone.'

'And that's possible?'

Echo nodded. 'You clone the IMEI — the phone's ID — to fool the app.'

'But wouldn't the cell towers know it wasn't real? Know that phone isn't there?'

'It doesn't ping through the cell towers. It's sent directly to the app. There's no actual real GPS involved at all.'

Hume stared at the board, shaking her head. 'But what's the point? What's the point of spelling out the name of the podcast? I mean, who's going to see it?'

'No idea.'

'Do we know what was on the hard drive Oliver stashed?'

'Jonas is cataloguing it as we speak. I'm going to check it out right after this.'

'And are we any closer to identifying the mystery woman who visited him?'

'No. Nobody seemed to be close to Oliver slash Freddy, and there are no CCTV or door cameras in the area.'

'What about an e-fit? Can we get somebody to her?'

Echo grinned ruefully at his boss, head tilted. 'An e-fit artist? The last one of those on the Met retired during lockdown. And now with all the CCTV and image-capturing equipment . . .' He opened his hands and spread his fingers.

'So no ID?'

'If it wasn't Melissa then we've no idea. A young woman in a cardigan and glasses doesn't really narrow it down.'

'Okay. What about the people outside the house on Aquinas Street? Do we know for certain it's the same people whom Beatrix Stevens saw in Wilbraham Place?'

'The DNA matches, but it's not registered on any databases we've searched.'

'Try and find the clearest shots of them we have and send it to whoever is interviewing the van dwellers. Maybe it's the same people who were photographing Oliver's vehicle — though God knows why.'

Echo made a note on his tablet.

'And why was he calling himself Freddy?' Hume mused.

'I checked with the petrol station down from Tressillian Road. Oliver occasionally used the facilities there. He rented a key to the shower rooms. The name he gave was Freddy Best.'

Hume stared at him.

'What?' asked Echo when he saw the expression of disbelief on his boss's face.

'Freddy Best. That's a joke, yes?'

'No, why? Does the name mean something?'

'Frederick Best was a London journalist,' Hume said, tightly.

'Okay.'

'He's often cited as one of the originators of the Jack the Ripper letters sent to the press.'

'*The* Jack the Ripper?' said Echo, astonished.

'What's going on with this case?' murmured Hume, staring at the wall screen. She crinkled her gaze in concentration. There was something just beyond her reach. Something that tingled at the back of her neck. After a moment she said: 'Cardigan and glasses. Didn't we meet someone recently who wore something like that?'

Before Echo could answer, her phone rang.

'Mary Hume,' she said, still staring at the board.

'Mary!' Raine's voice buzzed cheerily in her ear. 'I swear you sound more authoritarian every time we talk. Is it something you practise with Robert? Like a master and servant thing?'

'What do you want, Raine?' she said. 'I'm kind of in the middle of it here.'

'I bet you are. How's the case?'

'Confusing. Is there a reason for the call?'

'Two reasons. Has Echo heard back from the demon dentist?'

'Hang on.' Hume looked over at her sergeant. 'Echo, did you manage to reach Ms Arnold?'

Echo nodded. 'Yes. She said she'd be happy to help and to set up an initial meeting.'

'Did you hear that?' asked Hume.

'Yes! That's brilliant news. I'll pass it on to Libby.'

'No problem. What was the other thing?'

'Have you ever heard of quantum entanglement?'

'No.' Hume was used to Raine's sudden changes in direction. 'But it sounds complicated. Is it something we need to discuss now—'

'The theory is simple,' said Raine, continuing as if Hume hadn't spoken. 'It's something Clara explained to me. Quantum entanglement is when two particles are linked together on a fundamental level. No matter where they are in space and time, each has an indelible and immediate effect on the other. They could be a million miles away or two hundred years apart. It doesn't matter. They can't help but react to one another. Like they're in a dance outside of anything else the universe is doing. It's a bit like love.'

'That's actually . . . quite profound,' said Hume, momentarily forgetting the case. An image of her daughter flashed across her memory.

'Isn't it?' Raine's voice was bright and breezy. 'Well, I seem to be experiencing the London equivalent. London entanglement.'

'I'm not getting you.'

'Everything that happens to me seems to be connected. And that includes you. We need to meet. Bring Echo.'

'You're not making any sense.'

'Like your case? Just meet me, Mary. It's important. Those unknown people you're searching for? The ones outside the murder flat?'

'Aquinas Street. What about them?'

'And at the tree? You think they're the same people, yes?'

'How do you—'

'You connected me to the hub, remember?'

'Right.'

'*So* you think they're the same? The young people taking pictures of places connected to Melissa Clarke's murder?'

'We don't know how, but yes, we think they're linked.'

'Well, I had some young people visiting my boat today, taking photographs.'

Hume straightened, fully attentive. 'You think they're connected to my case?'

'Jolene caught them on her security camera. Looking at them, they could be the people that the tree woman described.'

'Beatrix Stevens. But she never saw their faces, just—'

'Because they weren't just taking photographs. One of them carved a word into my boat.'

'What word?' asked Hume, but she didn't need to. She already knew.

'Deadtown. We need to meet, Mary. Like now.'

Hume didn't hesitate. 'Where?'

CHAPTER 33

Raine was about to leave when her phone pinged. Another email from Felice, the potential French client. Felice was going to be in the UK from tomorrow, the 31st. She explained that she was doing some research on a circus act that would be performing as part of the Halloween event on Blackheath Common and asked that they meet there.

> *Please come alone. I still do not feel safe. If you could share your mobile number with me I will ring at 9 p.m. and tell you where at the fair I will be.*
> *Felice*

Raine frowned. She was aware of the Blackheath event. Every year there was a fair, with a selection of rides and stalls supplied by one of the few traditional circus companies left in the UK. She used to go when she was a child. She thought for a moment, then fired off an email confirming the meet. As she was locking up her boat, she saw Jolene hovering outside, clearly eager for news.

'It's all systems go with the dentist,' smiled Raine. 'I'll message you her details later and you can arrange an initial consultation.'

'Oh, thank God,' breathed Jolene. 'I was worried it was going to fall through. And thank *you*, Raine. I don't know what we'd have done without you.'

'No probs. I'll catch you later.'

As Raine walked away, she wondered if that was true. Now that someone knew where she lived, she couldn't stay there. Not just for her own safety, but for Jolene's. The young men who had visited her may have seemed nice and clean-cut, far away from thuggery and violence, but Raine knew better. Violence was coming. She could taste it in the bitter air. Feel it in the oppressive lowness of the clouds that were building above the capital.

'London entanglement,' she muttered, heading for the tube station.

CHAPTER 34

'I can't believe I didn't know this was here,' said Echo, tucking into his dumplings with the plastic chopsticks, his face a picture of delight.

'Not surprising,' said Raine. 'It's a pop-up. It's here today; tomorrow it will be somewhere else. You have to follow them on Snapchat to find out where.'

Hume tentatively placed one of the small packets of meat into her mouth. It practically melted straight down into her stomach, leaving her tongue on fire.

'You have Snapchat?' said Echo, astonished.

'Of course I don't,' snorted Raine. 'How old do you think I am?' She took a bite of her own gyoza, first dipping it into the sticky sauce. 'I get Libby to text me.'

They were sitting on a bench outside Methodist Central Hall, looking out over the tips of Portcullis House and the Houses of Parliament. A few feet away a small queue had formed in front of the man serving the Japanese delicacies from a steaming vat attached to a trailer. When Hume and Echo had arrived, Raine had already bought them the food. She had insisted they eat before discussing anything.

Raine pointed with her chopstick. 'See that bench over there?'

Just to the right of the steps to the hall, a woman was sitting on a bench smoking a roll-up. So layered with clothes that she could have been wearing an entire charity shop. Beside her was a carton of dumplings. Hume suspected Raine had bought it for her.

'Cold day to be on the streets,' commented Echo.

'That's where they were going to put the Homeless Jesus,' said Raine.

Hume looked at her quizzically.

'You know. The statue of the homeless person lying on a bench with no shoes. You can see the holes where the nails went through his feet. Jesus as a homeless person. There's one in Manchester, too. Glasgow as well.'

Hume nodded. 'I thought it was somewhere else in London.'

'It is, but this was the first choice. It was opposed.'

'By the church?' asked Echo, admiring the grand building.

'Nah, they were keen. It was Westminster Council. They said it didn't fit in with the surroundings.'

Hume and Echo looked over towards the Thames. The top of the Houses of Parliament dark against the gritty skyline. Then they looked back at the rough sleeper.

'Unbelievable,' said Echo, disgust in his voice.

'I'd make a joke about the lifestyle choices of a crucified Jesus, but I'm trying to be a better person,' said Raine. 'Tell me about the case.'

'What did you mean about London entanglement?' asked Hume, wiping her fingers on a napkin. Her tongue felt slightly swollen from the chillies.

'Later. First I want to hear about Deadtown. Did you get the security feed from Jolene?'

'Yes. Jonas is running it through the databases. You said they were students. Maybe we'll get lucky and they've been arrested on a march before.'

'*They* said they were students; I didn't. I very much doubt they are. Did you see the way they were using the phones?'

'What do you mean?'

'Well, they all seemed to be taking a picture of the same thing: the front of my boat. I checked but there's nothing there. Nothing of note, anyway.'

'I'll get Jonas on it,' said Hume. 'Maybe he can check the phone angles. See what they were really photographing. So . . . London entanglement?'

Raine nodded. 'Don't you think it's weird? That everything seems to connect? It's happened in the last couple of cases. Patterns seem to bring us together.'

'But it's not surprising, is it?' said Echo, who had just finished his last dumpling and was peering forlornly into his carton. 'I mean, you and the boss have a personal connection, a professional connection, and an ongoing connection with the London crime scene. It would be amazing if you didn't cross over occasionally.'

'Yes, but this seems more,' said Raine. 'And now this Deadtown thing. Do you have any idea where the video clips originated?'

'None,' said Hume, frustration clear in her voice. 'We can't trace them. Once they've gone through a third party like Reddit or Discord the origin data is lost.'

'What about the stuff from the journalist's van? Oliver.'

'There are multiple encrypted files on the hard drive,' said Echo. 'As well as what seems to be notes on future or abandoned episodes of the podcast. Maybe if we can get past his firewall, we'll have an idea if it's connected.'

'It must be, otherwise why hide it?' said Hume.

'Anything else from you, Raine?' asked Echo. 'You're plugged into our data hub. Has anything popped out?'

'A couple of things, but nothing helpful yet. If these suspects, whoever they are, are taking photographs, "why" isn't the only question.'

'What's the other question?'

'Where? Where are they posting them? All these people taking pictures, they must be sharing them somewhere. I think if you can find out where you'll be halfway to finding why.'

'Definitely worth following up,' said Echo, tapping into his tablet. 'If we cross-reference what they are photographing as an image search, maybe it will throw something up.'

'And the finger fragment from the furnace?' asked Raine.

'Melissa's. Which, as that's the only physical evidence of her murder, makes the abattoir the primary site. And now that we have an actual body part, I can probably get you an official research status on the case.'

'Make me legit?' Raine flashed a smile. 'How dull. Did you have any luck with my name?'

'Your name?' said Echo, confused.

'Not her name,' clarified Hume. 'The name she gave us. I'm sure I asked you.' She turned to Raine. 'No. Nobody has heard of him. Are you sure . . . ?'

'He has something to do with Heather's disappearance, I just don't know what. Nothing with immigration?'

'No.'

'What name?' asked Echo.

'Joseph Banner,' said Raine. 'I've asked around but he's thin air. Nobody's heard of him.'

'Maybe he changed it,' said Hume. 'Before he moved here. Maybe Ridgeway knows him from the bad old days.'

'I have,' said Echo.

'Have what?' said Hume, confused.

'Heard of him. Joseph Banner. I have.'

The two women stared at him.

'What?' said Hume. 'When?'

'He's on the drive.'

'What drive? You mean the drive from Oliver Bell's van?'

Echo nodded.

'Are you sure?' said Hume.

'Pretty sure. I think it was in the archive index. To do with an old episode or something. I'll have to check when we get back. But yes, I'm pretty sure.'

'London entanglement. I told you.' Raine stood up. 'Everything's coming together.'

'Where are you going?'

Raine smiled. 'The thing about everything coming together is that it's easier for me to pull it apart. I'm going to find a phone.'

'What phone?'

'One I should have found a year ago.'

CHAPTER 35

Raine decided to walk to Piccadilly Circus tube station, cutting through St James's Park. Hume had given her lots to think about. The whole murder of Melissa was weird. It was as if there was a massive piece of the puzzle missing, and without it nothing made sense. And the fact that Melissa and Oliver had once done some work on a story involving Joseph Banner . . . It was like unseen forces were creating a nexus around her.

'Bollocks,' muttered Raine as she walked. It was just London. The finite area where she worked. There was bound to be crossover, as Echo had said. Repeats and reruns of people she'd tracked and captured over the years — both as a police officer and then as a private detective.

At the entrance to the park, a vendor was selling Bulletproof Coffee from a handcart. She bought a cup and headed for the Blue Bridge, which would take her to The Mall, and then on to Jermyn Street. She watched the steaming liquid, careful not to spill it. There was no sip lid, as the oil and molten butter concoction made the drink too thick to drink through it. She crossed over the bridge and glanced down at the lake. It looked as black and still as a dead bird's eye. To her left she could no longer make out Buckingham

Palace. The air seemed to be leaking moisture. Not quite rain and not quite mist, but something in-between, darkening the day. Raine hunched her shoulders against the weather and hurried on.

As she walked, she mused on why the youths had been photographing *her* boat. Up to that point, she had only touched the case peripherally, accessing the data using the link Echo had set up. She hadn't done any actual investigating herself. But now there was a thread that pulled back to Heather, she was going to have to ramp up.

Stepping off the bridge, she walked towards the edge of the park, passing the toilet block. Adam Pirie stepped out from behind the red-brick building.

'Hello, Raine with an "e" on the end,' he said pleasantly.

Raine slowed to a stop. She felt the point of a blade press against the side of her neck.

'Don't fucking move,' a raspy voice behind her whispered.

Raine didn't move. 'Well, well,' she said brightly, matching Pirie's tone. 'I thought you would be all locked up by now.'

Pirie's smile widened. There was no humour in it. 'My lawyer pointed out that all the evidence was circumstantial. There was nothing to stop me being bailed. He's quite expensive, but worth it.'

'But you'll defo go down once I testify,' said Raine. An arm snaked round her, even as the knife bit in harder. She felt a hot tear of blood slip down her neck as the blade pierced her skin.

'Not going to get the chance.' The voice behind her sounded bored.

In front of her, Pirie glanced around the empty park. The toxic mist had driven away any last strollers, and the black sky had doubled the gloom caused by the weather, reducing visibility to a few feet. Seeing the park deserted, Pirie reached into the inside of his jacket and pulled out a stubby pick-axe.

'Now let's not do anything hasty,' said Raine, putting a twist of fear in her voice.

'Nothing hasty going to happen here.' Pirie smiled nastily. 'Going to take my time, for what you did.'

'Come on, Adam,' Raine said softly, trying not to move her head. 'You know I had to. I couldn't leave it. You nearly killed that girl.'

'Fuck her,' spat Pirie. 'Literally. Once I've finished with you, I'm going to let my man there have her.'

Behind her, Gravel Voice snickered.

'And you know what?' Pirie licked his lips, his tongue obscenely red against his cold skin, 'I think I'll watch. Make a video. Maybe sell it.'

'Did Joseph Banner send you?' Raine asked.

Pirie looked back at her blankly. 'Who?'

'Just checking.'

The arm around her chest tightened.

'Don't!' pleaded Raine, panic in her voice.

Pirie smiled and began to edge forward.

'Please! I don't want to die in—' Raine threw the contents of the coffee cup she had been gripping over her shoulder. There was a scream as the boiling mixture of water, coffee and oil hit its target. Raine stomped down on her assailant's inner shin, then lifted both her feet, dropping to her knees. The pressure of the blade disappeared. She threw her head back, smashing it into the man's crotch. The knife dropped by her side even as she launched herself upwards, her shoulder catching him under his chin as he doubled over. His head snapped back and he was unconscious before he hit the frozen ground.

Raine turned just as the pick-axe arced down towards her out of the sleet. She felt it stab into her side, scraping down her ribs. The tip dragged against the bone, causing it to vibrate in her body. She cried out and pushed herself against Pirie's frame. The pick-axe twisted sideways. Raine felt it rip through her skin. Pirie pulled at the handle in an attempt to release it, but it was slippery with her blood, and trapped between them. Raine hooked his ankle with her foot, tipping him backwards.

She fell with him, pushing under his chin so his head hit the hard ground first. Raine head-butted him on the bridge of his nose. She staggered to her feet, throwing the pick-axe out of reach. Gravel Voice was attempting to stand. His jaw was broken where her shoulder had connected with it and his face was a mess of burns. Raine stepped forward and kicked him in the side of his leg, just above the boot line, snapping the tibia. She spun back to Pirie, but he was still on his back, face a ruin of blood and snot, hand blindly searching for the axe, several feet beyond his grasp. She limped over, plumes of white pain issuing from her mouth with each step. Then she brought her boot down and smashed it onto his fingers. Pirie let out a hissing scream and passed out.

'Just so you don't try to film any teenagers,' Raine whispered, moving a few feet from him and sagging onto her knees. She looked down at her side. Her waistcoat was in tatters, and there was a rip in her shirt where the axe had penetrated. The fabric was dark and sticky, steam rising from it.

'That wasn't very nice,' she muttered, glancing at the two prone figures before lifting the damaged area of her shirt. There was a wet ripping sound as it came away from her skin. Raine could only lift her arm about halfway, but it was enough to see the gash in her side. The pick-axe appeared to be new. No rust or dried blood on it. Less chance of infection, then. She reached into her shoulder holster with her left hand and removed her phone. She put it on the ground and pulled up Echo's ident.

'Raine?' he said when he answered. 'What's up? Have you thought of something—'

'Track my phone.' Her voice was little more than a harsh whisper through the pain. 'I've just been stabbed and need some help.'

'What? Stabbed? Raine where are—' Echo's voice dialled out of cheery and into urgent. Raine cut across him.

'There's two men here requiring hospital treatment, plus me. I'm in the park. Track the phone.' Raine's vision began to darken, cobwebs of pain knitting across her sight. She thought she might pass out. 'They're unconscious but I don't know for how long.'

'I've got you on screen. Close to Memorial Walk. Hang on, Raine. Mary's called the paramedic. Two minutes.'

Raine clamped her hand against the wound in her side and looked at Pirie. He still hadn't moved, but she could see blood flowing from his shattered nose, and the movement of his chest as he breathed. She hadn't killed him.

'Shame,' she whispered, wincing as her lungs pushed against her ribs. She didn't think any were broken, there was none of the telltale crunch and grind that would indicate a break, but if small shards had fractured and got into her bloodstream, she could be in trouble. As the painwebs increased, she saw a flashing blue light through the gloom; a paramedic on a bike entering the park. She could hear Echo's voice from the phone lying on the hard ground, telling her he and Mary were crossing Blue Bridge and could see her. She smiled at the unconscious Pirie. 'My blood and your fingerprints are all over that axe,' she said. Or maybe she only thought it, she wasn't sure. She was feeling dizzy, spaced out. 'Don't think your lawyer will get you out of this one.' Raine lay down on her back and concentrated on the sky. Her skin was numbing from the cold, causing the pain in her side to recede. She closed her eyes.

'Raine!'

Hume, Echo and the paramedic arrived at the same time.

'Hang tight, love,' said the paramedic. 'My name is Aziz. Can you tell me what happened?'

Raine opened her eyes. The paramedic was gently probing her midriff.

'Those two attacked me,' she said, unnecessarily pointing in the general direction of the still bodies a few feet away. 'One of them is Pirie. I don't know the other one. Might be Crack-Mouth.'

'Pirie? The county lines guy?' queried Hume. 'I thought he was arrested.'

'Made bail.'

'Do you know if you have another wound?' said Aziz. 'This one is nasty, too deep for Dermabond, but it looks clean.'

Raine glanced down once more. He had cut away her shirt, exposing her side. There was a deep gash from the side of her right breast to just below her ribcage. 'That was a brand-new shirt!' she said.

'Sorry. You're going to need an X-ray to make sure there's no bone damage, but I think you were lucky.' He pointed at the pick-axe. 'It looks like he attacked you with the pointy end. If he'd used the flat side . . .' Aziz left the sentence hanging, his meaning clear.

'The pointy end?' said Raine, eyebrows raised despite the pain. 'Is that a technical term?'

'You'd better call for an extra ambulance.' Echo was examining the two men. 'There are multiple breakages here, as well as some nasty burning.' He turned and fixed his eyes on Raine. 'What—' he began before Hume cut him off.

'Bag the axe and the knife. Call for the ambulance and SOCO.' She glared at her sergeant, then at Raine. 'We'll secure the scene here, then come and see you in the hospital.' She glanced at Aziz. 'Which one will they take her to?'

'St Thomas. It's the nearest with A&E.'

'I don't need to go to hospital—' began Raine, before seeing the look on Hume's face.

'These men were trying to kill you, Raine. One of them stabbed you with a pick-axe! You are going to the hospital.'

'It's just a scratch,' said Raine. The cold had completely numbed the wound.

'You could have died.' Hume's voice shook with emotion. 'They could have butchered you and stuffed you in the toilet like something to throw away. Is that what you want as an end? Do you think that is what Clara would want?'

Tears were diamonding Hume's eyes, making them glitter in the damp air. 'You're all that I've got left that connects to her. If you die too, I'll have nothing.'

* * *

Half an hour later Hume and Echo sat on a bench, watching the SOCO team cataloguing the site. The mist had retreated to the pond and the team were sticking plastic orange flags in the ground, marking where the men must have been waiting for Raine. Breaking down the chain of events that had almost led to tragedy.

'I can't believe she got away with such minimal damage,' said Echo, sipping the hot borscht he had bought from a vendor on The Mall. He didn't mention Hume's emotional outpouring. It had been too raw. Too personal. 'I mean, those men weren't messing about.'

'She was lucky,' murmured Hume, sipping her coffee. Not the Bulletproof version that Raine had disabled one of the men with; just the normal London industrial shot that kept the city's wheels turning. 'But one of these days she won't be.'

'In fairness, she didn't go looking for trouble this time,' said Echo. The scene had collected several ghoulish sightseers, standing behind the hazard tape and taking photographs. The injured attackers had long since been removed, but that didn't seem to detract them. They took selfies and stood around in the rapidly cooling day waiting for something else to happen.

'She doesn't need to; it seeks her out. She's like nature's red flag. Everything wants to attack her.'

Echo kept quiet. He suspected that seeing Raine injured had triggered other memories. Memories of Hume's daughter. Memories of other times when the injuries had been much worse. The consequences so much bleaker.

'I mean, all that bollocks about London entanglement,' said Hume suddenly. 'It's just a way of disguising her death wish. She throws herself in front of cars and calls it karma. It's so . . . heedless of those who care for her.' The detective took an angry sip of her coffee. 'She has no thought for others. Just makes fun of her mortality like she's one big punchline. I lost someone too. It's not all about her.'

'I think that's a bit harsh, boss,' said Echo, his voice soft.

'Do you?' said Hume, her tone clipped. 'Well, you've known her for about five minutes. I've known her for over five years, and let me tell you something about Raine . . .'

Echo held his breath. He didn't want to be here. He didn't want to hear any secrets about Raine. Hume was upset, and anything she said now she would surely regret later.

'Guv . . .' he began.

'I know, I know. Don't worry, I'm not going to embarrass you. I just sometimes feel that . . . What is going on there?'

Echo was confused. 'Sorry, what?'

'Over there. What's going on?'

He turned to observe the SOCOs. There had been two small tents erected to cover where Pirie and the other man had lain to protect any evidence.

'No, not there. Over there. By the bridge.'

When Echo shifted his gaze he could see a couple of teenagers; they were laughing, seemingly unaware of the police and SOCOs behind them. And they had their phones out.

'What are they filming? I thought a crime scene would be more interesting than an old bridge. Like being on Netflix.'

Echo smiled. 'They're not filming the bridge. They're probably playing Pokémon Go.'

'Pokémon?' She watched as one of the teenagers moved in a semi-circle, phone outstretched, then let out a yelp of triumph. She noticed he was wearing an oversized sweatshirt with a Japanese manga character she didn't recognise printed on it.

'Yes. It's a game where you—'

'I know what Pokémon Go is,' said Hume. This wasn't strictly true. She knew that it had been a craze a few years ago. There had been reports of people stepping into traffic, following digital animals on their phones. 'All right,' she conceded. 'I sort of know what it is. I'm not fully aware of the details. What are they doing exactly?'

'It's AR. Augmented Reality. The player looks through their camera app and it shows what you'd normally see, but then overlays it with a Pokémon. A little cartoon creature you need to catch.'

Hume's brow creased. 'But how does the phone know that the Pokémon or whatever is there?'

'You sign up to an app and share your location. The app then uses it to put a digital image directly on the screen.'

Even as Echo said it he felt the tension increase in his boss.

'You need to share your location,' she said slowly.

Echo turned to watch the youths, laughing and pointing their phones. 'Jesus,' he whispered.

'Those people who went to Aquinas Street and Oliver's van. What if they weren't taking pictures?' said Hume slowly. 'What if they were watching something that wasn't there? These digital creatures. Pokémon.' She stood up, feeling some of the pieces slipping into place. The missing details that had made the case seem so bizarre. Hume looked at Echo. 'Someone designs them and decides where they go?'

Echo clambered to his feet as well. 'Yes, and they could be anything. A historical character. A dinosaur.' He paused for a second. 'Even a short action sequence.'

'Like someone being murdered?'

Echo looked back down at the couple, pointing their phones and laughing as they captured another image. He nodded. 'I'm not sure. I think so. If you had the skills.'

'That's it, then,' said Hume grimly. 'That's what we were missing. Whoever's behind this didn't kill Melissa for revenge. She was murdered as entertainment. "*Deadtown*" is a game.'

CHAPTER 36

Raine walked out of St Thomas's Hospital angry.

Angry at her present self for being caught off-guard by Adam Pirie and his drug-addled henchman. Angry at her past self for not seeing the links with Heather's assault. Angry at her future self for what she was about to do.

Because she couldn't let it go. She knew that Frankie Ridgeway had given her Banner's name because he expected her to be killed, but she couldn't let it go.

Just like she couldn't let Clara go.

It was a form of arrogance, she understood that. A refusal to let the universe dictate to her. Accept that there was something beyond her control.

But if she allowed Clara to be dead, closed off from her then what did she have? Nothing. Her whole life was wrapped around her wife. Clara was warped and wefted into every fabric of her being. If she allowed herself to accept her passing, to grieve, then she would be severing the link to the only thing that mattered to her. The only reason for her being alive. The only thing that stopped her from giving up.

Which, if she were to be brutally honest with herself, was kind of what she had been doing. Placing herself in danger. Being reckless. Trying to join Clara.

But seeing Mary Hume's face . . . the concern and love on it. The heartbreak etched into every line on her skin.

Maybe it was time to let go. To stop using the tears she had shed over Clara to be the ink she used to write the rest of her life.

She pulled out her phone, wincing as she did so. Her wound had been cleaned and tightly strapped. X-rays had shown there was no break, no structural damage to the bone, but it hurt like hell and she was going to pay it forward. Anger and pain and frustration had formed a white-hot singularity of fury at her centre and it needed release.

'DI Conner!' she said as the call was answered.

'Raine,' said Conner, his voice full of warmth. 'How are you?'

'There . . . you've barely spoken and you've already made me feel all cosy on a cold day.'

'Pleased to be of service. Is this a social call to compliment my dulcet tones, or is there some other point?'

'Some other point.' Raine paused in the doorway of a closed-down shop, allowing the river of London pedestrians to flow by. 'You know how I've helped you in the past, catching all those nasty drug dealers and gangbangers, thereby contributing to keeping the city safe from villains?'

'You make yourself sound like Batman, but yes. We're very grateful.'

'Good, because I'd like a teeny-weeny favour.'

'How teeny?' Conner's voice became cautious.

'Nothing too much. I went to visit Luke Parsons.'

'Luke . . . ?' It was clear Conner didn't recall the name.

'The roadman who was caught with a sack of drugs and attempted to kidnap an ex-police officer,' Raine reminded him.

'I remember now. Didn't he store his drugs in a children's Wendy house?' The disgust was clear even across the ether of the phone call.

'Yes, but he's on a redemption arc now,' said Raine brightly. 'And he's given me permission to check out the phone he had on him when he was arrested. I thought it would be with the rest of his possessions in storage at the prison, but it wasn't there.'

'If it was used as physical or digital evidence it might have been destroyed post-conviction. Sorry, Raine.'

'That's the thing: because of the pandemic, there's a massive backlog in the courts. He hasn't gone to trial yet.'

'Really? Well, if that's the case, and the phone was evidence, it should still be here.'

'That's what I'm hoping. If you can find out where it's being stored, would it be possible for me to take a butcher's? I don't need to remove it. Just need to get an app off it. He says he can't remember the password, but it should just open, meaning the password is on the phone. All I need is to switch it on and copy the app and the password.'

'What's this about? Every time you do something that hits my radar, people either get arrested, start a riot or destroy parts of London. I don't think the Met's reputation can take it.'

'Nothing like that. It's just a missing-person case. I think there might be some intel there. That's all.'

'Is this about the dead girl last year? What was her name?'

'Heather. Yes, but I don't think she's dead.'

'Raine,' DI Conner sounded weary, 'she took two shotgun barrels to the head. You don't get much deader than that.'

'I don't think that was Heather. I think it was someone made to look like her. Can you help me?'

Raine listened to the silence as Conner considered her request, until finally: 'Where are you?'

Raine didn't think it would help her cause to explain that she'd just come out of hospital. 'Nearby. I could be with you in fifteen minutes.'

'Fine. I'll see if I can locate the phone in the Material Evidence Unit. If it's there I'll leave a note at the desk. You'll be taken back and allowed access.'

'It might need charging.'

'Fine. It will have been processed already. But no removal, okay?'

'Cheers, Inspector. I owe you one.'

Raine folded the phone, ending the call.

Twenty minutes later she was in a small windowless room in the basement of Chapel Hill Police HQ, staring at Luke's mobile. It was a cheap burner, and the battery was dead. She had snagged a charger from the duty officer, and after plugging it in she was in business. The device had switched on, requesting a four-digit code. She tapped in the code Luke had reluctantly given her. Once opened she swiped to the app screen and located the tracking app. In settings, she requested a password change. The app sent a verification code. She entered the code and changed the password. She then pulled out her own phone and downloaded the app. She signed in using the new password and the app opened, displaying one pulsing blue dot.

Track-tile 34t#11

The tile was a tracking device with a two-year battery. About the size of a credit card and almost as thin. Luke had said he'd slid it into Heather's bag that night. Pushed it through a rip in the lining at the bottom. It seemed unlikely that it hadn't been discovered, but there it was, showing her at a location in South London.

Raine closed Luke's phone and checked the app was still functioning on her own, then left the building. She sent a quick 'thank you' text to DI Conner before heading back to her boat.

CHAPTER 37

Echo was pacing in front of the murder board. He was excited. Wired. 'I've done some simple manipulation of the video clip that was sent to us. It's not perfect, but here's how I think it could work. Melissa was tied to the chair and murdered, exactly as we saw.' He stopped and touched the screen, pulling the video clip of Melissa into the centre and expanding it. 'But the rest is bogus. She wasn't murdered in Aquinas Street. She was killed somewhere else.'

'Explain.' Hume sat on the edge of her desk, staring at the screen. 'Because it certainly looks convincing. When I stood and held up the tablet that night the image fitted perfectly.'

'I know, and it's the same chair. The DNA and prints prove it,' said Echo admiringly. 'It's beautifully done.'

'So how could she have been killed elsewhere?'

Echo swiped at his tablet. On the screen the room disappeared, leaving only Melissa on the chair, the background blank. 'Remember, at the beginning, I said the quality of the image was low grade? I think it's because it's a composite. Trying to hide the digital meshing.'

'Echo, speak English, for God's sake!'

'It's like the game. Pokémon Go. Or Jurassic World. Augmented Reality games that map something from the virtual world onto a real-life topography, only here it's a real image that's been grafted onto the location footage.' Echo became aware of the confusion on his boss's face. 'Think a sophisticated version of the backdrops people use for Zoom.

'Right.'

'AI algorithms have made all this stuff super accessible. I can't believe I never put it all together before. Bitz practically told me days ago.'

'Bitz? How did—?'

'The other night, when I was trying to work out the meaning behind the map-logging. It was Bitz who told me about GPS spoofing. She even said it was popular with AR games.'

'How? How does messing with the GPS help?'

'It lets you cheat. The digital images aren't there in real life, obviously. They only get activated when the phone is in the right geographical area. So, if you can make your phone think you are in different places, you can collect the Pokémon without actually needing to . . .' Echo fell silent.

'What?' asked Hume, her eyes shifting from him to the board. 'What is it?'

'The GPS markers.'

'What about them?'

'You said it yourself,' Echo said, staring at her. 'You said it was like someone was playing with us. Taunting us.'

'And?'

He pointed at the board. '"Deadtown" is spelled out in letters formed from virtual routes. What if there are GPS markers around London? Like in the AR games. Those people with their cameras. What if they all have the same program? The same app?'

Hume felt the skin at the back of her neck goose-bump.

'You think they're like signposts? The Deadtown geo-markers have . . . what did you call it? Digital overlay?'

'Yes. Maybe, with the right app, a person could see what we saw with Melissa. That if they went into the house on Aquinas Street, they'd see her have her throat cut in front of them.'

Echo pulled up the feed of the youths entering the Aquinas Street house. Saw them laughing. Holding up their phones.

Hume felt a chill shiver through her. 'No wonder we never saw the body removed. It was never there.'

'But the killer must have been, at some point,' said Echo. 'To map the room and position the chair.'

Hume nodded. 'Go back further, if you can. With the door video footage. See if we can find out when the chair was placed.'

'Guv.' Echo began tapping at his tablet.

Hume surveyed the smart screen again, then turned back to Echo. 'What's the point of those games? Pokémon and whatever they are called. Why do people play them?'

Echo shrugged. 'Fun. You connect with a virtual community. See how many you can collect. Some creatures are rarer than others.'

'Fun,' she repeated, as she resumed assessing the board. 'These other sites. Like the Soho pub and the tree. Do you think they are part of the game?'

Echo brought up an image of the tree, with the scarf tied round the branch. 'Maybe if you had a phone with that app you wouldn't just see the scarf. Maybe you'd see something more.'

'That's why they cut the branches away!' said Hume suddenly. 'To allow a straight shot up to the scarf. What do you think you'd see?' She turned to Echo. 'If we had one of those phones, what would we see?'

They stared at each other, both thinking of the awful possibilities. The very real chance that there could be more murders. More bodies.

'How do these games make money?' she asked, after a few moments. 'I think if you go to all this trouble, it isn't just for revenge, and it isn't just for one person. Not some feud. Setting up a game, if that's what it is, needs a different motive. How are they monetised?'

Echo frowned. 'I don't see how they could be making money. It would require substantial marketing, but via illegal channels, of course, because of the nature of the material being sold . . . Unless the game we know about is some sort of teaser.' He frowned in thought. 'Like a trailer to a main event.'

'What about the flash drive from Oliver Bell's van? There must be something on it that opens this up for us.'

'Hoping to be in soon. We've managed to unlock some of it. As I said, there seems to be archived source material for work-in-progress episodes. That's where we're starting.'

'Good,' said Hume, as she got to her feet. 'We really need answers quickly. Did you learn anything more about Joseph Banner from the drive?'

'Another archived case, it looks like. From some time ago. As soon as I have anything I'll send it to Raine.' Echo paused before asking, 'How is she, by the way? I'm surprised she hasn't messaged me for information herself.'

'I'm not sure. She's gone off-grid. She left a message saying she'd be in touch, but after that . . .' Hume sighed. She was worried, but pushed it to the back of her mind. 'I'll try to catch up with her later.' She turned to Echo, closing down the conversation. 'I want you to set up a watch on the Deadtown locations we know. The pub and the tree. All of them. If we're going to break this open, we need to get hold of one of those phones.'

CHAPTER 38

Raine sat on the deck of her boat, sipping the coffee from her Nespresso pod. She was wrapped up warm against the dying day, with thermals, combats, fingerless gloves, a thick black jumper and a beret.

During the night she had moved her vessel back to its former berth on Regent's Canal. She didn't want to put Jolene and Libby in danger, in case someone came in search of her.

And Raine was certain they would. Either the Deadtown gamers or Joseph Banner, whoever he was. Hume had sent her through some intel about the bizarre murder video, and the hypothesis that it was a game Melissa Clarke had come across in her research, that she had been killed while investigating. DNA from the finger fragment found in the incinerator was a positive match to Melissa. Her partner on *Deadtown*, Oliver Bell, had also been murdered. Perhaps many others, it seemed.

Raine glanced down at her phone, propped half open on the table beside her. The blue dot had not moved. It was stationary at an address in Hackney. According to the app data, it hadn't moved for months. Which meant one of three things.

The GPS device had been discovered and tossed, which would make it a dead end.

The bag was at the address, but it wasn't with Heather. Because Heather had said it was precious to her, so surely would be using it. Which meant she might be dead. Like her sister.

Because that was who must have been shot and dumped by Ridgeway outside Heather's office. Raine didn't know why yet, but it was the only thing that made sense. The thing that explained the similarities to Heather. It also explained why the corpse's face was blown off.

Absently, Raine moved her boot over the deck's surface, making rough patterns in the grime. Watching the blue dot again, which continued pulsing on her phone like an infection. Then she swiped it away and sent a text to Hume.

Mary
I love your daughter.
I love you.
But I can't come.
I just can't.

Raine closed the phone, her eyes hard and unblinking, and continued to watch the day expire.

* * *

Hume and Robert sat in a quiet corner of the bustling restaurant. As she stared down at Raine's message on her phone she felt her heart breaking.

'Not coming?' asked Robert gently.

'She says she can't.'

Robert didn't know how to help the woman in front of him. The person he loved more than anything in the world. 'It must have taken a lot for her to even send the message.'

Hume nodded. Robert reached over and took her hand. 'Have I ever told you the parable of the Backwards Angel?'

'Angel?' She looked up from the phone at Robert's face. Older than when she had first met him, but still with the kind eyes she'd fallen in love with.

'Old Babylonian myth. It was carved into a stone tablet found in upper Egypt. My team translated it a couple of years ago. The angel is out walking in the garden one day when they suddenly realise how awful the world is.'

'What garden?'

'Doesn't matter. It's written on pottery so doesn't say. Probably a metaphor meaning the world. Anyway, they are there, walking, and have this epiphany.'

'So is there more than one angel? You said "they".'

Robert shook his head. 'Babylonian angels don't have a sex.' He paused, thinking. 'Actually, I shouldn't think any angels have a sex. Or sex. Which is a bit of a shame because I'm sure the wings would add a whole different level to it.'

Hume sighed. 'Get on with the story, Robert.'

'Fair enough. Anyhow, the point is, the angel pinpoints a time in history where the world went wrong. The one thing at the one time that started the world on its path to destruction.'

'Just one thing?'

Robert nodded. 'Just one decision that messed everything up. Like chaos theory. One flap of a butterfly wing that caused a chain reaction ending in the collapse of the world.'

'Wow,' said Hume, interested despite herself. 'What did the angel do?'

'It decided to go back,' he said, taking a swig of his wine. 'It thought if it could go back it would stop the one thing, the one decision that ruined everything, then it could save the world from becoming broken.'

Hume took a sip of her wine. 'So it went back?'

Robert nodded. 'It asked God's permission, and He said sure, but you can't take everything with you.'

'What did that mean?'

'He said that the angel was an expression of the experiences it had accumulated over its existence, and so for every year it went back, it would lose a year of memory. Become less. A year's worth of thoughts and feelings and knowledge subtracted from its essence.'

'That seems . . . cruel.'

Robert nodded. 'God's a bit of a bastard like that. Anyhow, the takeaway is that the angel began to walk backwards through time, remembering less and less about the future, until when it came to the era of the terrible decision, it couldn't remember what that decision was. It remembered that a decision had to be made, but not which way to make it.'

'So what happened,' asked Hume. The restaurant seemed to have reduced around her. 'What did the angel do?'

'It made the wrong choice. The decision that started all the trouble. It became the instigator of the end of the world.'

Hume sat back, annoyed. 'Well, that's depressing. Where's the moral in that?'

Robert reached forward and stroked the back of Hume's hand. 'You can't change the present by living in the past. All you can do is envisage a better future to make the present liveable.' He raised her hand to his lips and kissed it.

'So what is this?' said Hume, gesturing around her. 'Am I living in the past?'

'No. You're acknowledging its existence, but you are here in the present with me. Always. Now and in the future.'

Hume felt the tears coming. 'And Raine?'

'She's the angel trying to fix things. All you can do is be there for her when she turns around and starts walking forward. That she didn't come tonight has nothing to do with you, or Clara. It's just Raine lost in the past. But I know when she finds her way back you will be there for her.'

Hume pushed her wine aside, wiping away her tears with her other hand. 'There's no way all of that fitted on a pot. You just made it up, didn't you?'

Robert took the olive out of his drink and ate it daintily. 'Might have. Doesn't make it not true, though.'

Hume smiled at him. 'And that, my dear, is why I love you.'

CHAPTER 39

Hinges squeaked in protest as Raine opened the metal gate. The front garden was divided by a short path, the grass that might have grown on either side long gone. In its place was rubble and weeds. The two bay windows that faced her were cataracted by street grime and a dirty crust of morning frost. One of the front-door panes had broken at some point, replaced with a square of plywood. Raine thought the property was so decrepit, squatters would turn it down. She glanced at her phone, once again checking the blue pulse throbbing on the screen. Satisfied, she navigated the cracked path and pressed the bell. Somewhere deep in the house, there was a distant buzz, like that of a giant insect stuck under a glass jar.

Raine bounced on her toes as she heard someone approaching. She kept her hands loose beside her, fingers curled tight, forefinger knuckle prominent.

The door opened, revealing a tatty-looking man in his sixties, wearing an ill-fitting pair of joggers, slippers and a jumper that was the colour of old microwave dinners for one.

'Morning!' said Raine. 'I was going to ask you not to hit me 'cos my ribs are still sore, but now I see you, I think I'll be all right.'

'Do what?' said the man, confused. His accent was pure unreconstituted London.

'No worries,' said Raine. 'I'm guessing you're not Joseph Banner?'

'No, love.' The man peered over her shoulder. 'You're not from the council, are you? Only the noise is doing my nut. I've been on at them and they said they'd send someone out.'

'I know!' said Raine sympathetically. 'It's a disgrace, isn't it? Do you know where Joseph is? Or Heather?'

'I think you've got the wrong house, darlin'. My name's Gilbert. Ain't no Heather here.'

'Right. How long have you been here, Gilbert? Only I was told to pick up a bag that was left. I thought Heather would still be living here. It's a tapestry shoulder bag. Bit like a carpet bag. Have you seen it?'

Gilbert gazed at her, his face slack. Raine wondered if he was on medication, or was just beaten down by one problem too many.

'Social supposed to come round once a week to check I'm all right . . .' He shrugged, suddenly hopeful. 'Are you the social? Only I've run out of tea.'

'Tell you what, Gilbert. You put the kettle on and I'll go and get us some tea bags from the Spar. How about that?'

Gilbert's face lit up. 'T'riffic.'

Ten minutes later she and Gilbert were sitting in the saddest kitchen Raine had ever seen. Everything was grey and covered with a thin film of old cooking oil. Even though she had washed the cups several times there was a rainbow skim of oil on the surface of her tea. She gently pushed it away.

'So, Gilbert. Who lived here before you?'

'No idea,' he said, taking a slurp of his tea. 'Place was empty when they moved me in.'

'And when was that?' Raine wondered how she could search the house without raising suspicions. The man appeared vulnerable, and she didn't want to upset or confuse him more than she already had.

'Must be twenty years now.'

Raine blinked. 'Really? Are you sure?'

'Oh yes,' said Gilbert, nodding. 'They knocked down my house on the Island when they redeveloped the place. Made a blasted mess of it if you ask me.'

Raine nodded. The Isle of Dogs had been completely gutted in the late nineties, with half the old-time Londoners thrown to all corners of the capital.

'Anyhow, they sent me here. Don't know anybody anymore. Spend my time doing crosswords and watching telly. That's when I can hear it. Bleeding noise.'

'Okay, Gilbert. Did anybody live here with you, maybe a year ago? A lodger, perhaps?'

'No, love. It's just me and the telly. My wife died ten years back. She was the one used to keep it proper.' He stared at her, a look of complete defeat on his face. 'I'm not very good on my own. Are you going to call on me regular?'

'No kids, Gilbert?' said Raine, dodging the question. 'I'm not seeing any family pictures.'

'Never bothered,' said Gilbert. 'Too much hassle. We was happy with each other.'

Raine walked over to the sink and poured her tea down the furry plughole, preparing to leave. There was nothing she could do here. From the window above the sink she could see that the back garden was worse than the one at the front. Ghosts of old white goods poked up out of the rubble. A septic-looking carpet was propped up against the gate. 'You need to get the council in to clear your back garden, Gilbert,' she said. 'Or you'll be getting a visit from the vermin brigade.'

'That's what I keep telling them,' said Gilbert angrily. 'But all they ever do is shout at me.'

'The council can't do that. You should—'

'No, not them,' said Gilbert. 'They're useless. Even when you can get through, all they do is put you on hold or make you feel stupid. Nobody has any pride in their work. Always somebody else's job.'

'Gilbert, I wonder if you'd mind me having a quick shifty round your gaff? Heather needs her bag and—'

'I'm talking about them upstairs. Always banging about. Never a thought for me beneath 'em. It's doing my trolley.'

Raine glanced up at the drooping ceiling, then back at Gilbert. 'Right,' she said. 'Silly me. The house has been split into two, yes?'

Gilbert nodded. 'Year or so back. The landlord did it.'

'Not the council?'

'Nah. The council pays for me, but it's private.'

'So is there another door?' asked Raine. 'Because I didn't see one at the front.'

'Metal stairs at the back. The least they could've done is made it stone. Clanging all night long, it is.'

'Right.' Raine smiled gently at the old man. 'Gilbert, why don't you make yourself another cup of tea while I go and have a word with them? See if I can't sort out the noise problem.'

Gilbert smiled, revealing a mouth full of gaps and bits of old food.

Raine opened the kitchen utensil drawer. She quickly searched through and then took out a corkscrew.

'Why do you want that?' asked Gilbert, confused.

'In case they have some wine,' she said, slipping it into her pocket.

* * *

The door to the first-floor flat opened before the bell had finished chiming. The man who stood on the threshold was thickset with a severe buzzcut and cruel eyes. One hand was wrapped around the edge of the door to prevent it from being pushed open.

'Yeah?' The tone was confrontational. His gaze flicked behind her, checking she was alone.

'Hi!' said Raine 'Is Heather in?'

'Nobody here called Heather.'

'How about Joseph Banner? Is he in?'

'Never heard of him. I'm busy.' The man began to close the door.

Raine put her foot in the gap. 'Don't think so.'

The man looked down at her foot, then back up at her face. 'Stroll on, or I'll—'

Raine removed her foot and pulled the handle towards her. The man gasped as his fingers, still clutched around the edge of the door, were crushed. Raine put her shoulder against the door and pistoned it open, smashing it into the man's body. He fell hard onto his backside. Raine ran forward and kicked the hammer out of his left hand.

'Word of advice, mate: never try to hide a weapon behind a door with glass panes. It just doesn't work.'

'You broke my fingers!' hissed the man.

'Can you tell how sorry I am?' said Raine.

Instead of answering, the man surged to his feet, reaching for her throat. Raine punched down into his thigh, the corkscrew sticking out from between her fingers sinking into the muscle. The man collapsed, then let out a gasp as Raine pulled out the corkscrew. Before he could say anything, she reversed her grip and punched him in the side of his head. The man's eyes rolled back, and he lay still. Raine pulled a handful of zip-ties out of a pocket of her combats.

'You know, these are fantastic,' she said conversationally to the unconscious man, lacing several together so she could secure his wrists. 'They come in packs of twenty for a fiver, and are practically unbreakable.' She dragged him over to the cast-iron radiator, grunting with the pain in her ribs, and used more zip-ties to attach him to the pipe. Softly, she patted his cheek. 'You sit tight while I do some exploring.'

Raine stood up. She was in a hallway with three doors leading off it. She tried the first. A neat toilet and basin greeted her. In the corner was a shower with no curtain. Everything was sparkling clean.

The next room was a small galley kitchen. Like the bathroom, it was meticulously clean. After a quick once-over, she moved on. The last room was a bedroom. Or at least it would have been if it had a bed in it. Instead, there was just a mattress on the floor, with metal rings bolted to the floor next to it. In the corner was a flimsy cupboard. Raine noted that the window was boarded up and there was a solid lock on the door. When she opened the cupboard she found nothing hanging on the rails, but a mound of stuff lay piled up at the base. Bags and coats and other items of clothing.

Near the bottom of the heap Raine spotted Heather's bag: empty. The shoulder strap was ripped. Reaching in she felt with her fingers along the base seam until she located the GPS tile. She took the bag back into the hallway. The man had regained consciousness and was struggling to free himself.

Raine held up the bag. 'Where's the woman who had this?'

He glared back at her. 'You're in a world of trouble.'

'Don't think so.' Raine walked back into the kitchen and started opening drawers. In the third one she tried were a selection of passports. She took one at random. It was dark green; issued by the Islamic Republic of Afghanistan. Inside was a photo of a woman in a hijab. It wasn't Heather. Raine looked back into the drawer. There were at least a dozen passports. She checked a few more then returned to the man who was still scrabbling uselessly at the zip-ties round his wrists.

'So what are we talking about? Trafficking?'

He scoffed. 'Trafficking? You've got no idea.'

Raine squatted in front of him. 'Of course I've got no idea. That's why I'm asking. You clearly keep prisoners here. I think it's reasonable to go with trafficking.'

When the man made no reply, Raine sighed and pulled out her phone. 'Last chance before I call the cops. Who's Joseph Banner?'

At the mention of Banner's name an ugly smile spread across his face.

Raine reached forward and frisked him while he squirmed helplessly. From his pockets she pulled a pack of cigarettes, a

Zippo lighter, a roll of banknotes, a phone in a flip case, an Oyster card, plus a butterfly knife.

She worked the knife mechanism, releasing the blade. 'Naughty,' she whistled, admiring the clean steel. 'Where did you get this — the Army? Love the buzzcut, by the way. Very butch.'

'What do you want?'

'I want you to give a message to your boss,' said Raine. 'Tell him Raine wants to meet him. Tell him I want Heather. Tell him Frankie Ridgeway gave me his name.'

She reached forward with the knife. The man shied away until he realised she was cutting him free of the radiator. Then she smashed his phone against the wall.

'Hey!' he shouted.

'So you can't call for back-up straight away and have me killed. I'll leave you the Oyster card, though.'

The man stood, his hands still tied behind him. He was completely unintimidated. 'I'll see you again.'

Raine slipped the ruined device into his pocket. 'Stroll on, mate, before you get arrested. I'm about to call the cops. Deliver my message to Banner. I want to meet him. I want Heather.'

He dead-eyed for a moment longer, then turned and walked out. Raine watched the door to make sure he wasn't coming back, then took out her own phone, fired up the tile tracker app and watched as the blue pulsing dot made its way down the street. She had slipped the GPS device from Heather's bag between the back of the man's phone and the flip case just before she'd smashed it against the wall. As he couldn't ring his boss and had no money, she hoped he would use his Oyster card to lead her there. She minimised the app and tapped the ident for DI Conner.

'My second favourite inspector!' she said when he answered. 'Not including Inspector Gadget. I've got a bit of a treat for you.'

CHAPTER 40

Hume sat watching Raine's empty boat, back in its Regent's Canal mooring. She had knocked, but there was no answer. She had walked up the bank and along the path to sit on a bench and phone Echo. 'Any updates?' she asked as soon as he answered.

'We've put a watch on all possible locations, but nothing yet.'

'Damn. We need one of those phones. What about Oliver's flash drive?'

'Slightly better news. Melissa and Oliver were definitely investigating Joseph for a story. We're not sure of the details yet but, judging by the size of the file, it was something big.'

A flash of movement caught Hume's attention. She turned to see a young man and woman walking up the towpath, chatting animatedly, white vape clouds trailing behind them.

'Good. Let me know as soon as you have something definite.'

'Wilco; I'll hopefully have more later. Did you locate Raine?'

One of the pair on the towpath, the woman, was dressed in grunge wear, with a baggy cardigan over a jumper. Her glasses were round. Hume's brow creased, as she remembered her thoughts about Oliver's girlfriend. Anwen, his neighbour, had said the visitor wore a hippy cardigan and small glasses, and Hume was certain she'd recently seen someone wearing exactly that.

'No, but I found her boat. It's back on Regent's Canal. I've left a message.'

On the towpath, the youth took his phone out to snap a picture of the canal.

Hume squinted. *Not the canal. Raine's boat. The youth wasn't taking a selfie or framing a picture of the canal. He was focused on the boat.*

'Well, I'm sure she'll be in touch.'

'You need to send a couple of officers to me,' said Hume quietly.

'Sorry?'

'You remember where Raine's boat used to be. I need some back-up. How long?'

There was a moment's silence before Echo came back on the line. 'There's a patrol car at King's Cross. I've alerted it. What's going on, boss?'

'Have you got it?' said the young woman. In the still, cold air, her words carried well. 'Was it there?'

'Hang on.' Her companion moved his phone around until it was pointing at the cabin of Raine's boat. 'Yeah, I've got it.'

'Nice! Show me.'

They crowded together over the phone, pointing and laughing at whatever was captured on the device. But it wasn't the kind of laugh where you see something funny. It was a nervous, almost awestruck laugh. An adrenaline-release laugh. Like in a horror movie just after the jump scare.

'If we're lucky we're about to have access to one of the spoofed phones,' Hume whispered to Echo. She stood up and walked down the small slope to the path, treading carefully on the weeds and grass. The pair were so engrossed by whatever was showing on the young man's phone that they didn't hear her approach.

'If you change the time settings, you'll be able to get it on yours,' Hume heard him say.

'Fuck off, Reuben!' The woman nudged him with her shoulder. 'Why would I want that on my phone? What if someone saw?'

'Excuse me,' said Hume, walking up behind them.

They both started, the woman almost dropping her device. 'Blimey, you gave me a shock,' she said, smiling anxiously.

'Sorry,' said Hume, smiling back. 'I don't mean to intrude, but I'm a bit lost.' She looked around her. 'Do you know which direction I should head in for King's Cross station?'

'Sure,' said the woman, relieved. She pointed down the path.

Hume's eyes followed where she was gesturing and nodded gratefully. 'Oh, that's great. It's easy to lose your sense of direction, don't you think?'

Reuben looked up and down the canal, then back at her, grinning. 'Not really. There's only two of them.'

His friend laughed, but it was strained.

'Yes, but you must have been lost, too, no? That's why you were checking your phones. I saw you moving them about.'

A patrol car pulled up on the bridge behind the couple and a PC got out. Hume gave a slight nod of her head.

'What? Oh no, we were just, erm, getting a shot of the canal.'

'Right,' said Hume, glancing out over the water. A duck was savaging an old kebab wrapper that was slowly submerging. 'Well, it is beautiful. Can I see the pictures?'

'I deleted them,' said Reuben, taking a step back and pocketing the phone. 'They didn't come out right.'

Hume smiled. 'Ever heard of Deadtown?'

Shock and alarm registered on their faces. The woman nudged Reuben. 'We should go.'

'I think you'd better stay,' countered Hume, taking out her warrant card.

Reuben turned and ran — straight into the police officer from the bridge, who had quietly positioned himself behind them.

'Now, would you mind showing me what you were so engrossed by on your phone?' asked Hume calmly, turning her attention to the young woman, who looked like she was going to faint.

'My parents are going to kill me.'

'It's not real, anyway,' Reuben said. 'Just a game.'

Hume held out her hand. 'Then we can get this all cleared up, can't we?'

There was a moment of resistance, then the young man's shoulders slumped and he reached into his pocket. 'Honest. It can't be what it seems.' He handed over his phone.

'Just a game,' nodded Hume, as she fixed her eyes on the screen. 'I get it.'

The camera app was open, along with a *Deadtown* banner. It wasn't in the same style as the poster in Melissa's flat. The font was more trashy, with saturated eighties video game colours. Hume held up the device and framed Raine's boat. All that was visible was a digital image of the vessel. Hume frowned. 'Shouldn't there be a body or something?'

'He's already captured it,' said the woman. 'It'll be in Collections.'

'Ah, of course.' Hume couldn't immediately see how to navigate the app but didn't want to hand it back to Reuben in case he deleted everything. She focused on the young woman. 'But you haven't, have you? Collected it. You were going to change the timing settings to get it. That's what your friend told you just before I arrived. What does that do, exactly?'

'Stacie.' There was a clear warning note in Reuben's tone. The woman blew out a dismissive breath between her teeth.

'Shut it, Reuben. If it weren't for you, I wouldn't be here in the first place.' Then she turned back to Hume. 'I only downloaded it because I was with him. I don't even like puzzle games, and this one's stupid.'

'That's because you're only at the first level,' said the young man petulantly.

'Whatever,' said Hume, concentrating on Stacie. She gave her an encouraging smile. 'Can you show me on your phone? It will count for a lot if you're cooperating. Helping us.'

'Sure.' Stacie, suddenly eager, took out her phone and flipped it open. She held it so the screen could be seen by Hume. 'The body-bot resets after thirty minutes. That's so a group can't all capture it at the same time.' She swiped into settings and changed the clock, putting it forward an hour. As soon as she reopened the *Deadtown* app, the phone buzzed.

'That means there's a body nearby,' said Stacie, before correcting herself. 'An avatar, I mean. Not a real body.'

'Right,' said Hume. 'So how do you capture it on screen?'

'It's called "reaping" in the game,' said Stacie. 'You just point the phone in the right direction to find it. This one is on that boat.'

Hume watched as the woman turned to point her phone at Raine's boat. On the screen, lying on the deck, was a man. It was impossible to tell his age because his head was a matted pulp of flesh and bone. No features remained.

'Jesus,' said Hume.

'It can't be real,' Reuben repeated, his voice small. 'It's like street theatre, yeah? Nobody's actually . . .'

Hume swiped the screen, removing the image. A menu appeared.

Knives
Hanging
Fire
Drowning
Bullet
Falling
Impact

'What do these words signify?' she asked them. Neither replied.

Thinking of Melissa, Hume tapped the avatar next to 'Knives'. The screen immediately changed to show the outside of the block of flats in Aquinas Street. A night scene. In the corner of the screen was a red 'record' button. 'Did you film this?' she asked Reuben.

'No.' His voice sounded pleading. 'It's just what comes through—'

'When you point the phone. Yeah, I see.'

The scene continued into the house from the camera's viewpoint. It was exactly as Hume remembered it. The tatty wallpaper. The dim lighting. The chair in the centre of the back room. Only the chair wasn't empty. A woman was seated, her face covered by her hair. Hume knew it was Melissa. It was the final scene Hume had viewed on the tablet. After Melissa's throat had been cut. The woman was slumped forward, her hands and feet taped to the chair. The river of blood down the front of her dress.

Hume felt her heart tighten with revulsion. She stared up at the young man. He couldn't meet her gaze. 'And the others? Fire? Hanging? They're all like this? Different ways to be murdered?'

He nodded. 'If you collect enough tokens, you get to watch the actual . . . thing.'

Hume was silent.

'The re-enactment,' he finished.

Stacie made a dismissive sound with her teeth again.

'Where did you get this . . . game?' asked Hume. 'Where did you buy it?'

Reuben looked puzzled.

'Did you download it?'

'No, we found it.'

Now it was Hume's turn to be confused. 'What do you mean?'

'We found it. There was a card with a QR on it. Like a business card. We scanned it, thinking it might be an address or something. Like maybe we could get a finder's fee. We got the game. We didn't mean to do anything wrong.'

A horrible feeling crept over Hume. 'Where was the card?'

'It was in the front pocket of a bag we found.'

'Where was this bag?'

'In the street, in Soho. It had blood on it. We thought it was from a mugging or something. We handed it in,' said Stacie, her eyes wide.

'And where did you hand it in?' asked Hume.

'Charing Cross Police Station.'

CHAPTER 41

'What do you know about Afghanistan?'

Jasper's smile creased his face into a map of happy memories. 'Love Afghanistan. Used to go there regularly.'

'Jasper, you never cease to impress,' said Raine, amazed. 'Afghanistan? How did that work?'

Jasper waved his hand, causing smoke from his Black Sobranie cigarette to make small vapour trails in the freezing air. They were sitting on a bench opposite the Bank of England headquarters in Threadneedle Street. Nearby, the Walkie-Talkie skyscraper loomed. To their left was the faded grandeur of Mansion House and The Monument.

By Raine's feet was her army satchel. 'This was back in the seventies before the Soviets invaded,' Jasper said. 'It was a completely different place, then. Very popular with the counterculture movement.'

'Wow. I never knew. So what were you all doing out there?'

'Smoking hashish, mainly,' mused Jasper, examining his cigarette. 'A bit of art dealing. It was a stop-off on the way to Pakistan. The old hippy trail.'

Raine looked at Jasper, shaking her head. 'One day I'm going to get you to write everything down. Whereabouts in Afghanistan? All I know about it is from the news.'

'Kabul. Me and my girlfriend. We used to buy goods from Chicken Street and import them back to the UK. It was a sweet deal. There were a few of us doing it. The culture was fantastic.'

Raine's brow furrowed. 'I've seen pictures of your girlfriend. I'm trying to imagine her in a burka, and it's just not happening.'

Jasper shook his head. 'No. This was way before the Taliban and all that shit. Women had equal rights under Muslim law. At least in the cities. No burkas. Not even a head covering if you didn't want it. Afghanistan was very progressive that way.'

'Why was it called Chicken Street? The place where you got your gear?'

'Haven't a scooby,' said Jasper. His face took a sad turn. 'Such a shame what happened to that country. I cried when they blew up those Buddhas.'

'What Buddhas?'

'The Buddhas of Bamiyan. Sixth-century statues as big as Nelson's column. Holy site. People used to come from all over the world to visit them. Taliban dynamited them into dust.'

'Why?' said Raine, shocked.

'Because they could. It was all about control. Same with the women. But instead of blowing them up, they shut them down. Shut them in houses. In clothes. In their own heads. Not even allowed to go to school. Fucking criminal.' Jasper carefully stubbed his cigarette out on the sole of his boot, then placed the dead butt in the metal sweet tin perched on the bench by his side.

They sat in silence, the dark sky adding a danger in the air that was reflected in Jasper's memories. Eventually, the old man stirred.

'Happy days, those were. We had a battered camper. We'd rock up at a market, pile it up with bags and rugs and dope, and we were sorted for the summer.'

'What sort of bags?' asked Raine.

'Handmade. Beautiful. You couldn't get anything like it in the UK at that time. We used to sell them at the festivals.'

Raine reached into the satchel by her feet and pulled out the stiff cloth bag that had belonged to Heather. 'Something like this?'

Jasper reached out, his gnarled hands gentle as he took it for closer inspection. The smile on his face was unreadable. 'Yes. This looks Afghan to me. The patterns are unique.'

'What I thought,' said Raine. 'So if this belonged to, or was made by, an Afghan woman who was, say . . . twenty-five years old, what would the situation have been like when she was a baby?'

'In Afghanistan?' He took out another smoke from a battered metal case and lit it. He took a deep drag, then stared at the glowing tip. 'That would put you right in the middle of hell. The country had been broken by the Soviets, then ripped in pieces by a power grab after they left, which left it open for the Taliban coming over from Pakistan. They shut up all the women and ran the country like a playground for bastards until the bombing of the Twin Towers.'

Raine tried to frame another question. She knew there was something there, something important, but couldn't quite see it.

'But I'm not the person to ask about this kind of stuff,' said Jasper. 'All I was there for was the drugs and the culture. The politics passed me by.'

'Okay, Jasper. Thanks.'

'I've still got a couple of connections from that time, though,' he said thoughtfully. 'They had to leave Afghanistan fast. Settled in Newcastle, I think.'

'Why did they have to leave?' asked Raine. 'Was it the drugs?'

'No. This was later, during the first occupation. They were helping translate for the Army. They'd go on missions with the soldiers and interpret. That kind of thing.'

'Right.'

'When the allied troops left and it all went to shit, they had a price on their heads. Considered traitors for helping the

Brits and Americans. We promised anyone who'd helped us a home here for them and their families.'

'And did we keep our promise?'

'For some,' he said. 'Others, we just left there to get killed. Same as now.'

CHAPTER 42

Hume, Echo and Chief Inspector Rockall were in Hume's office, the interactive data-screen on the wall split into a tree of information boxes.

'A game?' said the DCI.

'Maybe. Or the prototype. We don't think it has been released yet.'

'Dear God. Are you saying that someone's developed . . . what? A modern-day snuff movie?'

Hume grimaced. 'We're not sure. What we think is that, in the course of her investigations for her crimes podcast, Melissa uncovered something bad and was killed for it. Oliver too.' Hume nodded at Echo to explain.

'A lot of this comes from the archived files we discovered in Oliver's van. Melissa's *Deadtown* podcast started about five years ago, as a standard internet journal about murders in and around London — mostly historic cases. Nothing special, but it had enough subscribers to keep its head above water. She ran it as a side-hustle. Her main job was archiving old newspapers at the London Library. Digitising and cataloguing. That sort of thing. She had worked there straight from uni. Degree in Internet Journalism.'

'That's where she got her first stories,' cut in Hume. 'The London Library. The early episodes of *Deadtown* are all historical crimes, going right back to the eighteenth century.'

'The site was part pandering to murder-geeks, and part travelogue,' continued Echo, swiping various titles of episodes up onto the screen. 'She would film herself on the streets, pointing out where the crimes had happened, supplementing the first-person walk-around with images of the city at the time in question.'

'Seems like it would be popular with people visiting the capital,' said the DCI.

'Exactly. So far, so normal,' said Hume. 'A couple of years ago she joined up with Oliver. He was fresh out of a digital media degree and could add lots of value to the site. Glossing the thing up with audio and clever visuals. He redesigned the UI for mobile-first and made the whole thing more interactive.'

'How?' asked DCI Rockall.

'They hired actors to play the characters. Press a button and talk to this poisoner. Swipe to see the confession of this nightclub hostess from the noose. That sort of thing.'

'All a bit gruesome,' muttered the Chief Inspector.

'But quite popular,' said Echo. 'Then things took a left turn.' He swiped again, bringing up a photograph of a man in his thirties. He was sitting outside a cafe with a cup of coffee and a sandwich. The photo was slightly blurred, clearly taken surreptitiously.

'Joseph Banner,' said Hume.

'The person Raine is interested in?'

'Yes, sir. It seems Melissa was building a profile on him. Compiling background for a future *Deadtown* episode.'

'Which never saw the light of day,' added Echo.

'So who is he?' asked the chief. 'Presumably, he was involved in a London murder somehow, or he wouldn't be of interest to the show.'

'Oh yes, he was involved in murder, all right,' said Hume grimly. 'And not just in London. We think it could be Banner who had Melissa and Oliver killed.'

CHAPTER 43

Somebody's broken into the game.

Probably the police. Trying to work out who set it up. How many are playing.

Good for them. It'll be such fun to watch them scuttle around. By the time they really know what's going on, I'll be long gone. Off to set up a new game. A proper game.

Because this is just proof of concept. The real fun's to come.

The beauty is the algorithmic intimacy of it all. There is no exit road from the images once you've seen them.

The boys at Instagram understand. Snapchat. TikTok.

No delete button for the eyes. No closing time. No end. Ever.

Once you pop you just can't stop.

The addiction of murder, one step removed.

It's a bestseller waiting to happen.

CHAPTER 44

'Joseph Banner is a private military contractor,' said Hume. 'God knows how Melissa got on to him, but she did. He specialised in getting non-government personnel out of war zones, particularly across South West Asia and Africa. She has interviews with aid workers from the Iran–Iraq war. Political refugees from Afghanistan. Saudi Arabia. The DRC. Anywhere that required people to be evacuated and had employers willing to pay.'

'A mercenary? But why would that be relevant to a London murder blog?' asked the DCI. 'I can see how the MOD might be interested, but why Melissa Clarke?'

Echo swiped and an image of a man came onto the screen. The image was grainy. The man was smiling, his head covered by a shemagh. 'Abdul Jamil. He was an interpreter for the coalition during the occupation of Afghanistan. The Taliban put a kill order on him. The British government wasn't getting him out, so his relatives in the UK paid Joseph Banner to do the job for them. Over the years Joseph had built up an extraction network to remove people from the country and smuggle them across borders to wherever they could afford to go.'

The DCI studied the man on the screen. Someone who had put his life and his family's lives at risk with the promise of protection. Someone who had ended up in the care of a gun for hire. 'You're talking about people-smuggling,' he said, turning to face them.

'Yes. But if it was just that . . .' Hume grimaced. 'Smuggling people into a country they'd practically been promised they could go to anyhow. It wasn't what Melissa was interested in.'

'So, what *was* she interested in?'

'He was playing both sides,' said Echo. 'According to Melissa's research, as well as being paid to smuggle people into this country, he was taking money from the Taliban to find people here too. People who they felt had betrayed the cause.'

'What do you mean?'

'The Taliban would torture names out of the citizens they arrested, searching for people they considered traitors and the destinations of collaborators who had fled. Once they had the information, they would hire Banner to find them and bring them back. Or sometimes just kill them here in the UK.'

The DCI's face was tense, muscles bunching and twitching under the skin as he contained his anger. 'Why wasn't he on our radar?'

Hume shrugged. 'The military might have been keeping tabs, but we'd never know. They hold everything close to their chest.'

Echo broke in, unable to restrain himself. 'The thing is, sir, he was also branching out. Diversifying. According to Melissa's notes, he was also paid to locate people who had escaped the regime. Specifically, women. He would track down daughters who had been sent to relatives over here. Nieces and cousins. Kill them or take them back. Whatever was paid for.'

'Why didn't Melissa expose all this? Surely this would have catapulted her into the big time?'

'It's not clear,' said Echo. 'The research is in the files, but they don't take it any further. Maybe they were still gathering data and when they had enough, or had verified enough to publish, they would have gone public.'

'Perhaps Banner got wind of what they were doing,' suggested the DCI. 'And then had her and Oliver killed.'

'And now the podcast name is being used for some kind of digital interactive murder game — another money-making enterprise for him,' added Echo.

Hume intervened. 'There's also an outside chance that her death had nothing to do with Banner at all.'

The DCI turned to her. 'How do you mean?'

'There was a domestic situation with a man who lived with Melissa's mother. It seems Melissa may have accused him of sexual abuse. We're chasing it up.'

'All right,' sighed the DCI as he stood up. 'Keep me in the loop.'

'Sir. We've still got Jonas on the decryption of the remaining files,' said Hume. 'Echo's going to do a follow-up interview at Tressillian Road. We need to establish who Oliver's girlfriend slash mystery visitor was. We're talking to his parents, plus friends and acquaintances, of course. Whether he was murdered for the same reason as Melissa, or for something different, the mystery woman might be in danger. Or, she might even be the killer.'

'Right,' said the DCI. 'And what about you?'

'I'm going to see a man about a house.'

CHAPTER 45

Raine sat in Klute's — a cafe-cum-bookshop — happily tucking into her greasy spoon special. Danny Brin sat opposite her, a solitary mug of tea in front of him.

'So you think that Heather was meant to be taken back to Afghanistan?' said Brin.

'Not sure,' said Raine, scraping the remains of her egg off the plate with a soggy piece of fried bread. A dribble of yellow yolk trailed down her chin and she licked at it happily. 'Maybe. The information Echo has from the podcaster's notes isn't complete; they're still decrypting. My best guess is she was smuggled out of Afghanistan as a kid when the Taliban first came to power. Her accent was fully British. Maybe her sister got left behind. Maybe her parents could only afford to send one. Or the relatives could only take one. I don't know. But something happened when the allies went back in. Maybe her parents worked for them. Whatever. The upshot is, Banner was paid to take her. Or kill her. He used the sister as bait and then either grabbed her, or she went into hiding.'

'She must be important for them to go to all this trouble. To use Ridgeway.' Brin took a sip of his tea. It was the colour of burnt copper. He nodded with appreciation. 'What brand is this?'

Raine grinned. 'Gunpowder Tarry. Strongest tea in London. Chinese smoked leaves. Blow your head off if you have more than a cup.'

'Lucky I'm only on my second, then,' said Brin, taking another sip.

Raine pushed her empty plate away and took a slug of her own tea. 'I don't think it started with Heather. I think Banner had always used Ridgeway. That's how he got in with the traffickers. How he managed to get passports and immigration certificates.'

'So what are you going to do?'

Raine smiled, a glint in her eyes like a blade in a dark alley.

'We are going to fuck up his world and, if she's alive, get Heather back.'

'How? There's just the two of us. From what you've told me, this Joseph Banner is some kind of hard-arsed mercenary. He's probably got ex-military working with him. SAS types. If we pile in there, he'll tear us to bits.'

'The guy at the flat was probably ex-military. He had the haircut and everything.'

'Then shouldn't we call in—'

'But the flat was clean. It didn't look like it had been used for a while. I think the guy was low-level. Just there to keep an eye on it. I'm guessing Banner's ready to move on. That's why we need to boogie. We can't wait for the MOD.'

'If they're getting ready to scarper, they'll be on high alert.'

'Ah, I've thought of that,' said Raine. 'What they don't realise is we've got a secret weapon.'

'Which is?'

She took a sip of her tea. 'You know the reason the Tarry here is so good? They never wash out the urn. They just keep topping it up and adding more. The thing is coated with about a hundred years of tannins.'

'Is there a point to this?' sighed Brin.

She looked at him, a slight smile question-marking her face. Brin felt a ripple of fear in his spine. There really was something strange about her. Wrong. Like one of those distorting fairground mirrors.

'I'm the same,' stated Raine. 'London's made me that way. From when I was born to now. Every day I live in this city it fills me up with itself. It paints me. There's very little I don't know about it. Not deep down. Banner? He may be some top-notch mercenary fucknut somewhere in the world, but in London . . . ?' She raised a dismissive shoulder. 'A thug is just a thug, no matter how you dress it up. And in this city, against us, the thugs always lose.'

Brin closed his eyes. The woman was insane. 'We'll be slaughtered.'

CHAPTER 46

'No, cariad, it wasn't her.'

'You're certain?' said Echo, slightly disappointed.

Anwen nodded. 'Positive. The woman who came calling was . . . neater, somehow. I don't know how to explain it.'

'No problem, Anwen. I thought it was worth a shot.' Echo folded his phone, shutting off the image of Anita Straw he had acquired from St Andrew's University. 'How are things here? Settling back down?'

'Yes. Your lot took Freddy's van away. Since then,' she shrugged, 'it's all gone pretty well back to normal.'

They both looked at the spot where Oliver Bell's van had been parked. Already the space had been filled by another vehicle: a black Transit. Unlike Oliver's, this one seemed well cared for, with scripted lettering on the side advertising the owner's services as a web developer.

Then Anwen pointed at the koru tattooed on the scapha of his ear. 'Would you be willing to model for me, Etera?'

Echo blinked. 'Sorry?'

'I'm a painter. I teach, too, sometimes.'

'Then why are you here?' he asked, interested. He nodded at her van. 'If you're mobile, you could be anywhere. Painting anything. Why be in London?'

'Maybe *painter* was the wrong term,' said Anwen, frowning. 'Documentor, perhaps. Or witness. The people you meet on the outskirts of life . . .' She frowned. 'They're interesting. It seeps out of them, whatever it is that makes us live this way. Not fit in. It colours them. Shapes the way they move. I like to paint the colours. Draw the shapes.'

'I understand,' said Echo, thinking about Bitz. About the way he saw her in his mind. All exploding colours and frenetic, dynamic lines firing off in different directions. She was like a firework.

'And even though you're a policeman, I see it in you, too.'

'Okay,' said Echo.

'So, I'd like to paint you, if that's all right.'

Echo smiled. 'Well, I'm flattered, Anwen. Let me think about it.'

'Naked, if possible, as well as clothed. That way I get the full sense of how you see yourself.'

To Echo's credit, the smile stayed firmly in place. 'Right.'

'You can keep the glasses on, if you want.'

Echo looked at her keenly, then reached up and touched his glasses. 'Are these similar to hers?'

Anwen stared back at him in confusion. 'Who?'

'The woman who visited Freddy?'

Her face cleared. 'Oh, no. They were much smaller and completely round, which is quite unusual. Expensive, I think.'

'Do you always need the subject in front of you, Anwen? When you sketch?'

Anwen laughed. 'No, love. I'd be a rubbish painter if that was the case. Look around you! My subjects are transitory by their nature. I take photos. Or sometimes quick sketches. Fill in the details later.'

'Do you think you'd be able to sketch a picture of the girlfriend for me?'

Understanding spread across Anwen's face and she nodded. 'Make me a cuppa, Etera, and I'll do it for you now.'

* * *

Garrett's Estate Agency was far more upmarket than Hume had expected, but she shouldn't have been surprised. When she had entered, the manager, insectile in his movements, had looked at her like she'd come to rob the place. Even after she'd shown him her warrant card he had maintained an aloofness, as if she could infect him with her lack of money or status.

'So, the woman who dealt with the property still hasn't returned to work?'

'Miss Jenson, no. But since the pandemic we don't require our people to keep traditional office hours.'

'Our people?'

'Colleagues.'

'Right. But she must phone in or something?'

The manager, Mr Pottingrew, replied in a distinctly patronising tone. 'All our people are self-employed, Inspector. They don't "phone in". We supply them with properties that have come on the market, and then they . . .' He paused, micro-shrugging one shoulder. 'Well, let's just say that all our colleagues have their own set of contacts. Clients who they feel would suit the properties.'

Hume kept her face passive, swallowing down her bile. 'I understand, but you must have a list of who has visited the property, surely?'

Mr Pottingrew smiled, but not with his eyes and barely with his mouth. 'As I said, *Inspector*, we allow our people—'

Hume cut across him. 'Which of them is she?'

'I'm sorry? Which one is who?'

Hume pointed at the wall behind the manager's desk. She was tired of speaking to this man, with his prejudice and assumed privilege. On the wall were various headshots of men and women. All of them clean-cut and professional-looking. Hume suspected they'd never had to struggle in life, then reprimanded herself. She didn't know them, so shouldn't judge. 'Them. Are they your "people"?'

Pottingrew nodded curtly, dislike and resentment radiating off him.

'Which one is Miss Jenson?'

The manager pointed to a photograph on the top right of the wall. It showed a woman, perhaps in her twenties, with a pixie cut and expensive skin. 'This is she. We were lucky to get her. She's not long returned from the Middle East.'

Hume walked around the desk and stood in front of it, staring up at the photograph. 'You've got to be kidding,' she breathed.

'I'm sorry?'

Hume took out her phone and snapped a picture.

'I really don't think you can do that—' began the manager, before Hume turned to face him. Seeing the expression in her eyes, he took a step back.

'I really think I can. Now, unless you want me to get a digital search warrant and go through your accounts, I suggest you get me Miss Jenson's address and client list.' She turned away and focused again on the estate agent's wall. On the image of Miss Jenson, smiling with her perfect teeth, expensive-looking cardigan and eyes shining behind the round glasses.

Hume sent the image to Echo.

* * *

Echo was studying the picture Anwen had sketched of Oliver's girlfriend when his phone buzzed. He opened the attachment from Hume and looked at the image she had sent through. Then he compared it with the sketch Anwen had drawn for him.

It had to be the same woman.

Echo was about to phone Hume when he got a call from DC Jonas.

'We've identified the body,' said the DC breathlessly when Echo answered.

'Which body?' Echo gave an apologetic smile to Anwen and walked a few feet away.

'The body on Raine's boat. Well, not on her boat, but you know what I mean. We know who it is.'

'How? The face was completely obliterated.'

'By the tattoo on his neck. It's a butterfly.'

'Jonas, there must be hundreds of people in this city with butterflies on their—'

'It's Peter Holt.'

'Who's Peter Holt?'

'Remember you asked me to chase up Melissa's old flame? The one in the papers?'

'Right. He said she'd had some mental trauma when she was younger.'

Mrs Clarke's former partner flashed across Echo's brain. Abuse would certainly classify as mental trauma. He still hadn't managed to locate 'Derek'.

'Well, we found him — Peter Holt. Tracked him down through social media. He lives in Canning Town. I sent some officers to invite him in for interview.'

'And?'

'The place had been ransacked. There was broken furniture and a fair amount of blood. Looked bad, the officers said.'

'But no sign of Peter?'

'No.' Jonas's voice was full of ghoulish excitement. 'But there was a photograph of him.'

'And he had a butterfly tattoo on his neck. Yes, I see. Good work, Jonas.'

'Shall I let the boss know?'

'I was about to phone her. I'll pass the intel on, and make sure she knows who got it.'

'Cheers, boss.'

Echo ended the call and immediately pushed the button for Hume.

'It's the same woman. The estate agent,' he said, as soon as he was connected.

Hume clenched her fist. 'That's it, then. She's the link between Oliver, Melissa and the Aquinas Street flat.'

'There's more,' said Echo, and he told her about the probable abduction and murder of Peter Holt.

'This is spiralling,' said Hume when he had finished. 'First Melissa. Then Oliver. And now this Peter Holt. But why?'

'Melissa seems to be at the centre, with anyone connected to her being targeted. If it is Banner, it's pretty brutal.'

'What about the outlier? Derek Evans, Pauline Clarke's ex-partner. If he's the killer, maybe he's just flipped. Sees anybody who knew her back then as culpable in some way.'

There was dead air for so long that Echo wondered if he'd lost connection, before Hume's voice came back down the ether. 'Send someone to Pauline Clarke's flat. Now. We need to make sure she's all right.'

* * *

Pauline opened the fridge and pulled out the half-empty bottle of Chablis. She just had time to have a glass in the bath before he arrived. She smiled to herself. To think, after all this time, he was coming back to her. It was more than she could have dreamt of.

Taking her glass, she read the email again.

Dearest Paulie,

I'm sorry I haven't been in touch. I was so broken by what Mel said about me I had to go. I thought you believed her, you see. But now she has recently told me (I won't say how) that you didn't know anything about the fantasies she was harbouring about me. The poor girl was ill. It would make me so happy if I could call on you and we could clear the air. I have thought so much about you over the last few years. I always considered you my soulmate.

If you would like to meet up then I could call for you at 6 p.m. tonight. I am back in the area for work.

Please reply with yes!
Forever yours,
Derek

Pauline had replied. She had told him she completely understood, and that it would be lovely if he called by. Then she'd started her bath running, plans already whirring through her head. *Did he want to meet up to explain properly why he left? Ask for her forgiveness, perhaps?*

She took another glug of wine, smiling. *Or did he want to do more than explain? Maybe rekindle.*

The doorbell chimed.

Pauline glanced at the kitchen clock: 5.30.

Surely that couldn't be him already? She walked to the door, stopping to check her appearance in the hall mirror, using her fingers to tease out her hair a little. She stood a moment longer, examining her eyes.

They were hard, she thought. Harder than they should be. They didn't reveal how she felt inside. How she'd always felt. Scared and alone and out of her depth. What they did was reflect. Reflect the world and all the difficulties it had thrown at her.

She tried a smile.

The doorbell chimed again.

Pauline attempted to keep the smile in place as she walked down the immaculately clean hallway. She took a deep breath and opened the door, the smile still there.

Not that it mattered. The punch that greeted her as soon as the door was wide enough wiped the smile away. She didn't even have time to say anything. Just felt the shock reverberate through her skull. The second punch, straight into her throat, took her breath away, even as her sight began to dim. She felt herself stumbling back into the flat.

The third punch she didn't feel at all.

CHAPTER 47

The temporary building didn't seem to be anything sinister. It was well maintained and the two people that had entered were smartly dressed professional types.

'Are you sure this is the place?' asked Brin sceptically. He and Raine were crouched behind a low wall opposite, surveying the premises.

'It's where Soldier-boy from the flat came after I let him go,' said Raine. She glanced away from the buildings as a jet came in to land. The industrial estate was only a couple of miles from London City airport and the sky traffic was constant. Raine waited until the noise abated before continuing. 'And it makes sense. As well as the commercial airport there's a private jet centre.'

'Swanky. And why would our guy be interested in a private jet centre?'

'Because, if you've got the money, that would be the best way to get someone in or out of the country. If Ridgeway could provide legit passports and papers, then there's no need to smuggle people in via boats. And if you hire a personal jet with, say, a high-end chauffeur business, then the wheels of immigration are pre-greased, as it were.'

'A high-end chauffeur business like that one?' said Brin, pointing at the container office across the road. Outside the building two top of the range Mercedes executive cars and a Transit van with blacked out windows were parked. A sign by the gate proclaimed the business to be CHARON COURIER SERVICES.

'Exactly. And if you're some scary extraction service gone rogue, then this would be the perfect cover venture.'

'So what are we going to do?'

Raine re-examined the image of Joseph Banner that Echo had posted on the information hub about Melissa Clarke's murder. She hadn't seen him enter or exit the building, but that didn't mean he wasn't there. Or that there wouldn't be some information about him. Or about Heather.

'What do you think?' Raine asked Brin, standing. She unhooked her satchel and pulled out a selection of fireworks.

'Raine,' he said, eyeing the explosives. 'You don't even know how many people are in there. What are you going to do, trick or treat them into surrender?'

'Two cars, so two drivers. Someone to man the phones, and maybe Joseph, if I'm lucky. Four people max.'

'Or maybe a few extra people with guns, to protect their investment,' muttered Brin.

Raine held out a hand to help him up. 'You know I'm a solutions kind of person. I manifest a result in my mind and then actualise it.'

'What the hell are you on about?'

She shrugged. 'It's the sort of thing Jolene says. I think it means if you decide you're going to win, you keep kicking people until you do.'

'And you think that will work in real life?'

'Let's go and see.'

Brin watched Raine as she strolled across the road towards the chauffeur offices. Swearing under his breath, he got up and followed her. The two of them walked through the open double-gates to the compound and past the executive cars.

'How much do you think one of these costs?' asked Raine, running her hand along the Mercedes.

'V-class EQV? Not much change out of a hundred grand.'

Raine was shocked. 'That's more than my boat! What's it made of, gold?'

Raine walked around the Mercedes nearest the office, appraising its sheened metallic body. 'Where's the exhaust?'

'It's electric.'

'Well, how am I supposed to stuff some bangers into it as a distraction, then?' Raine raised her eyebrows at him, as if he'd made them electric on purpose.

'You can't. Let's just call your police friends and hand it over to them.'

'Hand what over? All I have is a blue dot on a phone. There was nothing in that flat to connect it to this place, and by the time they've chased through all those passports they'll have closed down and reopened somewhere else. I told you the flat looked like it was being mothballed.'

'No, but I'm sure with their resources they can— Oh, you've got to be kidding . . .'

Raine had taken out her boat key and was scraping the paint off the car in a long line from front to back. 'You know, considering how expensive the car is, it scratches just the same as any other.'

'Was that really necessary?' Brin sounded personally affronted.

'Yes,' said Raine, knocking on the office door. 'Now shush. I'm actualising.'

The door opened and a smartly dressed young man looked at her enquiringly. 'May I help you?'

Raine offered one of her most dazzling smiles, while noting the nametag pinned on his suit jacket. 'Hi, Brian! We were just walking by when we saw two dodgy characters keying your ludicrously expensive car. We thought you'd like to know.'

Brian glanced past her at the Mercedes, the smile dropping off his face. 'Jesus!' He stepped past them to the car. 'It's ruined!'

As he passed by, Brin grabbed him in a choke hold. The man struggled, his legs spasming, arms flailing wildly. After several seconds Brin lowered him to the ground.

Raine walked into the prefab office. One man sat in front of a monitor, his back to her, playing Sudoku while eating lunch out of a Tupperware bowl. Another, sitting at a desk in the far corner, also seemed preoccupied with his computer screen. The remaining occupant was the same guy Raine had encountered at the flat where she found Heather's bag. His hand was bandaged, and he had his chair tilted back with his legs up on the desk. His jacket was undone, revealing a shoulder holster beneath. His eyes widened in recognition. 'You!' He reached left-handed into his jacket.

'Hi!' grinned Raine. 'Trick or treat?' She ran forward and kicked his chair. As it crashed backwards, he managed to get the gun free, but had no opportunity to aim. His head hit the desk behind him with a loud crack, and he slumped unconscious to the ground. Raine reached down to pick up his gun, just as Brin burst in. 'What happened?'

'I actualised my manifestation,' said Raine, looking a little smug. 'Where's Brian?'

'I locked him in the car,' said Brin, eyeing the unconscious body.

Brin and Raine heard a strangled whisper. 'I think . . . I think you've killed Stephan.'

They both turned towards the speaker, the man who had been playing Sudoku.

'Better call for an ambulance, then,' said Raine. 'And the police, in case they need to arrest me. Where's Joseph Banner?'

The man made no move to grab the phone on the desk in front of him, simply staring back at her as if mesmerised.

She gestured to his colleague: 'Or maybe you could phone Joseph? He'll know what to do.' Then she pointed the gun at each of them in turn and nodded at Brin. 'Please tie them up and put them in the car with Brian.'

'Sure.' Brin pulled out a handful of zip-ties from his pocket.

Once he had marched the two men out of the office, with their wrists securely bound, Raine turned her attention to their desks. On the surface the set-up seemed normal. An itinerary of pick-ups and drop-offs. Future clients. A list of the best hotels and restaurants in London. Everything a high-end chauffeur service might require. Plus a firearm.

Raine examined the gun she'd picked off the floor. The serial number had been obliterated, probably by acid. Then she looked down at the body. His chest moved a little as he breathed. Taking no chances, she zip-tied his hand to one of the legs of his desk.

By the time Brin came back in, Raine was looking through the office computer files.

'Anything interesting?'

'Nothing obvious,' said Raine. 'What have you done with our new best mates?'

'They're locked in the back of the Mercedes, with no access to the driver's compartment. I'm pretty sure Brian was calling the police, though.'

'I doubt it.'

'Banner, then?'

'Doesn't matter. What we have here is a list of pick-ups and drop-offs. Airport to hotel. Hotel to airport. All seemingly legit.'

'It might matter if his boss calls in reinforcements.'

'He won't,' said Raine. 'Except maybe to burn the place down. He'll know we'll have called the police ourselves. We're right next to an airport in the centre of London. The place would be crawling with cops in minutes.'

'If you'd actually called them.'

'Exactly. This is interesting. They also do pick-ups from the airports at Biggin Hill and Northolt, ex-RAF bases. Used by the super-rich as quick getaways from London.'

'Or to smuggle in people with enough money,' added Brin.

A mobile began to ring. Raine looked down at the unconscious man at her feet and swiftly removed the device poking out of his pocket. 'Kidnap and Abduction R Us!' she announced. 'How may we be of service?'

'Raine.'

The voice that slithered out of the earpiece was flat; expressionless. Like all the life had leaked out of it, leaving only the dead remains.

'Joseph! So happy to hear your voice. Where's Heather Salim?'

'Dead. I took her last year. Blew her sister's brains out in front of her and delivered her back to the Taliban. She paid the price for her traitor parents. Everything you've done has been for nothing.'

Raine closed her eyes. The room seemed to tighten around her.

'And now I'm going to come for you, Raine. And for your pet policewoman. For all your little friends.'

'Raine,' said Brin softly.

Raine took a deep breath. Held it. Let it go.

'No,' she said, her voice quiet but firm as she opened her eyes again. 'I don't believe you. Heather texted me.'

'I texted you. Tried to goad you into—'

'No,' she said again. 'And now you've threatened me, which was a really silly thing to do.'

Joseph's chuckle sounded like a bag of hammers being thrown down a well through the earpiece. 'You stupid bitch. I'm going to enjoy killing you.'

Raine cut the call. 'Definitely got some anger issues,' she said, opening drawers and searching through loose papers. She glanced at the man on the floor. 'Better call the cops and an ambulance.'

'Raine, I don't think—'

'Then you should go. You don't want to be here when they turn up.'

He took a step forward, unsure. 'You'll be okay?'

She smiled at him. 'I'm always okay.'

You're really not, he thought, but nodded, heading to the door.

Raine watched the door close behind him, then focused back on the papers in front of her. At first she thought they were itinerary sheets. Records listing where drop-offs and pick-ups had occurred, but then she frowned, recognising one of the addresses. It was the house in Aquinas Street. She stared at it a moment, then reached back into the desk and pulled out another sheaf of papers. She looked at the bold, scripted heading.

Garrett's Estate Agents
Exclusive properties available pre-market
Exclusive land opportunities for bespoke redevelopment

'Well, well,' said Raine softly. According to the documents, it seemed that Charon Courier Services had bought property all over London, using Garrett's as their agent. The house on Aquinas Street. The property where Gilbert lived. As she read through the list, she came across another name she recognised. After a moment, she pulled out her phone and sent a message to Hume.

CHAPTER 48

The images of Peter Holt and Pauline Clarke had been added to the smart board, their faces staring out at Hume like an accusation of failure.

'And there's no clue as to where Pauline Clarke's been taken?'

Echo shook his head. 'None. The blood at the scene suggests she was alive when she was taken, but other than that . . .'

'And nobody saw anything? No door camera footage this time?'

'Sorry, guv.'

'So we've got nothing,' said Hume grimly. 'We just wait until video footage showing her being slaughtered turns up on one of the murder phones.'

'Murder phones,' said Echo. 'Catchy.'

'Should we assume that whoever murdered Melissa and Oliver has also taken Pauline Clarke?'

'If Banner did kill Melissa and Oliver, then he's a good contender. The people he worked with, the Taliban, are renowned for wiping out whole families because of a grievance against one person.'

'So Banner learns that Melissa is planning to expose him via her podcast. He has her and her business partner killed and then goes after her mother too?'

'Only what the old-school gangsters used to do, isn't it?' said Echo. 'And that's what the Taliban are, when it comes down to it. And the people he does his trafficking deals with. Gangsters.'

'And what about this murder game? How come the app hasn't been discovered by many more punters? I thought apps had to be in a repository or something. An app store.'

'No. It's part of Web3.'

'Ah,' nodded Hume. 'Web3. Thought so.'

Echo ignored her. 'In this case there is no centralised index where the app is stored. It uses blockchain technology to— Ow!'

Hume had thrown a ball of paper at him.

'No talking about blockchains. We've discussed this before. No blockchains. No Bitcoin. No indecipherable tech talk. If you want to talk like that, do it with Bitz. Tell me in plain language.'

Echo blushed. 'There's no way to trace the designers since there's no external directory.'

Hume looked at him in triumph. 'See? That wasn't so hard, was it?' Then she sighed, before moving on to the next thing on her mind. 'Have we had any luck tracking down the estate agent — Deborah Jenson?'

'No. We now have her home address, but she hasn't been there for a couple of weeks. We have additional confirmation that Oliver and Deborah had met, though.'

'Really? Other than your van lady's statement?'

Echo nodded. He swiped at his tablet and opened up a video file on the murder board. A smartly dressed woman with a pixie cut and round glasses could be seen on the screen, shaking hands with Oliver Bell. 'This was pulled from the door camera on Aquinas Street. Once we had Deborah's diary, we cross-referenced. There also seems to be a connection between Deborah and Joseph Banner. Some of Garrett's clients have bought properties abroad, including in the Middle East. It seems Deborah spent time out in Egypt and Saudi Arabia. New housing and such. It seems that the properties were rented to NGOs.'

'How does that connect her to Joseph?'

'According to the files Melissa had on him, he had extraction houses in all the hot spots. Places where he could store people before moving them out. Lots of money to be made if you have the right connections.'

'We need to find her. Whether she's innocent or working with Banner, she might be in danger.'

'Or dead,' said Echo.

'Or dead.'

'Boss!' Jonas bounded into the room. 'We've found him!'

'Banner?' Hume was immediately on high alert. 'Where is he?'

'No, sorry. There's no sign of him. We're checking the airports and such but no luck yet.'

'Who have you found, Jonas?' asked Echo.

'Derek Evans.'

It took Hume a moment to locate the name in her head. 'Pauline Clarke's ex? Where is he?'

'Stepney. He changed his name to Martins. That's why it took so long to locate him.'

'Have you got an address?'

'Yes, but that's not all, guv.'

Hume raised an eyebrow.

'He's served time. For assault on a minor. He was released from Wandsworth Prison three months ago.'

Hume felt a surge of adrenalin. 'Great work, Jonas. Echo, you and I will go and interview Mr Martins while—' Her phone vibrated. 'It's Raine,' said Hume, scanning the ident, relief in her voice. 'She's fine.' But she frowned as she read the message.

'What is it?' asked Echo.

Hume glanced up. 'Get Garrett's on the line. Find out who owns the properties in the industrial estate where Melissa was cremated.'

CHAPTER 49

Hume looked at the dilapidated building through the windscreen of the armoured van. She, along with the tactical team, was parked at the corner, hidden by overgrown shrubbery and the bones of abandoned machinery. The old abattoir where the remains of Melissa had been discovered was on the other side of the industrial estate. If anything, this part was even more run down.

'We can't detect any hidden surveillance systems,' whispered the SCO19 officer sitting next to her. He was wearing an earpiece that relayed a real-time rundown regarding the imminent assault on the building. 'Just a chain and padlock on the gate.'

'Cameras?'

'Just one above the door.'

'No others?' said Hume, surprised.

'Too many electronic deterrents would do the opposite. Draw attention to the place.'

Or maybe Raine's wrong, thought Hume, feeling a heavy stone of tension in her stomach. *Maybe Banner isn't here and this is just a derelict building with minimal protection to stop squatters; and when we storm it, all we're going to arrest is a couple of rats and a family of foxes.*

'Although the lone camera is in itself suspect,' continued the officer. 'Also, the metal shuttering on the windows is recent. You wouldn't go to that trouble if you were just protecting property. Not property round here, anyway. The physical buildings won't be worth anything. It's the land that will have value. They'd tear everything down for redevelopment.'

Hume continued to assess the exterior of the building. A property search had shown the connection between Banner's various businesses and the old abattoir where Melissa Clarke's body had been cremated. A further search had revealed that the entire estate was owned by the shell company that Banner operated. Almost all the buildings were in such a state of disrepair as to be of no interest. This one, however, although appearing to be the same as the others, was different. For a start, like the abattoir, it still had an electricity supply. It was possible that the supply was merely to power cameras or background heaters to keep the building from completely collapsing, but the shutters worried her. Metal shutters were mainly used in vacant housing to stop squatters. She hadn't seen them used in commercial properties on decommissioned industrial estates. Boarding and bars would normally suffice. The way this was set up was more . . . sinister. Like there was something in there that didn't want to be seen.

Hume's phone vibrated: it was Echo. 'Raine was right. Charon Courier Services is a subsidiary of Charon Enterprises. They own the house on Aquinas Street. Deborah Jenson fudged the paperwork. They also own the flat where Raine found Heather Salim's bag, and a number of other properties around London. Jonas is having them all checked out.'

Hume mused about Oliver Bell and Deborah Jenson. Had he approached her, or was it the other way round? Maybe they'd seen an opportunity and gone behind Melissa's back to make a deal with Joseph Banner. Banner certainly had the skillset to commit varied and filmable murders. And, she thought grimly, a ready supply of bodies from his trafficking and contract-killing business.

'Okay, good,' said Hume. 'What about Derek Evans?'

'I'm pulling up outside his address now. It's a sheltered accommodation complex for newly released prisoners.'

'It'll be interesting to find out why he changed his name. I'm going to be incommunicado for the next hour or so, but message if anything urgent crops up.'

'You'll be the first to know if he confesses to Melissa's murder,' said Echo.

Hume ended the call and contemplated the building in front of her once more. The SCO sat quietly beside her. Finally, she nodded.

'We go in, but quietly. If the place is full of civilians caught up in some trafficking scheme, I don't want any twitchy fingers on triggers.'

'Ma'am.'

Hume winced at the honorific but didn't correct him. The SCO spoke softly into his collar mic, confirming the operation as green.

Hume watched as the tactical officers approached the building. They came in from the side, out of the view of the camera above the door.

'The camera is a standard domestic unit,' the officer explained quietly. 'It sends the image via Wi-Fi to a monitor or to the cloud. Like the door cameras you see everywhere. Once the team leader is within ten metres, she'll activate the Deauthor—'

'What's a Deauthor?'

'You see the thing she's holding? Like a mobile?'

The lead SCO officer was tapping on what looked like a smartphone. Hume nodded.

'That's a handheld Wi-Fi signal disruptor. It will stop the camera from transmitting any data. Sound or images. It won't block the Wi-Fi signal in the building itself. You can get jammers that will do that. Eliminate the signal for a whole street if needed. But if they just disable the camera then it might not alert anybody inside. If they shut down everything it would be immediately noticed.'

Hume watched the SCO give a thumbs-up, then another officer crept forward and examined the lock. The man beside Hume put his hand to his ear, listening. Hume checked his nametag: Burrows.

'The lock is a standard mechanical code punch; not a problem. But the officer thinks the door is bolted from the inside. There's less movement at the top and bottom.'

'Which means there are occupants,' said Hume, feeling the excitement. 'So are they going to break it down?'

'That would alert whoever is in there for sure,' said Burrows. 'SCO have been listening in and think there could be a hostage situation. They can hear whispering. Some crying.'

'Shit. So what happens next?'

'They're going to remove the door wholesale. The door is metal but the frame is wood. They're going to cut through at the hinges and slide the door out.'

'Won't that be just as noisy?'

Burrows shook his head. 'Battery-powered jigsaw with a muffled casing. If they position it right, it should only take about thirty seconds. They'll time it in with the crying. There's also some other industrial noise in there. They think it's worth a shot. If they go in with the door ram, they lose any chance of surprising the occupants, and it would make a hostage situation more likely.'

Hume could feel the tension bite as the officers worked silently in the cold, still air, with armoured personnel crouched by the door. She was aware that they were going in blind, with no knowledge of what might lie within. There could be men with guns, or it could just be a holding pen, waiting to transport people either back to Afghanistan or on to slave labour here in the UK.

'They're in,' said Burrows, cutting through her thoughts.

Several officers took hold of the door and slid it outwards. Immediately Hume stepped forward, speaking softly. 'Right. Come on. We'll follow behind as they secure.'

* * *

Physically, Derek Evans was the direct opposite of Pauline. Where she had been all angles and anger, he was almost smudged. As Echo gazed at him, he seemed to blur, as if he wasn't fully present.

'I don't understand,' he said, his voice soft. 'What is it you want again?'

Echo and Derek were sitting in the communal area of the sheltered accommodation where Derek lived. It was brightly lit and warm, and on the low table between them two cups of anaemic tea were slowly cooling.

'How long have you lived here, Mr Evans?' asked Echo.

'About three months, and I don't go by Evans anymore. It's Martins now. I changed it.'

'And would you mind telling me why that was, sir?'

The man looked uncomfortable. Echo noticed that his nails were bitten, and his right leg seemed to move independently from the rest of his body; jittering as if an electric current was running through it.

'I had some problems. In my old life. Spent some time in jail. Then hospital. When I came out of . . . of where I was. In my head . . .' He tapped his head for emphasis. As he did so, his shirt sleeve slid up, revealing scarring on his wrists. 'I wanted to make a total separation. A rebirth. There were some things in the past. Some . . . mistakes.' Martins sighed. 'I just needed to start again.'

'Could you tell me what you were in jail for, Mr Martins?'

Martins stared at him for a long moment, and Echo felt a slight shiver. The man's eyes seemed to look right through him to somewhere else. There seemed to be a deadness there. A disconnect.

'Assault of a minor. I served seven years.'

* * *

Hume tightened the straps on her combat vest and slipped quietly out of the vehicle, following Burrows. The brittle weeds crunched under her feet as she approached the building. Ahead of them the lead officer gave a signal and entered the premises. A few minutes later Burrows, having heard confirmation in his earpiece, gave the thumbs-up.

'They've secured the floor. There's activity on the upper level, but they're waiting for instructions. They're unsure what it is.'

As soon as she crossed the threshold, Hume smelled it: the high copper odour of blood and despair. It was a thickness in the air, as if the pain couldn't disperse, souping the molecules until they were thick enough to taste.

'Careful,' Burrows warned in a whisper.

A soft keening sound was coming from a doorway to the left. Hume moved past the SCO and entered. The space was dark and reeked of unwashed bodies. The walls were covered with foam-backed MDF panelling, effectively soundproofing the room. The entry team had brought a small battery-powered LED light on a squat tripod, and the faces that were lit up from behind the cage in the centre of the room were streaked with terror. The cage was probably large for what it was designed for — containing dogs — but not for the people crammed into it.

'The entrance to the cage is deadlocked,' whispered the officer beside them. 'But the bars are standard. We'll have them out in a jiff.'

Another officer arrived by his side and began whispering to the men and women behind the bars. He seemed to go through several languages before looks of comprehension replaced the fear in their faces.

'Persian-Dari,' he said, turning to look at Hume. 'Afghanistan.' He returned his gaze to the caged people and began to speak urgently. After a moment they moved back from the front of the cage.

A moment later a third officer joined them and began to cut through the bars of the cage.

'Try to get them out without making too much noise,' she said. The interpreter nodded and began talking softly again, explaining what was happening.

Hume and Burrows left the room and made their way to the bottom of the stairs.

'There's two other rooms on this level, both with prisoners,' whispered the team leader. 'Eastern European. Not malnourished, but pretty battered.'

'What's happening here?' whispered Hume. 'Is this some sort of temporary stop-off?'

The SCO leader shook his head, pointing upwards.

Hume saw that there was a set of wooden stairs against the wall. She nodded. As they began to ascend, she could hear the murmur of voices. One was clearly female with a London twang. The other was male. Hard-sounding and flat.

'For fuck's sake, how difficult can it be?' the female voice said. 'I need her to be still so I can map her. I don't care how you do it, just stop her moving!'

An image of the estate agent, Deborah, flashed through Hume's mind as they began to ascend. The SCO was in front, her gun held hard to her thigh, the muzzle pointing down. Hume followed behind.

'Hit her again with the hammer. We'll get a more natural reaction when she starts to wake up.'

The stairs above led to an open trapdoor. The SCO held up three fingers. Then two. Then one. Hume took a deep breath then followed the woman upward.

* * *

'I didn't mean to push her, I just wanted to get away. She'd been goading me. Calling me names.'

The man in front of him still seemed disconnected. He could barely function, even in sheltered housing. He had clearly suffered some trauma, either in prison or beforehand, that had profoundly affected him. So much so that he had changed his name. Tried to separate himself from his past. Echo wondered what that event might have been.

'When she fell, she hit her head. There was blood everywhere.'

'Sorry? Who fell?' Echo leant forwards.

'I was blamed, of course. Fair enough. I did push her. Maybe it looked like I was attacking her. That's what the judge said.' Martins stared at Echo, diamonds behind his gaze. 'Maybe I even did, a bit. I was so messed up in those days. Drinking. Pills. My life was a car crash.'

'Where were you last night, sir?' asked Echo.

'Yes. I'm in a much better place now. I've learned to control my anger. Understand why I feel certain things.'

Echo thought back to his and Hume's interview with Melissa's mother. About the concern he and Hume had felt for Melissa from comments the mother had said.

'What sort of things?'

'Fear, mainly. And anxiety. I had spent so long running scared, you see.'

'Last night, Mr Martins. Where were you?'

'What?' The man seemed genuinely confused. 'I was here. We have a curfew.'

Echo nodded. There was something about the man, but he couldn't quite put his finger on it.

'What can you tell me about Pauline and Melissa Clarke? It's my understanding there were some difficulties when you lived with them?'

The air seemed to change around them. Become more charged. Martins blinked slowly.

'Melissa Clarke. Is that what this is about?'

'How do you mean?'

'She's evil. A stone-cold psychopath. She's the whole reason I'm like this.'

The leg began to vibrate more. Echo felt the back of his neck tingle as he watched.

'There were problems?'

Martins spat out a gob of laughter. The bitterness was so palpable it was like he'd hawked up bile. 'Problems? She hated me. Lied to anybody who knew me that I was . . . was . . .' He couldn't finish his sentence. 'There was something wrong with her. Even when I left, she followed me. Tracked me down on the Net. Doxed me. It was like a game to her. Just because I tried to put boundaries on her behaviour.'

'Sorry, Mr Martins. Are you telling me she harassed you? She was a child, no?'

'She was a monster,' said Martins simply. 'Something was broken in her head. She's the reason I pushed that girl. I couldn't stand to be near them. They're all liars.' Fat tears began to drip down his cheeks. 'I just couldn't stand it.'

Echo stared at him for a moment. At the smudgedness of the man. The emptiness behind his eyes. The leg in perpetual motion. Then reached for his phone.

* * *

It took Hume a moment to realise what she was looking at. Against the far wall was a desk with three large monitors. To the right was the corner of the room which had been painted white, including the floor. Around the area were tripods with digital cameras and boom mics. She understood it was an ad hoc studio but couldn't get the rest of the images to tally. Just outside the painted area was a trestle table with various instruments laid out. Saws and knives and what looked like a car battery with crocodile clip attachments. Pauline Clarke was cowering on the studio floor. A man stood over her, a hammer in his fist. He was clearly getting ready to hit her with it. Another woman stood in front of him, her back to them, a camera in her hand. She was filming the assault.

'That's it. Now get to work with the hammer. I want to see the bitch's brains.'

The man raised the pinball hammer, getting ready to strike. As he adjusted the shaft, he turned slightly and saw the SCO, with her weapon pointed directly at his chest. Hume hadn't even seen her raise it.

'Police!' shouted the SCO, her arm rock steady. 'Armed officers! Place your weapon on the ground, kneel and put your hands on your head. I repeat. Armed officers!'

Hume felt a stab of relief as the man carefully knelt and placed the hammer on the ground. Below them she could hear an increase in noise as the prisoners were released. Her phone vibrated in her pocket.

'You too!' shouted the SCO to the woman with her back to them. 'Turn around, place the camera on the ground, and put your hands behind your head!'

As the woman slowly turned, Hume felt the shock vibrate through her.

Melissa Clarke glared back at them, hate radiating off her. Her hair was different: short and black, cut into a gradual fade, but it was her.

'Put down the camera and hands behind the head,' repeated the SCO.

Melissa did as she asked, all the time fixing Hume with a bold gaze. She no longer wore glasses. Her eyes were a muddy blue rather than green. Hume's attention flicked to the woman's hands as she raised them on to her head; saw the bandage that held her fingers tightly together, spots of blood still seeping through.

'You can't fake DNA,' said Hume, nodding. Recalculating. Recalibrating.

Melissa smiled. 'But you can fake just about everything else. How did you find me?'

'Your partner. Joseph Banner. He wasn't as tidy as you. He left crumbs.'

Melissa's smile turned into a frown. 'Right.'

'The video of you being murdered was a scam? A fake?'

Melissa sneered. 'Of course it was fake. I'm standing here, aren't I?'

As the SCO began to move forward, Melissa dropped to her knees, shielding herself behind Pauline, who screamed in terror. Melissa snaked her arm around her mother's throat, and Hume saw the glint of steel.

'Come on, Melissa. There's nowhere to run.'

Hume heard the sound of footsteps on the stairs behind her.

'It's all changing,' said Melissa, a smile on her face.

'What is?'

'The world. Do you know how easy it was to put my face on the estate agent's body? All it takes is a camera and a bit of generative AI. Oliver showed me.'

'But why?' asked Hume. Beside her she felt the SCO's presence. Arm steady. Waiting for the shot.

'Heritage journalism is dead. Even the internet. Nothing's real anymore.' The woman seemed to be talking to herself. Hume could see the knife cutting into Pauline's throat. See the blood dripping off the blade.

'What do you mean?'

'Russia. China. They're all at it. Changing the narrative. Altering reality. It's impossible to tell fake news from the real thing. Everything is just entertainment. When I found Banner, it seemed like the perfect opportunity. He was killing people anyway. Why not repackage it for the masses as entertainment?' Her brow creased. 'It's not ready for release yet, obviously, but it definitely works.'

'It was your bag that the students handed in?'

Melissa nodded. 'It was meant to make you think I was dead. So I could start again with Joseph in America.' She pointed at herself with her other hand. 'New face. I thought cutting off a bit of my own finger would be the clincher. DNA proof I was dead. Silly me.'

'No, I don't see. Why abduct your own mother?'

'You're not listening,' said Melissa, her voice cold. 'Nothing's really real. She's not my mother.'

'What? Of course—'

'She stopped being my mother when I was twelve.'

Hume looked at her as the final piece fell into place. 'Derek.'

'Yes, Derek. And she knew. Like I said, Detective, nothing is ever what it seems. And underneath reality . . .' she shrugged, looking sad and young and broken, 'it's all fake.'

'If you surrender yourself now—'

Hume never got the chance to finish her sentence. Melissa pulled the knife across her mother's throat. As the blood fountained out, the SCO fired. A red rose caused by the bullet bloomed in the centre of Melissa's forehead, before mother and daughter fell forward to the floor.

All Hume could do was watch.

CHAPTER 50

The gym wasn't the kind that encouraged personal trainers or building core strength through Pilates. It was rough and stank of sweat and anger. There was an old-school punching bag suspended in the corner, a set of weights in another, and no sign on the door to tell anybody what went on inside. The space was lit by bare bulbs hanging from the ceiling, revealing the utilitarian starkness of the grey walls. Normally busy with clientele from the twilight industries, the gym had only four people in it at present.

Raine and Jolene sat on the wooden bench that stretched the length of the room. Brin and Libby faced each other in the centre of the room, where some practice mats had been laid out. Brin was wearing shorts over leggings and a muscle vest. Libby was dressed similarly.

'She looks like a tiny version of him,' whispered Jolene to the detective, her voice tense.

'Worse things to look,' answered Raine pleasantly.

'I'm not going to teach you self-defence, Libby. Being in school, you probably know more than me. Lot of bullying. Lot of grabbing.' Brin spoke quietly, but his words carried. Libby nodded, eyes wide.

'And you live in London, so you know about the street. Keeping yourself safe. Where to go and where to not go.'

Libby nodded again.

'What happened to you throws a person. Makes them doubt themselves. Second guess every corner. Turns the city into a place of shadows and traps. You get me?'

A third nod.

'Happens to everyone. Don't care who they are. It's an affront to the body. To the soul. The first thing you need to do is re-find yourself. The authentic you. Everything else is window-dressing.'

A door at the back of the gym opened, and Raine glanced round to see Hume silhouetted in the threshold. She leaned over to Jolene. 'Just stepping out,' she whispered.

'No problem,' Jolene whispered back, eyes never leaving her grandniece.

Raine smiled at Hume when she reached her. 'Mary. I heard what happened. That was beyond sick.'

Hume nodded. 'Another week and they would have left the country to set up the real thing. We found passports and fake IDs at the warehouse. Still trying to locate Banner, though. Anyway, you must be glad to finally get the truth about Heather Salim.'

Raine clicked her tongue. 'Don't know about the truth. I still don't know where she is, or even if she's alive or dead.'

'You've done all you can.'

Raine shrugged, noncommittal. 'Did you ever find out why the leaves, by the way?'

Hume nodded. 'It was all in Oliver's files. They were using the prototype game like a dummy run. Seeing what worked and what didn't. The leaves were a kind of in-game bonus. Same with letter-tagging around London. Very popular with the gaming community, apparently. The leaves lead you to the tree. The tree leads you somewhere else. They'd made a whole points system.'

'Where did all the leaves come from?'

'We found an online invoice for an order of saplings from an internet nursery business in Melissa's hard drive. She'd tried to delete it but, as Echo says, nothing ever truly goes away.' A beat. 'So what will you do now?'

'Kind of why I wanted to see you. I got a couple of emails offering me a new case. I'm going to meet with them tonight.'

'Really?' Hume raised her eyebrows. 'Shouldn't you take some time off?' She looked pointedly at Raine's ribcage. 'You must still be hurting.'

'Only if I breathe hard,' said Raine, smiling.

'What do you want?' sighed Hume.

From the gym room came a scream of triumph. The two women looked through the open door. Brin was lying on the mat, Libby above him, her fists clenched.

'That's right!' shouted Brin. 'And when they're down, don't hesitate. Don't aim for the balls. Kick them in the knee-cap and run. Remember, they can't hit what they can't catch!'

'Jesus,' said Hume. 'By the time that bouncer has finished with her, she'll be a walking bomb.'

'Hope so,' said Raine, nodding approvingly. 'And Brin won't teach her to attack; only defend.'

'Thank goodness for that.'

'Probably by attacking first.'

Hume turned her attention back to Raine. 'So tell me what you want.'

'Just a small favour.'

CHAPTER 51

The air was so brittle with cold that Banner felt he could break it off in chunks and use it as a weapon. The chemical vapour trail of candyfloss, kiddivape and generator diesel only seemed to solidify it. The ground was rock hard, despite the thousands of people tramping over it, the cold November air barely above freezing.

Banner looked down at his phone. The blue dot that showed him Raine's whereabouts was stationary. He looked up and across the park. He saw her standing by a food kiosk, buying a steaming plastic cup of some drink. Coffee, maybe. Banner smiled. Probably coffee. The woman was a caffeine junkie. He'd have to be careful. He'd seen what she'd done to Pirie. And to Ridgeway. Ridgeway had used his phone call when he was arrested to speak to him. To warn him she was coming.

Ridgeway was stupid. He thought he was doing him a favour sending her to him, but he'd nearly blown everything. The woman was a fucking cluster bomb.

Still, no worries. Banner felt the comfortable weight of the knife nestled in its holster under his shirt.

As punters streamed onto the heath, Raine disappeared from his sight, hidden by crowds and the thick fingers of white vapour from various smoke machines, fracturing the light from the laser beams that shone out into the night. Blackheath fair was in full swing.

Even though Banner couldn't see her, he wasn't worried. He was tracking her on his phone. It didn't matter where she was, he'd be able to find her.

He smiled. And after tonight it wouldn't matter at all. He was leaving. He'd done everything he needed to do here. The game worked. He didn't need Melissa Clarke anymore. There were Melissas all over the place. All that was needed was a supply of bodies to map faces onto and you could have any murder you wanted. It really was a brave new world, and he was in right at the start. And the variations were limitless. You could theme the murders according to whichever city you were in. Like an exclusive edition. Better yet, because he'd proven the concept as viable, he'd have no problem franchising.

New York. Moscow. Tokyo. He had contacts everywhere. There was no reason *Deadtown* couldn't go international. Global.

But first he had to settle the score with private detective soon-to-be-dead Raine. The bitch had nearly skittled the whole thing. She was like a virus. And all because of that Muslim girl.

He'd suggested they meet by the waltzers. Or Felice had. A connection to an old client. The suggestion of a woman in danger and a new case. It was so easy.

He hoped Raine would go for the waltzers. Somewhere noisy and full of people. Somewhere he could stab her and nobody would notice. He knew how to do it. Had been trained how to do it. Through the back to sever the spinal cord so she couldn't move. Then, if no one was looking, he could punch her in the throat. If he did it right, he would crush her windpipe. Watch her choke to death in front of him. The noise and the people and the rides and everyone bundled up. No way would he get caught. And best of all, no CCTV on the heath. Nothing to trace back to him.

He pushed off the railing, following the little dot on his phone. Banner almost chuckled. The stupid bitch had fallen for it full tilt. The tale about her ex-client. The new life in France. The shared confidences. All culled from her laptop, stolen by Ridgeway to find Heather Salim. Then, once she had shared her number with Felice so they could stay in contact, it had been a piece of piss to start tracking her phone.

At the memory of Heather, Banner's smile slipped. He had thought dumping the sister would break Heather. Make her run. But she had just hidden herself deeper.

Fuck her. He had the game now. He could leave the warlords and wankers to their medieval madness. He had a brand-new income stream.

But first he was going to kill Raine.

The blue dot veered off left. Banner looked up. Through a gap in the throng he saw her, the black beret unmistakable. He picked up his pace. It looked like she was heading away from the main rides and up towards the area where the fairground staff kept their caravans. Perfect. Most of the roustabouts were old-school travellers. If they found a body on their patch, they'd more likely bury it somewhere than bring the eye of the law down on them.

As she stepped away from the crowd and slipped between two caravans, he followed, slipping the knife out of its holster. As soon as he entered the trailer compound, the noise of the fair lessened, the trailers creating a barrier. He saw Raine ahead, holding her phone to her ear. He felt his own mobile vibrate in his pocket. He grinned, his teeth white and feral in the night. She was trying to reach Felice, the woman he had pretended to be. Wondering where she was, if she was near. It was perfect. She was half turned away from him. The knife would find its target and slide in before she even knew he was there. He moved forward silently.

'I just had to check if it was you first,' said a voice behind him.

Banner spun round. Raine was leaning against the caravan, her hands in her pockets. She wasn't wearing her beret, but rather a black shemagh round her neck like a scarf.

'Evening, Joseph,' she said. 'Just how much of an idiot do you think I am?'

He stepped forward, knife poised.

'You know, this would normally be the time I break something,' said Raine, conversationally. 'Probably your arm. But I'm trying to grow as a person, so I'm just going to give you a devastating look instead.'

Banner paused, confused.

'Plus all the police officers that have you surrounded would have to arrest me if I hit you.'

'What are you talking about?' snarled Banner, taking another step forward.

'I wouldn't do that if I were you,' said Hume. He turned to see the detective inspector removing the beret from her head.

'That's the trouble with misogynistic fuckbuckets like you,' commented Raine pleasantly. 'You see the clothes but not the woman beneath. The woman in this case being someone who is about to put you in jail.'

Banner looked from one woman to the other. He could kill one, no problem, before the other even moved. He'd survived war zones. A couple of bitches were no barrier. Then he could lose himself in the crowd.

'I should warn you there are a couple of policemen with tasers behind you as well,' Raine commented. 'They only let me be here as bait. You've no idea of the disclaimers I had to sign.'

'Drop the knife, then kneel down with your hands clasped over your head,' said Echo, coming out of the shadow of the trailer, the taser pointed out in front of him.

Banner let the knife fall but he didn't take his eyes off Raine.

'That email from Felice's address that you sent,' she continued amiably. 'It came in from an old address and was bounced to me. There's always footprints.'

'Still stored in the hard drive of the computer at the courier office,' added Echo. 'You sent it from there and then deleted it, but never wiped it from the register.'

Raine finger-gunned Echo cheerily. 'I thought the email looked suss, so I asked Echo to check for digital markers. He followed the footprints back to Charon Couriers. Nice name, by the way. The man who transports the dead. Very meta.'

Banner nodded, like she had given him a compliment. He began to kneel, then grabbed the knife and lunged towards Raine. Echo fired the taser, but the momentum kept Banner going, the knife held out in front of him. Hume's boot shattered his wrist as she kicked him, sending the knife skittering across the frost-bitten ground. Banner ended up at Raine's feet, his broken hand twitching as 10,000 volts passed through his spasming body.

Raine looked from the man on the ground to Echo and Hume. 'My heroes,' she said, smiling. 'If I wasn't already married I'd suggest we form a throuple.'

'For fuck's sake,' panted Hume.

'Wow,' said Echo. He was still standing in a firing pose, the taser in his hand. 'I've never actually fired one of these. What do I do now?'

'I think you should stop pulling the trigger before you fry him,' said Raine. She squatted down next to Banner. 'I don't know where Heather is, or even what her real name is, but you know what? I don't think you do either. I think that's why you kept tabs on me. Why Ridgeway never let me go. Why my boat was tagged in *Deadtown*. I think you always thought I'd find her eventually.

'She's safe. She sent me a message after you killed her sister, so I knew you didn't have her. Would never have her. That she was in hiding. And right after they cart you away, I'll send a message to her phone. She never answered my earlier messages, but I'm going to try again. Tell her you're nicked. Your whole organisation is shut down. That she doesn't need to hide anymore.'

Banner attempted to speak, but his throat muscles were locked.

Raine put her hands in her pockets and walked away, ducking under the cordon that had been erected to keep the public and fairworkers away. Hume and Echo watched her go.

CHAPTER 52

'Echo! Bitz! So glad you could come!'

Bitz waved, the cold November air glinting off her spider-bite piercings. She was dressed in skater shorts with thick leggings, engineer boots and a grey tee shirt over a long-sleeved black top. The design on the tee was a childlike line drawing of an alien holding a red balloon.

'Nice upgrade,' Bitz said, admiring Raine's new boat.

'I couldn't keep the other one, knowing how it had been used. Even if no one was actually killed there, Melissa Clarke ruined it for me. It would have been like living in the middle of murder-porn.' Raine paused for a second. 'Although, bizarrely, it did increase the sale value, allowing me to afford this. You're the last to arrive. Come down.'

Raine's new boat was a 45-foot wide-beam, making it far more spacious than her last vessel. Unlike the utilitarian design she had previously favoured, this was much cosier, with wood panelling and large rugs covering the floor. Everything was still open plan, but as well as the bed there was a settee and beanbags. The micro gym was still there, but tucked into a corner.

'Still no cooker, I see,' said Echo, looking around.

'I may have mellowed on my decorating style, but I'm not ready to go full Gordon Ramsay,' said Raine. 'Except in the swearing department, natch. Help yourself to food. There's hummus and something made of pea protein that Jolene brought.' She looked at Bitz. 'And Wotsits.'

'All the food groups in one tasty snack,' the coder said happily, throwing herself down onto a beanbag and snagging a Red Bull from the table.

Gathered were Hume, Robert, Echo, Bitz, Jasper, Jolene, Libby and Danny Brin. Libby was looking at Bitz, whose mouth and lips were now Wotsit-orange, with something approaching awe. Robert admired Bitz's tee shirt.

'Is that how you see yourself? As an alien looking in?'

'Nah,' said Bitz cheerfully. 'I'm the balloon.'

Raine stood in the centre of the space and clapped her hands together. 'Right. I'm so glad you could all make it! As you can see, I've got new accommodation, which is just as well because it's too cold to be on the deck. The only person not here is Ms Arnold, the woman who fixed Libby's teeth.'

Libby smiled shyly when everybody turned to look at her.

'Although, as it is still light outside, she probably wouldn't have come. Does everyone have a drink? Good. Well, I'd just like to thank you all for what you've done for me over the last few months. The closing of this case has given me a little bit of closure, too.'

'Fuck me,' muttered Brin. Libby nudged him hard in the ribs.

Raine raised her glass of Coca-Cola. 'All the bad guys went to jail. None of us got too hurt,' she looked at Libby. 'Or if we did, it made us stronger, and we all live to fight another day. Cheers.'

There was a slight pause before Robert said: 'Was that Oscar Wilde?'

Raine shook her head. 'In his dreams. Think it was Austen. Please drink and eat everything; I don't want any food left on the boat.'

'Did you ever hear back from Heather?' asked Bitz.

'I sent a text telling her that Banner's in jail, but it just ghosted.' Raine shrugged. 'Hopefully she's far away and safe and Banner was lying about having captured her. If not, she's dead. Either way, I've done everything I can.'

There was silence until Libby finally spoke. 'What's your full name?'

Everybody looked at the young woman, and she blushed under the scrutiny.

'Libby!' Jolene whispered.

'I mean, what's the big secret? Why won't you tell anybody?' Libby persisted.

Raine gave her a dazzling smile. 'It's not a big secret, Libby.'

'So what is it then?'

'Actually, I've always wanted to know, too,' said Robert.

Hume flashed him a warning glance.

He shrugged. 'Well, I have.'

In the new, expectant silence, Jasper let out a laugh. After fifty years of smoking it sounded like he was dragging someone out of a coffin. Everybody turned to him in surprise.

'You mean you've never told them?' he said.

'Not on purpose,' Raine answered, primly picking up a cube of cheese and pickled onion on a stick. 'It's just never come up.'

Jasper started laughing again. 'Oh, that's priceless. I thought they all knew.'

'Knew what?' said Hume, sounding slightly put out.

'It's something awful, isn't it?' said Echo, smiling.

'No, not at all,' said Jasper, pulling himself together. 'You mean you really don't know?'

They all looked at Raine, then turned to Jasper.

'Can I tell them?' asked Jasper.

'Knock yourself out,' said the detective.

'So, you probably all know that Raine grew up on the canal, yeah? That her parents were . . .' He moved his hand in a see-saw gesture. 'Let's say they were eco-punks. They used to arrange warehouse parties and happenings around London.'

'Ace!' said Bitz.

'Really?' said Libby, staring at Raine wide-eyed.

Raine nodded. 'Got taught on a school barge. Spent most of my youth around bouncers and small-time criminals.' Brin and Jasper both nodded their heads in acknowledgement. 'Brilliant childhood.'

'Thing is,' continued Jasper, 'Raine's parents were basically hippies. New-age travellers. Romantics. When they had their baby, they wanted to call her something beautiful. Something primal and healing.'

'For God's sake, what's her name?' said Hume.

Raine smiled. 'You already know it.'

'What do you mean?'

'Her name's Raine,' said Jasper. 'She's a mononym.'

There was a pause. Raine took another piece of cheese on a stick and pulled it into her mouth with her teeth.

'What's a mononym?' said Jolene.

'There's only one name on Raine's birth certificate. No surname.'

'Really?' asked Robert, amazed. 'I thought . . . no surname?'

'The law says you need to put down the parents' names, if known, but you are perfectly entitled to just have the one for your child.'

'So you are just Raine?' asked Robert. 'One name. Nothing else?'

Raine nodded.

There was a long silence, before Libby finally said: 'That's brilliant.'

* * *

'I know how much it must have hurt,' said Hume quietly, later, touching Raine's arm. They were standing out on the deck, watching a freezing fog roll out from the direction of Camden across the black water. 'To sell the boat. Get rid of where you lived together. You and Clara. I know how happy you were with her.'

Raine stayed staring out at the canal for a moment, before turning to face Hume. She returned the detective's gesture, touching Hume's arm.

'I know why you might think that, Mary, but you're wrong. I did love her. Do love her. And the times we spent on the water were the happiest I've ever known. Sharing my life with Clara was everything. And when she was gone, the boat was all I had left.' She sighed and ran her hand through her hair. 'I don't know. I thought I could make her come back if I held on to it. That if I could hold the memories tight enough. That if I squeezed tight enough I could squeeze the death out of her.'

Hume looked at Raine, devastated.

'But I can't bring her back. The boat was part of that. Not letting go. But it's just a thing. A crutch. In the end, it became a kind of prison.'

Raine reached up and touched her chest. 'But she didn't really live on the boat. This is where she lives. In here.'

Then she touched Hume's chest. 'And here.'

Tears slipped from Hume's eyes.

'Plus I took the bed from the old boat, so I'm basically still sleeping with her,' said Raine, flashing a smile. She grabbed hold of Hume's arm. 'Come on, let's go back down before they start getting too comfortable.'

EPILOGUE

Raine sat on the deck of her boat, wrapped up in a fleece, beret pulled down hard on her head. Tiny daggers bit into her face, as if the fog that now shrouded the boat and canal was made up of ice. Her hands were deep in her pockets, her fingers wrapped around the key cache in which she kept a twist of Clara's ashes. Raine's guests had left, laughing and smiling, and she had laughed and smiled right back. She had managed to keep up the pretence until every single one of them had gone, and then she had turned off all the lights, opened up a camp chair and sat.

She didn't know what she was going to do next. She had come to a crossroads in her life. Should she attempt to rejoin the police force? Take the boat and just go travelling? Do something else entirely?

Because she hadn't been honest with Mary. Or at least not completely honest. She had let Clara go a little when she got rid of the boat. Felt little bits of her slipping away each day. But she had kept her in her broken heart, lodged among the shards of her grief. And now, with Clara slowly fading, she was worried there'd be nothing left behind. That she'd just be empty. That her choices would become more brutal. Her attitude to others colder. She was worried that by letting Clara go she might be killing the only thing that kept her going.

She looked along the towpath. It was deserted, with fog swirling and tunnelling along it. The canal beside was black and deep like an open vein. She closed her eyes.

What would it be like to just leave? Maybe forever?

When she opened her eyes again Heather Salim was standing on the path. She looked different from two years ago. Thinner. Harder. Her face was in shadow from the hijab. Raine couldn't tell how much weight she had lost beneath the cargos and baggy fleece, but she thought it might be a lot. Heather's hands were stuffed into her fleece pockets. The two women stared at each other for a beat, until Heather finally broke the silence.

'Hello, Raine with an "e". I got your message. You really stopped him? He's gone?'

Raine smiled at the woman. Her bones ached with tiredness.

'I really did. He's going to prison for a very long time. Nobody's coming after you.'

Heather's face was unreadable. She wrapped her arms around herself and shivered. 'Thank you.' Strands of fog clung to her legs, hiding her feet.

'No sweat. I've got your sister's bag. The one you had in that alley.'

Heather's drawn face broke into an answering smile. 'Really?'

'Yes. Do you want to come in and get it?'

Heather looked up and down the towpath, at the white cords of fog that seemed to weave around the emptiness of the night, like a secret wanting to be whispered.

'I promise not to pry,' said Raine softly. 'Tell me or don't tell me. I don't mind. I'm just glad that you're safe.'

Heather took a step towards the boat, then stopped, unsure.

'You can just sit awhile. Or sleep somewhere safe. Or turn away and leave. There's no charge.'

Heather looked at the detective, her expression full of conflict.

Raine held her breath.

'You have the kindest eyes, Raine. Has anyone ever told you that?'

'Not since my wife died.'

The night wrapped itself around the two women, blanking out the rest of the world for a moment. All sound was shut out by the fog. The city, normally so full of noise, seemed to be put on pause. Finally, Heather nodded, then stepped forward onto the boat.

'Have you got any tea?'

THE END

ACKNOWLEDGEMENTS

I am so happy that Raine and Co. have had another outing, but it wouldn't have happened without the following people.

Josephine, for never holding back or holding in.

Lula, for their attention to detail on the final read.

Gabriel, for averting the tech wreck.

Joseph, who always finds the time.

Wren. You're all caught up!

Dominique, for always being supportive.

Sally. Thank you for all your enthusiasm! I am so sad you won't get to read this one.

Anne-Marie, for all the hard, hard work.

Kate, Rachel, and the team at Joffe, thank you for sending her out again.

All of you who have joined Raine, Echo and the gang by reading my books.

Thank you. Really. Thank you. Characters don't exist until they are read.

Cheers!

Stephen

THE JOFFE BOOKS STORY

We began in 2014 when Jasper agreed to publish his mum's much-rejected romance novel and it became a bestseller.

Since then we've grown into the largest independent publisher in the UK. We're extremely proud to publish some of the very best writers in the world, including Joy Ellis, Faith Martin, Caro Ramsay, Helen Forrester, Simon Brett and Robert Goddard. Everyone at Joffe Books loves reading and we never forget that it all begins with the magic of an author telling a story.

We are proud to publish talented first-time authors, as well as established writers whose books we love introducing to a new generation of readers.

We won Trade Publisher of the Year at the Independent Publishing Awards in 2023. We have been shortlisted for Independent Publisher of the Year at the British Book Awards for the last four years, and were shortlisted for the Diversity and Inclusivity Award at the 2022 Independent Publishing Awards. In 2023 we were shortlisted for Publisher of the Year at the RNA Industry Awards.

We built this company with your help, and we love to hear from you, so please email us about absolutely anything bookish at feedback@joffebooks.com

If you want to receive free books every Friday and hear about all our new releases, join our mailing list: www.joffebooks.com/contact

And when you tell your friends about us, just remember: it's pronounced Joffe as in coffee or toffee!

Milton Keynes UK
Ingram Content Group UK Ltd.
UKHW030747100924
448141UK00004B/166